DISCLAIMER

This is a fiction. Names, Characters, Business, Events and incidents are the author's imagination. Any resemblance to any persons, living or dead or actual events or localities is purely coincidental.

This story explores the journey of a soul across time, memory, and lives. While it draws upon concepts such as reincarnation and spiritual continuity, these are used as narrative devices to deepen the emotional and philosophical arc of the characters.

The beliefs and events depicted are part of the fictional world and are not meant to represent the author's personal worldview.

Soul to Soul

by

ANAMIKA S YADAV

First Published in June 2025

ISBN: 978-9334-313-246

Cover Design:
Anuj Yadav

ACKNOWLEDGMENTS

This story wouldn't have taken form without the subtle guidance of many seen and unseen forces.

To the reader; if this story touched something deep within you, know that you are not alone. Stories heal because they remind us of the truth we already carry.

DEDICATION

To every soul carrying the weight of unspoken pain

Prologue

There's a strange certainty carried that this life is not the first, and it won't be the last. It's not something can be proved or explained easily, but the feeling exists, steady and quiet. A knowing that a soul have been here before in different forms, different stories. And that it returned now because something remains unfinished.

Not everything is remembered clearly. Some lives blur together, just flashes of emotion, moments of clarity, or an image that stays for no reason we understand. But the sense of purpose of something left to do is stronger than anything else. It pulls us forward.

No life is accidental. Every person we meet, every decision we make, becomes a thread in a much larger pattern. Most of us never see the full picture, but we each play a part in something far bigger than ourselves.

This time it's a coming back with more questions than answers. But I know this; I am here to remember, to understand, and to finish what was once started. Whatever that means, and whatever it takes.

SOUL to SOUL

I will return, I softly vow,
for my part is not yet done somehow.
The universe waits, a stage divine,
incomplete without this role of mine.

Through lifetimes vast, I've come and gone,
a fleeting star before the dawn.
Yet every step, each choice, each day,
adds a thread to the cosmic play.

The tapestry weaves, both bright and stark,
guided by whispers in the dark.
"I'll come again," my spirit pleads,
to sow the love, fulfil the deeds.

For every soul, a story to share,
each note a song, unique and rare.
Together we form the endless whole,
every piece vital, vital every soul.

So let the wheels of time unfold,
I'll journey back, brave and bold.
Until the script is fully spun,
and the play's last curtain has begun.

Ana..

Contents

The Doorway

As she rest on her back, eyes slowly closing, Kshipra feels a whisper of air brush her cheek; cool, ancient, familiar. Her chest grows heavy, not with fear, but with a longing that had lived too many lives. A thread tugged inside her, woven with love, regret and something unfinished. Not a memory, not a face, but a presence. If this door opened, she needed to know. Who was it that her soul returned for?

It is dark, darker than anything she's ever known. Kshipra feels her breath catch, her heart pounding in the silence. The world is still, empty. She reaches for something, anything... but there is only space. Her heart pounds and beats at a high pace. She is struggling to cope. A soft but crisp voice tries to calm her, "Relax Kshipra, it's dark, but you can see what needs to be seen. You are here for a reason. A reason you chose, and you will find the truth you seek. Slow down your thoughts, focus, and look for something that will lead you to the truth."

Kshipra still can't cope. She turns around, looking for something, but sees nothing. The voice speaks again, "Try moving ahead." Kshipra tries to take a step forward, but stumbles. "I can't see anything. How can I move? It's too dark, I'm falling!" she cries. The voice tries to give her courage, "No, just take a step at a time, and you will move and see."

Kshipra steps forward, one step, then another. Her gaze

focuses on something that seems like wood. She says with doubt, "It's something wooden, but what is it?" The voice guides her further, "Move ahead and focus." Kshipra tries to focus, hesitantly reaching out to feel it. She identifies it as a door. "Is it a door? A wooden door!" she exclaims. The voice responds, "Okay, look around. Can you see anything else?"

Kshipra turns in all directions, slowly scanning, and then says, "There are many doors, all wooden, and very old." The voice encourages her, "Look at each door and see which one is calling you." Kshipra responds, "they all look the same, nothing special about any of them." The voice says, "There are many doors, but only one is meant for you. That one will reveal the truth you seek. Move closer and find the door that calls you. Go ahead."

Kshipra's anxiety rises again. She moves her left hand forward to reach for a door but feels nothing. Fear grips her. "I can see, but I can't feel the door. I'm scared," she admits. The voice reassures her, "Don't step back. You must move forward."

Kshipra gathers courage and moves forward again. She walks anxiously toward each door. She feels trapped, surrounded by these doors. She takes several turns, her pace increasing with every passing moment, until suddenly her hand taps against one door. Her breath sharpens as she feels a cold current run through her spine, and tiny droplets of sweat form on her temples. A strange pull towards the door takes over her. Her feet seem to have life of their own, as she steps closer.

She notices the door is still closed, but a bluish light looks seeping from a thin crack. She opens the door and steps back, startled by the intensity of the blue light spreading out. Reflexively, her eyes close and she covers her face with one hand while holding the door with the other. The cloud of blue light seems to swallow her. She's pulled inside, her hair flowing freely as she feels she's stepped into another place. Slowly, she uncovers her face with a deep sigh.

The blue light dims, and a cloud of dust rises accompanied by the sounds of horse riders. The chaos around her becomes clear as she sees a huge mob running before her, chased by soldiers on horseback. A young girl, about 20, dressed in a half sari, leads the mob away from the soldiers, trying to save them. She's running with the crowd, holding some people's hands, pushing others, but not everyone follows. Some run in different directions.

The voice asks, "What do you see, Kshipra?" She responds immediately, "That's Arya. It's me! I want to save everyone. They're running in different directions, and I can't get them all to safety. British soldiers are chasing them."

The soldiers pull people they catch, hanging them from the trees in the jungle. The chaos grows louder. Kshipra mutters, "They'll kill them, and I can't stop it." She cries out. The voice tries to comfort her, "You did your best to save them. You can't do more. Whoever is lost was not your fault. Don't blame yourself."

Kshipra holds her head, recalling the dreams she's had since childhood, dreams exactly like what she's seeing now. She remembers lying in bed, restless, as the sounds of chaos echo. As a small girl, she cried after having the same dream. The jungle, the hanging bodies, the birds chirping wildly, and a small girl searching for her parents.

Tiny Kshipra crying in bed, scared as her parents tried to wake her.

She's brought back to that moment, and it's overwhelming. The mob vanishes, but the dust still lingers.

The voice asks, "Are you done, my child? Come back to the present." Kshipra breathes deeply, feeling frozen. "I can't move. I'm stuck," she says.

The voice asks, "What's holding you back? Can you still see anything else?" Kshipra replies, "No, everything is blurry. I can't see clearly anymore." The voice instructs her to focus, "Look around. What's still missing? Are you ready to come back?"

For a few moments, there's no response. The voice grows concerned, "Kshipra, you must return. Turn around and come back if you can't see anything more."

Finally, Kshipra responds, "I can't come back. He's here." The voice asks, "Who is he?" Kshipra hesitates, "I don't know, but he's here."

The voice pushes for clarity, "Is it your brother, your father or a friend?"Kshipra shakes her head, "No."

The voice continues, "Look closely. You know him. He's holding you back. Go to him and ask him what he wants."

Kshipra looks around and spots a poor man sitting in the corner. Their eyes meet briefly. Kshipra feels a deep connection at that very moment, and as she stares into his eyes, memories flood back.

She recalls cooking with her husband, Rajan, laughing together while soft music played. Suddenly, Rajan's face flips to that of the man sitting in front of her. Goosebumps rise as she realizes this man is Sujoy.

She continues to stare at him. He's dressed in a worn-out dhoti and kurta, a small cloth tied around his head. He looks tired, hungry, and very poor. Kshipra murmurs, "He is here. He looks at me with such hope."

The voice asks, "You know him. What does he want?"

Kshipra sobs, "He is poor, and he wants to marry me, but I can't. I want to serve my country, fight the British, but he thinks it's because of his poverty. I can't explain that it's not true. I love him, but I can't be with him."

She continues, "If I marry him, they'll torture him. He doesn't understand. He thinks I'm mean.

Kshipra walks towards Sujoy, "I loved you, but I

couldn't say it. They would have hurt you. We're meant to love each other. But if you don't value this bond, I will leave you and won't return not in this life, not in any other."Her tears fall as the pain releases.

She collapses, holding her knees, crying.

Voice echoes, "Is he still there? What's he saying? Stay with me, Kshipra."

Kshipra calms down slightly, wiping her face, standing up slowly, and saying, "He's gone. He's not here."

The voice gently insists, "Okay, it's time to come back now. Turn around and return."

Kshipra turns and looks at the door. Slowly, she walks toward it, holding the door and opening it wide. Just as she's about to step through, a young boy of around 8 or 9 laughs at her. She steps back.

The voice asks, "What's going on now? Has he returned?"

Kshipra answers "no but there's a small boy laughing at me, he thinks I couldn't save the villagers, and many were caught and hanged."

The voice urges, "Tell him you did your best."

Kshipra feels uncertain, "He's just laughing and running away. Who is he? I can't identify him."

The voice warns, "Don't focus on the boy. You've turned to return. Don't dig deeper. Come back now."

But Kshipra continues to look at him. The boy keeps laughing, turning back to look at her. She closes her eyes and suddenly recalls a memory, a photo frame with a boy around 9 years old, showing a mark on his forehead. She opens her eyes and breathes deeply.

She realizes it's the boy she knew, and her expression changes.

Kshipra's emotions swirl as she steps forward, her heart heavy with realization. The boy's laughter lingers in her mind, a haunting echo of the past. As she moves toward the stairs, the soft rhythm of her footsteps contrasts sharply with the chaos of her thoughts. A photo frame flashes in her mind once more, a small boy with a mark on his forehead, Sujoy fading bit by bit, and the dusty chaos of many running.

As Kshipra ascends the stairs, each step brings her closer to the present moment, offering glimpses of clarity. Yet, the image of the boy lingers, etched in her mind, pulling at her heart with a sense of guilt. He is not just a face from her past; he is someone she remembers from her childhood of present life though she couldn't place the connection before.

Now, as the fog of her subconscious begins to lift, the pieces of the puzzle fall into place. He is a symbol of something lost, something unresolved; one of the many lives she had tried and failed to save may be, she thinks.

Kshipra halts, her body freezes in the realization. She remembers a moment from her childhood when the British soldiers had chased her family, when she had tried to escape, and when everything had fallen apart. She feels the boy may be one of the many she had tried to protect. Yet, in the chaos, he had slipped through her grasp. His face, his smile, had been so innocent, and yet his fate had been sealed by the cruelty of those who sought to dominate.

Now, this very boy stood before her, an echo from the past, challenging her efforts. Had she failed him? Had she failed many? A sharp ache stabs at her heart, and a strong pull settles in her abdomen.

Kshipra hesitates, unsure whether to turn back toward the door, but the voice urges her again. "You must return. Don't get too much lost in the past. You've done all you could."

But Kshipra can't tear her eyes away from the boy. His laughter fades, and he turns, looking directly at her, his eyes full of sorrow. It's no longer laughter but a silent plea. Kshipra's heart sink, she feels she has failed him.

She opens her mouth to speak, but the words catch in her throat. The boy waits, his gaze never leaving hers. Slowly, she turns fully toward him. His expression has changed, no longer playful but full of understanding.

Kshipra's heart races as she reaches out, trembling, "I'm sorry... I couldn't save you."

The boy doesn't respond in words. He simply stares at her, his gaze deep, as if acknowledging the truth of her words. Then, he smiles and it's a sad smile and with it, he vanishes.

The boy is gone.

Kshipra stands in the silence, breathing in the stillness. For the first time, there's peace. Her chest feels lighter and her guilt though not erased but has eased.

The voice speaks again, more gently now, "You've acknowledged the truth, Kshipra. Now, it's time to let go."

Kshipra nods as her body slowly relaxes. She turns away from the boy's fading presence and faces the door. This time, there's no hesitation. She opens it wide, stepping forward into the unknown, ready to return to the present moment, to the reality of her life.

As Kshipra steps through the door, she feels the warmth of the present embrace her. The darkness that surrounded her is replaced with the soft, familiar light of the world she left behind. The past no longer holds her captive. She has faced it, understood it and tried to let it go.

Her journey is not over yet. There are still many doors ahead, many truths to uncover, but Kshipra is no longer afraid. With every step she takes now, many unknown faces flash before her, for this is just the beginning of something bigger to be revealed. Just as she climbs the last step, she hears the voice ask, "Were you able to make him understand?"

Kshipra opens her eyes, wiping the sweat from her brow as she returns to the present moment. She utters softly, "I don't know if Rajan understood how much I love him."

The voice, Lakshmi responds reflexively, "Only if that's the only thing bothering his soul, not otherwise."

The journey momentarily rests.
But the soul's story stretches far beyond what the heart remembers.

Return to purpose

There was this young girl Vasanti, A life not remembered, but deeply imprinted. A quiet beginning that held the first notes of a melody still playing through times.

Every morning Vasanti wakes hoping to feel different; less hollow, more whole. But beneath her smile, there's always a quiet whisper: Will I ever be enough to be loved without condition? She doesn't voice it. But it follows her like her shadow, clinging close.

At 16, she had been a bride, her laughter youthful but nervous, her steps tentative as she learn the role of a wife at this early age. The weight of expectation had been heavy, not just from her family but from the world around her. By 17, she had been pregnant, her body unprepared for the life growing inside her. She had dreamed of motherhood, but those dreams shattered quickly, like glass falling to the floor.

She could still remember the sharp pain, the cold sweat that clung to her skin, the way the world seemed to spin and blur, around her as she lost her first child. It was a cruel reminder that she was not ready, her body not strong enough for the demands of carrying life.

After the miscarriage, there is hollowness inside her, a vulnerability that remained long after the physical healing had begun. Her body had betrayed her, she thought and though she tried to move forward, something within her had changed.

Vasanti's fingers tighten on the shawl as she stands up, a small sigh escaping her lips. The breeze tugged at her hair, and for a moment, she close her eyes and imagine what it might have been like holding a baby in her arms, but it is just a dream, one that felt as distant now as the setting sun.

In that quiet moment, as night began to settle over the garden, Vasanti feels the weight of all she had been through, the vulnerability that had become her silent companion, and the long road ahead that stretched into the uncertain future.

Vasanti is tiny, her frail figure moving quietly through the house, trying to avoid the eyes that constantly watch her. Her hands are delicate, but they work tirelessly; washing dishes, sweeping floors, folding clothes always busy, always trying to keep up with the unending chores. But no matter how much she does, it's never enough. The house feels suffocating at times.

After the miscarriage, the weight of her world had only grew heavier. Her mother-in-law Radha's cruel words cut deeper, as if the loss of the child wasn't enough. "Look at you," her mother-in-law hisses, her voice dripping with disdain. "You couldn't even carry a child. You're useless."

The words strike like blows, cruel and unforgiving. Vasanti doesn't respond. She's learned not to. Radha's anger is sharp, and there's no escaping it. The woman has tormented her, mentally and physically, ever since the miscarriage. Every day is a new round of insults, a constant reminder that Vasanti is somehow to blame for something that was beyond her control.

Her husband Madhukar is distant, his eyes cold whenever they meet. There's no warmth between them, only a painful silence. He doesn't say anything, but she can feel his disappointment hanging in the air, thick and suffocating. He doesn't even try to comfort her. His silence says everything, she feels.

Vasanti never wanted anything more than to be a mother. Not riches, not praise; just a child to call her own. Her dreams were fragile, simple. Now, they lay shattered, like glass dropped on stone. And yet, every morning, she rises. Because if she doesn't, who will?

As the sun begins to rise, Vasanti steps out quietly with a small packet of rice tucked in her sari. She walks to the neighboring house, where an elderly woman sits on the steps, coughing softly. Without a word, Vasanti places the packet beside her and bows slightly. The woman's eyes glisten. Vasanti says nothing, but her hand lingers gently on the woman's shoulder before she turns away.

Back inside, she scrubs the utensils quickly, but her fingers move with a quiet satisfaction. For a moment, she feels like she still has the power to give, even if no one inside her house sees it.

It is a new moon night and Vasanti is restless for the whole of the night. Her eyes are closed but thoughts awake. She slowly gets out of her bed, looks at Madhukar's calmly sleeping face. Vasanti adjusts the coversheet lying on the bed over Madhukar then sips some water from the tumbler kept next to the bed on a side table. It is 3.45 am as she is looking at the sky, whose small portion is visible from the window near her bed.

A breeze carries the faint scent of incense from the shrine room. It coils around her, sudden and familiar, and her eyes close. Somewhere, deep inside, she feels her soul exhale.

On the other side, far off, as Arya's soul prepares to depart from her earthly vessel her essence trembles with a mixture of sorrow, loneliness, and a poignant sense of self-doubt, if she did enough? She had spent her final days in quiet isolation, the weight of unshared burdens pressing heavily upon her departing spirit. Drifting in the ethereal expanse, she seeks solace amidst the infinite cosmic tapestry.

Meanwhile, across the veil of existence, Vasanti traverses her own emotional landscape. Haunted by the silent ache of her first miscarriage, she carries within her a labyrinth of emotions left unexpressed. A profound sense of loneliness lingers, echoing in the depths of her being.

In the unseen realms where souls navigate beyond mortal comprehension, a subtle yet powerful resonance begins to unfold. Arya's soul, adrift and yearning for connection, finds itself drawn inexorably towards Vasanti's frequency. Their energies, like harmonizing melodies in a symphony of the cosmos, converge with a cosmic precision that defies earthly logic.

Something beyond words connects them. Arya's loneliness reaches out, and Vasanti's silent ache receives it. Their souls find each other, not through thought, but feeling grief folding into comfort, sorrow into shelter. A gentle pull, and Arya's energy nestles into Vasanti's womb, beginning again.

With each heartbeat and breath, Arya's essence merges gently into Vasanti's awaiting womb. Here, amidst the tender embrace of maternal warmth, their spiritual journey takes a defined turn.

The invisible threads of fate and emotion bind them together, offering both solace and renewal in the delicate embrace of new beginnings.

It is not cold but Vasanti feels a soothing cold current passing through her, it was not hot either but she feels warmth in her heart like never before. She feels strange. Her body feels cold and her heart warm at this very moment.

Somewhere in the universe, a frequency aligned in that dawn hourand it is a soul finding its womb for its rebirth, rebirth for a cause, for a desire for some accomplishment, not fulfilled yet but need to be fulfilled for sure.

Vasanti rests back on her bed but couldn't sleep. She doesn't feel uneasy as she usually does, what she feels is not known to that little girl. It is a strange and unknown feeling but soothing.

A couple of weeks and Vasanti shows symptoms of being pregnant. Her mother-in-law as usual taunts and Vasanti is quick in her response" I missed my periods and it's been 15 days. Radha looks at her, blank-faced, unreadable. Vasanti feels dejected, yet again.

Days pass, and Vasanti is also in a state of mind that her body knew she was carrying but her mind kept on recollecting previous experiences and all that Radha said to her. She feels a need for reassurance from someone, always.

It's a hot summer and Vasanti is almost 5 months pregnant. Her baby bump is tiny yet. Vasanti checks if Radha is asleep and slowly comes out of her house. She joins all the females sitting on the neighbouring varanda for a chat.

Before joining the verandah, Vasanti stops by Asha's

back window. She taps twice, softly. Asha opens it, startled.

"You look tired," Asha whispers. "I had to come out. I couldn't breathe," Vasanti murmurs. Asha hands her a mango slice. "Then eat this like a queen. Even queens need to hide sometimes." Vasanti smiles a real one for the first time in days. "Then today, I'll be a hiding queen."

Asha, her friend and next door neighbour passes a comment "Where is your old lady? How did she allow you to come out? Vasanti just smiles in response as all sitting there are aware of the reality. Vasanti takes Asha to one side and asks "See, can you make out if I am carrying or not? Asha gets upset, "How many times do you want to reconfirm? She eases a bit looking at Vasanti's sad face, "Relax Vasanti, you are definitely carrying. Did you get your period last 5 months? No! Why are you not able to believe it? You feel it, right? the baby is in your womb. Don't listen to that old female, she is a cruel person. Vasanti closes Asha's mouth with her palm and nods in non-acceptance for using such a word for her mother-in-law.

Vasanti's husband, Madhukar relaxes after dinner. Vasanti is still busy winding up her kitchen. She hears a loud argument between mother and son. She peeps moving slowly near the door to hear their talks.

Radha slowly wispers " She is too weak to carry a baby hence she had a miscarriage"

Madhukar replies" She was just 17, the doctor said at this age it's not right to deliver a baby. And you stop blaming her for that".

Radha continues" Why don't you marry a little older and physically fit girl, we will leave Vasanti, as it is I don't like her".

Vasanti's face drops and her heartbeat rises to hear this. Her gaze instantly gets fixed on Madhukar's face in search of his reaction to this.

He blasts "You said it for the first and the last time. Another time if you even think of it, I will take you and leave at your brother's place. I love her and won't leave her even if she is not able to have a baby at all. Keep this in mind forever".

Vasanti's eyes overflow with tears and heart with love to hear what she hardly expected.

Later that night, Vasanti finds Madhukar alone in the shed, checking sacks of grain, "You meant what you said?" she asks, voice trembling. He doesn't turn, but nods once. "I don't lie when I'm angry." She steps closer, her hands cold. "No one's ever spoken for me like that. Not even my own father."

Madhukar finally turns. "You're strong, Vasanti. But I forget, you're still just a girl."

The silence between them softens and something old and rough inside her cracks open, just a little.

 Madhukar is 12years older than Vasanti and rough in talk. Vasanti is always scared of him and always wondered if he loved her or not. Today after hearing this Vasanti is touched and happy like never before. For the first time, she felt the real support and love of her husband.

Days pass and a tiny little piece of moon is in Vasanti's arms and Madhukar is all above the seventh cloud.

There is a big celebration while the baby is named 'Kshipra', the river, symbolizing the flow, purity, natural beauty, sacredness, and the ever-flowing nature of a river.

Seasons of Innocence

Kshipra fills the life of Madhukar and Vasanti with all her charm. Vasanti is no longer the fearful wife she once was, Motherhood had softened her fears and reshaped her into someone quietly strong and Kshipra's presence in Madhukar's life changes his rough nature as well.

Days pass and Radha gets sicker and sicker. Vasanti holds no grudge against her and serves her at her death bed till her last breath.

Kshipra is 5 years old by now. Early this morning there is some sort of movement in the house. Kshipra is too small to understand what is going on but she does acknowledge that there is something which makes everyone happy even as Vasanti is been taken to the Hospital.

Kshipra holds a packet of biscuits sitting on her bed, trying to figure out when her mother will be back home.

Asha rushes in and hands over a small bowl to Kshipra "You have got a little brother dear, have this sweet".

This tiny little girl looks at the bowl and at her biscuit packet. Asha is not able to understand what she is trying to do. Kshipra keeps the bowl down and holds a biscuit packet, opens it, and makes two portions. She holds a portion in each hand. Asha looks with appreciation as such a small girl immediately shares what she had with her sibling whom she has not even seen yet. She didn't know what a brother meant yet, but in her heart, she already knew he belonged to her.

The divine bond is evident.

Both the kids Kshipra and Ajay grow in a gentle, loving and caring environment and along with Asha's kids Murli and Sudha almost of the same age. They fill the environment with joy and laughter in and around both the families.

They would go to school together, play together, and sometimes even work in the fields with their parents. They would sing, dance, and play in the water pits all day long.

Lots of times Ajay and Murli would go a bit far from their village and Kshipra would get tensed for Ajay. She would search for him, her anxiety would rise and tears roll. Her heartbeat would increase as if something bad had already happened to him.

It's a warm, lazy afternoon the kind that makes the whole village feel like it's drifting off to sleep. But for Murli, Sudha, Kshipra, and Ajay, it's the perfect time to head down to the water pits. Laughing, they race across the field, kicking up little clouds of dust behind them. Murli, as usual is the fastest and he reaches the edge of the pit first, diving in with a loud splash that sends ripples everywhere. Kshipra carefully dips her feet into the water and feels the coolness wash over her. She giggles as Ajay playfully splashes her and before long, the air is filled with the sound of their laughter, water droplets flying all around them. Murli and Sudha join in, creating a splash fight, each trying to outdo the others.

 Kshipra and Ajay, though, have their own way of enjoying the day. She leans back, watching him with a mix of pride and protectiveness. Ajay is her little brother, always looking up to Murli, trying to do whatever he does. She laughs as he copies Murli's antics but also keeps a watchful eye on him, ready to jump in if he stumbles.

As they dry off in the sun, lying on the warm earth, Ajay leans against Kshipra, eyes half-closed, feeling safe. Kshipra wraps her arm around him, watching over him quietly. It's a simple moment, yet its clear how much she cares for him and how protected he feels.

One day, Murli comes up with a wild idea. "Let's go to the big mango tree outside the village and get some fruit," he says, his eyes gleaming with mischief. Kshipra immediately feels a flicker of worry as it's farther than they're usually allowed to go, and the tree is known for its height. Ajay's face lights up, and he jumps up excitedly, eager to prove himself. "I can climb as high as Murli!" he says confidently. Kshipra's stomach twists with nerves. "Ajay, maybe we should stay closer to the village," she suggests, giving him a concerned look. But Ajay just shakes his head. "Come on, I'll be fine." They set off together, with Kshipra trailing behind, her heart pounding.

The boys race each other to the tree, and soon Murli is halfway up, laughing down at Ajay, who's determined to catch up. Kshipra stays on the ground, looking up anxiously as Ajay climbs higher and higher. When he finally reaches a branch near Murli, she calls up to him, "Ajay, be careful! Don't go too high." The moment stretches out as he leans out to grab a mango, the branch swaying slightly.

Kshipra's breathe catches, her heart thudding so loudly she's sure they can hear it. But then, with a triumphant yell, Ajay holds up the mango, grinning down at her. Kshipra feels a rush of relief, her heart calming down as she watches him climb down carefully. When Ajay's feet touch the ground, she rushes over to him, throwing her arms around him. "Don't scare me like that again!" she says, half laughing, half scolding. Ajay grins up at her, holding out the mango. "I got this for you." She takes the fruit, ruffling his hair with a warm smile. It's just a mango, but to her, it feels like the world.

Shadows of the Past

One such evening Kshipra returns back with Vasanti from the local market. She gets freshened up and calls for Ajay, but he doesn't respond. Kshipra looks for him all around the house but he is not to be seen. She checks up with Sudha and learns that Ajay and Murli have not been seen since the afternoon. Kshipra gets anxious at this. She gets out of the house not bothering to reply to Vasanti's call. Vasanti shouts a loud "Don't go they will come in some time" But Kshipra runs out of her house saying "Baba will get angry if Ajay is not at home before he comes".

Sudha, sitting on the platform of her balcony gives an unconvincing look as Kshipra looks at her. She knows Kshipra wants her to join but Sudha is not interested as usual. Kshipra searches them in fields and at all other friends' houses as well.

As time passes her heartbeat increases, she breaths sharply and feels a deep hole in her heart. Her mouth is dry and her eyes are wet. By this time she just roams around in the neighbourhood and doesn't have any energy to even talk to anyone. Her bare feet are peeled by now. She drags herself towards her house. Her watery sight catches a glimpse of her house verandah and she almost loses her senses as a crowd appears there. She is terrified with that all-white shade around. She rubs her eyes to get a better vision but tears refuse to stop blocking her view further. Her speed increases and she almost starts running towards her house. She runs as fast as possible and suddenly dashes with someone, her speed is so much that she gets thrown away into the bushes.

She tries hard to stand on her feet but is unable to. She raises her gaze and finds a hand to help her. Face is not seen but she has no other option but to hold it. She gets pulled out of the bushes while she is gasping. It's Murli, she starts crying uncontrollably asking him for Ajay. Murli wants to speak but Kshipra is inconsolable. He holds both her shoulders and shakes her rigorously, holds her face in his palms, and tries to tell her to calm down. She stops crying but is still sobbing intensely.

Murli shouts "What happened?" She points her finger towards her house looking at Murli. Murli turns around to see and finds 3-4 men walking away from her house. He questions again "What?" In reply, he receives a question from Kshipra "You too were with Ajay?" Murli replies "Yes we were together and went to a friend's shop inauguration. What is the problem?" By this time Murli understands what the problem is. He holds her hand and walks towards her house literally pulling her.

As they reach close he points at Ajay who is sitting with

his father and talking. She runs a few steps to have a bit more closer look at Ajay and her breath normalizes.

Murli comes and stands in front of her. She hesitates to look at him. Wiping the sweat on her face with her dupatta then waving it behind her right shoulder she mentions "I searched for Ajay all over and I couldn't find him". Murli interrupts "You couldn't find him so you assumed."

Kshipra looks at Murli with eyes wide open, an indication not to say anything further. Murli understands and responds to her with another look indicating "Don't worry, I won't tell anyone. Now you go home". She slowly walks towards her house giving herself some more time to wipe out the panic from her face.

Murli too goes home and post dinner as he lies on his bed; Kshipra's panic face still keeps haunting him. He cares for her. He recollects an episode from when they were all younger.

"Vasanti's nephews had an accident, and both the brothers died on the spot. She had to visit her brother immediately. She carried Ajay along as he was very young. Kshipra had a high fever, so Madhukar chose to stay back with her.

A few days later, Vasanti was supposed to return by the

afternoon. Madhukar had some work to do, so after putting Kshipra to sleep, he left for a while. Murli kept watch on Kshipra from the window of his room, knowing that she was unwell.

Kshipra woke up but remained lying in her bed. She kept checking the time anxiously. As the minutes passed, her anxiety grew. Despite being too weak to walk, she got up and left her room, stepping out of the house, desperately looking for Vasanti and Ajay to return. After some time, she sat on the verandah and slowly started crying. Before long, she was sobbing loudly.

Seeing this, Murli rushed to her, fearing something was terribly wrong. He tried to talk to her, but she just kept crying. Unable to figure out what to do, he hurried to call Madhukar. Both of them came running to her. Kshipra rushed towards Madhukar and hugged him tightly. He, too, was frightened by her condition. He asked, "What happened dear? Why are you crying?"

Kshipra didn't respond but slowly calmed down after a while. Madhukar gently held her and guided her back to her room, continuing to ask her what was wrong as he made her sit on the bed. Kshipra finally spoke in a soft voice, "I got scared. Mom and Ajay aren't back yet."

Before she could finish her sentence, Vasanti enters, holding Ajay. She made Ajay sit near Kshipra. Kshipra immediately hugged him and held him for a long time. Vasanti exchanged a glance with Madhukar, her face questioning and Madhukar explained, "Nothing, I just stepped out for a while. She was alone and got scared. She must have had some bad dreams."

Murli quietly watches the scene and then leaves.

While everyone slept that night Murli watched Kshipra still feeling restless as the lights of her room gets on/off several times throughout the night.

Murli gets disturbed while recollecting this episode and wonders why Kshipra gets this type of panic attacks.

Just then Sudha wakes Murli as it's already morning while he is remembering all these.

All four friends walk down to school the next day and Murli asks Kshipra about her behaviour last night. She ignores him. But he is persistent and daily asks her the same question whenever he finds her alone. Finally, she opens up.

Sitting on the bank of the river, their regular gateway; Kshipra hesitantly mentions that when time passed and her mother and brother still didn't return she got so panicked that she started feeling that they wouldn't return back at all. She briefs, "I was feeling as if their dead bodies are lying on the verandah and I was able to see all that. How will I tell this to anyone? Everyone will feel I have become mad". She continues "Many times I get very bad dreams like all dead bodies hanging on the trees in the jungle and there are lots of snakes and birds and I get so scared".

While describing her face is as tense as it would be seeing all this live. Murli holds her hand to calm her "You should tell this to your parents. It's not normal".

Years pass and Kshipra's panic attacks subside with time. She seems more confident girl than before. At least she can pretend so.

Roots & Wings

Over a period, Kshipra develops deep interest in farming and attempts several experiments with different crops. Not only in her village but all around her village farmers come to seek her help for how to do farming using less water, cross-breeding, etc.

The afternoon sun scorches the open field, but Kshipra doesn't slow. Her dupatta is tied tightly around her head, shielding her from the dust and sun as she moves in rhythm; hoe, twist, lift, breathe.

The plot small, barely a quarter acre, lent to her by an old widow in exchange for a share in the first harvest as Kshipra helped her yield the harvest. She refuses at first but eventually takes it as the lady insists.

While others her age go to towns looking for marrying into quiet domesticity; Kshipra stays back, hands in the soil. She reads every book on farming she can borrow, scribbles notes by lantern light, and rides her cycle to the Krishi Vigyan Kendra every week to attend sessions mostly filled with older men. At first, they smirk. Later, they begin to nod along.

The first yield is modest, but clean. She sells her vegetables at the weekly market and returns with a pouch of notes. She doesn't buy gold, or clothes, or sweets. She buys a goat, then two more.

In two years she purchases her first half-acre, barren and dry, but hers. She wants to register it in her mother's name.

Madhukar objects. "No, Kshipra. If you're doing this, building this with your own hands then own it. Don't hide behind her name. It's not about pride, it's about truth. Vasanti too insists for the same.

She listens quietly, as she always does when he speaks with that steady, serious voice. She says nothing.

By now Ajay has made up his mind and wants to move out of the village and explore a different world. He is fascinated with the side of the world other than farming. He would read the newspaper and all about the different business opportunities.

Sudha is keen on getting married and making her family while Murli is by now a trader, taking the grains from the village and selling them to the shopkeepers in the city.

This day Murli is expected to return from city, Ajay waits until late afternoon then reach out to Murli's house to check up on him. Ajay stands at the door, his hand gently knocking on the wooden frame. A few moments later, the door swings open to reveal Sudha, her face lighting up with a bright smile. There's unmistakable warmth between them, something unspoken yet deeply understood not only by them but also by both the families. The connection they share has grown over the years and is a open secret that everyone is quietly aware of but chooses not to address directly yet.

Ajay stands there for a moment, hesitating then asks, "Did Murli return from town?"

Sudha, her eyes sparkling with a mix of affection and curiosity, responds without missing a beat, "Yes, just now. Come in." She steps aside to let him in, and Ajay follows her into the cozy living room.
Ajay settles into a seat, and the conversation begins casually. They talk about the weather, the latest village gossip, and simple everyday things. The atmosphere is relaxed, but a subtle tension hangs in the air, a tension that only Ajay and Sudha seem to truly understand.

As they chat, Murli walks in. His presence is always larger than life, and he quickly begins talking about his recent trip to the city. "You wouldn't believe the things happening there," he says, his voice full of excitement. "The city life is fast, it's full of opportunities. There's always something new, something fascinating."

Ajay listens intently, his mind beginning to wander. Each time Murli talks about the city, about the business opportunities and the fast-paced life, Ajay feels a small spark of ambition light up inside him. He imagines himself there, in that bustling city, making a name for himself and building something of his own.

As Murli continues to share stories, Ajay's thoughts drift. Finally, he speaks up, his voice tinged with quiet longing. "I want to go there too," he says, his eyes downcast for a moment. "I want to start a business, but… Baba won't allow it. I don't feel any interest in farming, but he insists that I stay here and help with the land, just like Kshipra does."

Murli pauses, giving Ajay a thoughtful look. Sudha, too, seems to sense the weight of Ajay's words. For a brief moment, the conversation slows, as if all three are lost in their own thoughts, pondering the paths they've chosen and the ones they wish they could take.

They would always discuss this matter with no solution for this. But this time Sudha comes up with an option "Why don't you convince Kshipra first, she can convince your parents then we can start business and settle there".

Both Murli and Ajay look at Sudha with surprise for the later part of her sentence. A tiny, hesitant smile plays on Sudha's lips, a blend of awkwardness and hope.

But this idea clicks in Ajay's mind and he keeps on thinking over it through the next few days.

It's almost midnight and Kshipra notices while she gets up to drink water that Ajay is not asleep but is restless and just changing sides in an attempt to sleep.

Kshipra walks down to Ajay and sits on one corner of his bed "What is the matter? Why are you so restless?" Ajay immediately opens up "I don't enjoy working in the fields like you. I want to do something else, something different. I want to see life differently". Kshipra smiles as she is already aware of this. She says "Okay, let's talk this in the morning. Now you sleep it's too late" and she gets up. Ajay holds her hand and makes her sit again. Will you talk to baba about this, if anyone can convince him, it's you. If I say it will be out-rightly rejected. Kshipra puts her point of view "We are farmers Ajay and we can do this better. Business is not our cup of tea, and if you go and do something else, who will look after all this property baba has made? It is his hard-earned possession". Ajay in a slightly angry tone says "I thought you would help me but if you are not convinced then how will you convince them? You won't, right?

Kshipra knows his urge to start his business. She has been noticing this for quite some time. She suggests "Why don't you trade our own crops then, like Murli does. That will keep you very much attached to the farms and this house as well and just like Murli does you can spend a few days here and a few days in the city".

Ajay gives her an unconvincing look and pulls a sheet over his face with disappointment. Kshipra raises her hand to pull down the sheet from his face but then opts for leaving him alone for now.

Back to her bed Kshipra keeps on thinking about Ajay's words and she makes up her mind to speak to her father about it.

In the morning during breakfast Kshipra looks at Ajay who is attempting to behave indifferently, not at all looking at Kshipra, indicating that he is angry with her for not understanding him. She slowly looks at her father who is by now aware that something unsaid matter too rests there with them.

He looks at Ajay "What is the matter, why are you both so quiet". Ajay prefers to continue eating putting his head down but Kshipra knows that she has to speak. She mentions "our farm work is well settled and two people getting involved along with you is wasting one person's time and energy", Madhukar stares at Kshipra with surprise as she continues "I mean, I feel so. Why not one of us, either i or Ajay try out something else, explore some new field?"

Madhukar knows where this is exactly coming from. He asks Ajay "You too feel so? ". He replies in reflex action "Why not, it's a good idea. We can have another earning source and nothing wrong in making an attempt. Shall I try out something?" Madhukar argues, "Kshipra will get married in few years and I am also growing old. You will have to solely look after farms, if you try something else you will lose interest in farming and it will be difficult to come back".

Ajay further argues "What if my business settles well

and there is no need to come back?" Madhukar responds "If you are not interested to come back, what will happen to all our farms? Who will take care of this huge land?" Kshipra interrupts "Let him go and try out, I am here for now. We can take a call once Ajay sets up his business and we shall see how it grows".

Madhukar conditionally agrees "Fine, I give you two years. You can try it out whatever is in your mind. I will not even question you if you fail but then you will need to return to our family business if things don't work out favorably."

Kshipra nods, her face calm, but her heart uneasy. If Ajay leaves, and she too was sent away in marriage, who would stand beside their father in the fields? Who would protect the soil that held their childhood and their mother's sacrifices? This land is more than crops, it is everything their family had endured and survived.

 Supporting Ajay meant love.

But staying might mean loss. She stood in the middle, knowing whatever she chose, something may ache.

Vasanti is quietly listening to all this conversation. She looks at Kshipra and says "I am not convinced but does my opinion count? There is no need to try out something we don't have expertise in". Madhukar agrees with this but doesn't utter anything.

Madhukar enquires "Is there anything in your mind? Ajay replies "Yes, Murli introduced me to one cloth manufacturer who is from Surat. He will supply and we will have our retail shop of these garments. Initially one, then two, four, and many more! I will go and tell Murli that tomorrow itself I will join him and meet that guy" saying this Ajay runs out to meet Murli.

Madhukar looks at Kshipra saying "And you say, one of us can try something else", "Kshipra smiles as she looks at both her parents, then lowers her head and starts gulping."

Ajay starts his venture with initial funds from Madhukar.

He sets up his first shop and all are excited to see this. They all travel for the opening of Ajay's shop.

It's the day of his Shop's inauguration. Murli, Sudha, and their parents as well join for the event. It is a big day for Ajay and he is very excited about his new venture. Madhukar and Vasanti support but are skeptical about this.

Inauguration takes place and most of the guests leave.

Ajay is winding up while Sudha walks slowly towards him and murmurs "so, business is set, what next?" Ajay gives her a naughty smile and this is caught by Kshipra's eye.

Kshipra takes the initiative in this matter as well. She mentions it to Vasanti pointing her gaze at both of them "We all know they like each other then why not openly agree and break the ice. Let's fix their marriage".

Vasanti is instant in her reaction "What will people say if Ajay gets married before his elder sister?" Kshipra tries to convince "at least we can get them engaged for now". Vasanti almost shouts at Kshipra "don't impose all your decisions all the time."

Kshipra is well aware that her parents are not happy with her backing-up Ajay's decision to start this new business. But, she is confident, looking at his passion for doing something different. She feels once Ajay's business grows everyone will be happy.

Ajay and Murli decide to rent out a small place in the city so that they don't have to travel daily. No one is happy and convinced of this decision but it's convenient for them to work for extended hours and that is what matters for now.

Murli frequently travels to their village and makes it a point to meet Kshipra each time. Kshipra is also glad to meet him for her reasons. She would enquire all about Ajay and pack lots of homemade snacks for them.

This morning while Murli is about to leave, he stands beside Kshipra while she is busy packing. Sudha enters the room saying "enough Kshipra by now everyone knows that you cook well. It is not required to do all this every time. They don't stay in the jungle, it's a city and all this and much more and better than this is available there".

Kshipra would not mind Sudha's comments as she is aware of her nature. Kshipra just smiles saying, "Yes but the main ingredient will be missing from all of that, which is a sister's love. And you know how much Ajay likes my preparations". Sudha gives a weird look at Murli and is about to say something further but Murli interrupts "ok give all those bags to me, I will need to adjust in my bags and he takes all these jars of dry snacks and leaves.

Kshipra and Sudha watch him as he leaves. They both sit on the verandah for a long time remembering how nice the days were when the four of them would be together and always playing.

Kshipra holds Sudha's hand and reminds her one such episode while they were young. As they recollect, there go back to that day.

One evening, after dinner, Murli has another idea. "Let's go out to the field with lanterns and find fireflies!" he suggests, his eyes shining with excitement. Sudha, Kshipra, and Ajay eagerly agree. They each grab a lantern, lighting it carefully under their parent's watchful eyes before heading out. The night is dark, and the glow from their lanterns seems to create a little bubble of light as they walk across the fields together. Ajay sticks close to Kshipra, his hand clutching hers. The night air is cool, and there's a stillness that makes everything feel a little magical.

As they reach the edge of the field, the first firefly appears; a tiny spark of light in the darkness. Sudha gasps in delight, and soon more fireflies join in, creating a soft, blinking light show all around them.

Ajay's face lights up, his eyes wide with wonder as he reaches out, trying to catch one. Kshipra watches him, a gentle smile on her face. She's glad to be with him, to share this moment with him. She feels a deep sense of peace, standing there with her friends and her brother, surrounded by the magic of fireflies.

Murli and Sudha laugh and try to catch a few, but Kshipra just watches the lights, feeling grateful. She knew then, that no matter where life takes them, these memories will always be with them, filling their hearts with warmth and love.

As they walk back, Ajay leans against her, his head nodding sleepily. Kshipra wraps her arm around him, holding the lantern in her other hand, guiding him home safely under the starlit sky.

Sudha remembers, "and the way Ajay would always grip your plait". Kshipra feels that small pull and her head goes back a little, as they giggle over the memory.

Somehow both of them feel that those days are left

behind. Sudha says "When will we see those fireflies again?" Kshipra responds "May be never but, we will see something else, something different may be something better!

Madhukar and Vasanti watch the way Kshipra works in the fields. They are now keen on getting her married. Vasanti mentions to Madhukar "Ajay likes Sudha. Kshipra was suggesting if we can get them engaged. Let's first find a good match for Kshipra".

Vasanti recollects something and asks "Your friend's wife and his son were supposed to visit, when are they coming? Madhukar responds, "Yes tomorrow morning, please keep some snacks ready."

Next morning, Kshipra is aware that the guests will be arriving any moment. She rushes out with a bedsheet after wrapping all the preparation in the kitchen. She unfolds the sheet and tries to adjust it on the mattress but before its done Madhukar's friends widow Madhu and her son Rajan arrive at the doorstep. Madhu and Rajan are to visit a holy place and had dropped in just by the way.

Kshipra feels awkward as they walk in and she had not yet done with her arrangements. She holds the bedsheet in her hand itself and greets them. She recollects that the sheet is yet in her hand, she again makes an attempt to spread it, and looking at this, Rajan moves forward and lends a helping hand to Kshipra holding the other end of the sheet.

As Rajan takes his seat, he feels a quiet pull in his chest. Kshipra looks at him with a smile and in that brief moment their eyes meet, he feels as if he'd known her smile; her silences, something in him stirres, not attraction but an unsettling recognition.

Everyone look at both of them as they glance at each other with a slight smile on their face and gleam in their eyes.

For Kshipra, Rajan looked handsome like no one else. He is tall and dark. As she heard he was well educated and highly intelligent which appeared on his face as well.

Arranging snacks on the plate happens in slow motion as Kshipra's eye catches a glance of Rajan from the kitchen window. She notices that Rajan too is trying to peep in to catch a glimpse of her. She feels shy and smiles to herself.

Kshipra serves them tea and snacks with a calm expression but she knows what's going on inside her. Her heartbeat rises as she moves close to hand over a cup of tea to Rajan. Rajan feels her warm vibrations.

Not known to this world, there appears a natural connection between the two. Rajan's staring at her doesn't go unnoticed by all those sitting there.

Days pass to this episode but Kshipra still thinks about Rajan. She feels lost like never before. There is not even a single communication between Kshipra and Rajan but there was a lot which was exchanged. A lot that even both of them were unaware of. Kshipra's soft heart gets fill with love for Rajan day by day as he continue bothering her thoughts. Kshipra is unaware if the feeling is mutual.

Vasanti mentions to Madhukar that Sudha's mother talked about getting Ajay and Sudha engaged and then after Kshipra's marriage they can get married, "they are concerned as all the villagers are now aware of their liking for each other and hence we should consider this option".

Madhukar is not yet in agreement with this and he is adamant that only when Kshipra gets married Ajay's marriage or engagement is possible. Kshipra hears this standing outside the room and feels upset. She wants to go to them and disclose her feelings for Rajan but is not bold enough to do so. She is about to leave while Vasanti still continues "They also suggest if …" Vasanti hesitates to continue and looks at Madhukar. Madhukar knew what was coming next. He looks at Vasanti, both know Kshipra so well and the next suggestion was just to mention and nothing else, "They want us to consider an alliance of Murli and Kshi…."

The words rang in her ears like the thud of heavy

footsteps behind a closed door. Kshipra turns away quietly, but inside, her heart slams against her ribs. She had always feared this being handed over without being asked. But this time, it is worse.

Her soul wasn't silent anymore. Ever since she saw Rajan, something had shifted. He had looked at her as if he knew a version of her the world had forgotten. Maybe she was foolish, maybe it was nothing but something in her soul said wait. And she had no words for that.

Madhukar cuts in between "I don't want anyone's name to be taken with her name. Though they are friends, I know my daughter very well. She doesn't like him that way. Vasanti further mentions "She has to get married to someone and what if she starts liking him once we fix up the alliance? Possible, right?".

Listening to all this Kshipra closes her eyes for she always feared that this may come up some day. She looks at Madhukar from the distance with a slight smile on her face and watery eyes. She always knew her father knew her very well and this talk between her parents marked that yet again.

There develops a strange distance and tension between all these four friends now as there is no response on Kshipra and Murli's alliance from Kshipra's family. Once happy-go-lucky and free birds were now tied to some string that was difficult to untie and it poked too.

Kshipra notices behavioral change in Ajay towards her and this bothers her. She knew Ajay would not like her to marry Murli if she didn't like him.

Ajay spends more time with Sudha whenever he visits for a day or two now. Kshipra accepts this natural process but misses the affection of her brother more than anything else. She thinks to herself that any of her steps should not be a hurdle in Ajay's happiness and though she is not yet mentally prepared for this she decides to put it to Madhukar about her feelings for Rajan to dissolve the pressure of her alliance with Murli.

One evening when Ajay had just left after two day's stay at home, Kshipra comes to Madhukar who is staring at the distant road sitting on his rocker chair. Kshipra sits on the floor and rest her head on Madhukar's lap saying, "You miss Ajay being here with all of us?" Madhukar smiles at her but rather than answering her question he questions back, "What is it, you want to say something? I have been noticing this for few days".

Kshipra takes a sharp and deep breath "I don't like this thought of leaving you all and going to some other house". Madhukar laughs, "But that is how it is, every girl has to marry and go and have her own world". Madhukar puts it to her as he feels appropriate moment now, "What is your opinion on Murli? I don't feel you like him that way but still I want to hear your opinion from you." Kshipra gathers all her courage "If I can leave without you all with someone then that's only Rajan."

Madhukar is shocked to hear that, "Rajan!" he exclaims. How come you have met him only once if I am not wrong? Or is it that …? Kshipra interrupts "No, I have not met him again but I felt the warmth when I saw him that first and last time and felt as if I know him since ages". Madhukar places his hand on her head with an unconvincing smile on his face.

In a corner of the house, Murli hears the name Rajan, spoken in hushed tones. The sound hits him like a slap.

He clenches his fists, staring at the wall, unmoving. She barely knows him. What does he have that I don't?

For the first time, the childhood warmth he carries for Kshipra feels invaded and claimed by a stranger. He paces, unsure whether it's sadness or something darker forming inside him.

This isn't how it was supposed to go.

 It doesn't take much time for all around Kshipra to know what she wants. She has not even spoken with Rajan about this. It's a heart calling a heart. She is not even aware if Rajan also has the same feelings for her.

Vasanti is unhappy with this thought as they all know very little about Rajan.

Murli and Sudha are confused and see no reason why Kshipra opts for this.

The only person standing behind Kshira is Ajay and his opinion is clear, Kshipra likes Rajan and that is all that matters to him.

A week later, Madhukar visits Rajan's parents. While he returns, it's hot and humid and Madhukar looks very tired. He rests on his easy chair and sipping water looks at Kshipra saying "Your Rajan is very humble and caring" Kshipra smiles and looking down warns her heartbeat to calm down and not allow everyone to know how it feels to hear 'your Rajan' from her father.

Dates are finalized and willingly or unwillingly all are engaged in the preparations. Murli still wants to talk to Kshipra one last time expressing how all this is difficult for him. Kshipra too understands that there has to be a proper closure for this awkwardness that developed between them, before her marriage.

It's a mehendi day but still Kshipra manages to convey it to Murli to meet her at the river bank, which used to be four friend's regular gateway.

She reaches there and Murli is already waiting. Kshipra looks at him from behind. He sometimes just fiddles with the mud, picking tiny stones and throwing them into the river.

As Kshipra walks towards him, she recollects those days when the four of them used to be in this same place and this place used to fill with the laughs and giggles, playful arguments and all unrestrained joy that made those moments unforgettable.

They would pick up tiny stones and throw at an angle to hit the surface of the water so that it bounces and bounces and bounces many times before it sinks. Neither Kshipra nor Ajay or Sudha could achieve this, every time Murli's throw used to be perfect, and then they would jump and shout.

Kshipra is still witnessing Murli's perfect bounces till Murli's first ever miss brings her abruptly back to the present. Kshipra stands beside Murli and he is not happy that she witnessed this sink.

He sighs and looks at her feet not raising his head to look at her he murmurs "You saw? My stone sink before first bounce, it won't bounce again ever". She sits beside him and looking into his eyes she says "When all the conditions are favorable it will bounce as always". He smiles but his eyes don't, he looks at Kshipra and utters "I thought everything was favorable and it won't sink ever".

Kshipra responds "You are my best friend and you will be one always. I treasure your friendship and will always be your friend". Murli continues to look at her with filled eyes and moves his right hand towards hers. She too holds his hand but that slight hesitation now which never appeared before is quite evitable to both of them.

Murli recollects how they wandered all around holding hands without any hesitation. Unlike the stronghold back then this hold is so light that it is almost ready to separate, he feels.

Fearing the separation he holds her hand tight, she makes an attempt to take her hand back, but he holds still tight. She looks at him with an unuttered question mark on her face. Slowing swiping his thumb over her hand he takes a deep breath and says "Why this hesitation then?" She tries to pull her hand but he is not willing to leave. As tears roll down her cheeks, Murli leaves her hand with a jerk.

Kshipra cries as she feels that nothing is the same between them as before, it can't be. She feels the difference and so does Murli. They sit there for a long time without uttering anything. Both realize somewhere that the thread of friendship has lost its tie, unraveling slowly as distance and silence have loosened the bonds that once held it strong!

Both still hold the ends but the string may not produce

a sweet tune of friendship anymore.

Murli believed that Kshipra had always known how he felt, convinced that his emotions were clear to her all along. Kshipra, on the other hand, was certain that she had never felt anything of the sort, convinced that their connection was purely platonic.

In reality, both were right in their own way, yet neither understood that the threads of destiny were woven in ways they could not control or foresee.

Kshipra lies on her bed while this was her last night at her house where she had grown from a tiny little girl to a young lady. All these years, many episodes roll under her closed eyelids. The moon peeping in from her room window witnesses her face with a smile sometimes, and sometimes a calm teardrop. In between she recollects many mischievous episodes with Ajay.

Memory rolls and young Kshipra runs behind Ajay and she is not able to catch him. From the kitchen to all the bedrooms to Verandahh and to the Verandahh of Sudha's house and to their room where Murli and Sudha start cheering them leaving behind their studies and again out in their verandah where now Sudha and Murli also follow them. The entire atmosphere is filled with their giggles and suddenly Kshipra manages to hold Ajay's shirt from behind, all his shirt buttons break and the shirt comes down both his shoulders and then there is complete silence as by now they are in the middle of the road and apart from them there are many on goers witnessing this and everyone starts laughing, while Ajay starts crying trying to cover himself.

Kshipra doesn't realize when she too starts laughing loudly lying on her bed. Her eyes are still closed and Ajay shakes her to bring her to the present moment.

She opens her eyes and looks at him with that pleasant smile on his face he asks "What happened?" she smiles and just nods and hugs him. He knows the reason, that night Kshipra holds his hand throughout the night and he manages to lie down somehow without disturbing her. He too carries the same sentiments and his eyes, and his heart is filled with all the love and care she gave him for all these years and beyond.

While they were small and shared the same bed Ajay used to hold her hand and unless his cheek didn't feel the warmth of her palm he would not fall asleep.

Kshipra's wedding witness happy, sad, and angry emotions. She is not willing to leave Ajay while seeing off. Her last look is at Murli who stands with a blank face. She still wants to make him understand that she looks at him as a close childhood friend and that he should not forget this.

But for Murli, he looked at their relationship much beyond a friendship so, at this moment he feels dejected.That night, Murli sits alone by the old neem tree. He presses his palm to the earth, as if trying to ground himself. He remembers the days Kshipra would sit beside him, their laughter filling the air. Now, even the silence feels like a betrayal.

He doesn't cry. He doesn't speak. But something inside him begins to hollow. It's not the pain of lost love, rather it's the ache of being unseen, of being erased from a world he build.

The Embrace

Kshipra starts her new life.

Her family is small and it doesn't take much time for her to develop a good bond with her mother-in-law, Madhu who supports her while she continues working with farmers.

Madhukar sees his dreams and wishes coming true with Kshipra working with passion even after marriage.

Kshipra would do all her household work and go to the farms. Compared to her parent's farm, here it's not seasonal multiple crops, rather they have teakwood all over, and more than working on farming it's more of managing the estate. Kshipra misses the feel of the soil but that doesn't stop her from exceeding in her skills.

She works hard as always and Rajan and his mother Madhu are really happy about it. Their business grows many folds and Kshipra gets really busy. Madhu is proud of her but doesn't forget to remind her about her duty towards her marriage.

The sun filters through the tall trees of the teakwood estate, casting dappled light on the land below. A gentle breeze stirs the leaves, and the soft sound of workers tending to the trees hums in the background. Rajan sits on a rocking chair, his gaze focused on the estate. Madhu stands nearby, wiping her hands on her apron after finishing some chores.

Kshipra walks up to them, holding a small bundle of seeds in her hand. Her face is bright with excitement.

"I've been thinking," she says, her voice is full of energy. "I want to grow something small, like the crops I used to have back home. Just a little patch of land, nothing big but enough to remind me of the farm I grew up on."

Rajan looks at the seeds in her hand and then shifts his gaze to the vast teak forest surrounding them. He doesn't seem convinced.

"I don't know, Kshipra," he says, frowning. "This estate is for teakwood, not regular crops. If you start planting, it could interfere with the trees. We can't risk that."

Kshipra's excitement falters, but she doesn't give up. "It won't interfere. It'll only be a small patch, near the edge. We can plant simple things vegetables, grains. It'll be good for the soil, and I promise I'll take care of it."

Madhu, who has been listening quietly, steps forward and places a hand gently on Rajan's shoulder. Her voice is calm but firm, "Rajan, it's good for the heart to be connected to the things you always loved. A small patch of crops could make Kshipra happy. We can make sure it doesn't affect the teak trees."

Rajan hesitates, looking at his mother, then back at Kshipra. "But we've worked so hard for this estate. I don't want to risk anything. Your contribution has increased the work and now if you get diverted then this work will suffer"

Madhu's expression softens. "It's not just that Rajan, Kshipra needs something that reminds her of home. We've always managed the land well. A small farm won't change that."

Rajan looks at Kshipra, her face hopeful, and sighs. After a long pause, he relents, though still a bit unsure.

"Alright, but it has to stay small, Kshipra. And you can't take up too much of the land. I don't want to see you working too hard either."

Kshipra's eyes light up and a wide smile spread across her face. "Thank you, Rajan! It means a lot and I promise I won't take up much space or time either."

Madhu chuckles giving Rajan a knowing smile, "See? That wasn't so hard."

Rajan shakes his head with a soft laugh, "Fine, but you both make sure it doesn't interfere current work."

Kshipra grins, "Deal!"

The three of them share a laugh, the tension easing as they stand together, a quiet sense of understanding settling between them.

Kshipra wakes up before dawn, as she always does. The house is still wrapped in a quiet, peaceful silence, and the early morning light softly fills the room. She gently gets out of bed, careful not to disturb Rajan, who is still sleeping soundly beside her. Her fingers touch the smooth fabric of her sari adjusting the pleats as she does every morning. The gentle movement of her pallu slipping behind her right shoulder is automatic, a comforting habit that feels like a quiet anchor to her day.

As she steps out of the bedroom and walks down the hallway, she hears the faint sound of the kettle boiling in the kitchen. She knows that Madhu is already up. Kshipra enters the kitchen, finding Madhu standing by the stove, preparing tea. "Good morning, Ma," Kshipra greets her softly.

Madhu looks up with a smile, her face lighting up as she sees Kshipra "Good morning, my dear. You're up early again."

"I've always been an early riser," Kshipra replies, sitting down at the table. "I thought I'd join you for tea before Rajan wakes up."
Madhu nods approvingly "It's nice to have the quiet early mornings, isn't it? There's something peaceful about the stillness before the day begins." She pours the tea into two cups, handing one to Kshipra. "You have got used to life here, I see." Kshipra nods with a smile, taking the cup from her "It's a big change, but I'm glad to be here."

They sit in silence for a few moments, savoring the warmth of the tea and the stillness of the morning. The sounds of the workers beginning their day in the fields float in from outside reminding Kshipra of the responsibility that lies ahead. Madhu speaks again, her voice thoughtful "Rajan's always been a hardworking man. He's built this place with his own hands. His father did the same before him.

Kshipra looks up from her cup, intrigued. "I've noticed that about him," she says. "He doesn't talk much about the estate, but I can see how much he cares for it and for the people who work here."

Madhu nods. "He does and now, with you by his side, I think he's even more determined to make this place thrive. You're a good match for him, Kshipra. I can see it in the way you work together. You're more than just his wife; you're his real partner."

The words settle in Kshipra's heart, warming her. She had never imagined herself in this role, but with every passing day, she feels more connected to Rajan, to this estate and to Madhu, of all.

Later in the morning, Rajan comes into the kitchen, looking as though he's been busy in the fields already. His shirt is slightly damp from the heat, but his smile brightens the room as soon as he sees Kshipra.

"Good morning," he says, walking over to kiss her forehead. "Did you sleep well?" Kshipra looks up at him,   smiling warmly. "Yes, just fine. I was up early, though, helping Ma with breakfast."

"Good," Rajan replies, his voice is filled with quiet affection. He glances at his mother then back to Kshipra, "I'm glad you're here. It feels like everything is just right."

Kshipra smiles, feeling a swell of gratitude for the life they are building together. It's been less than a year since their marriage, but already, everything feels natural like they've known each other for much longer.

Later that day, Kshipra walks through the fields with Rajan. The sun is high in the sky, casting long shadows across the earth. She admires the way the crops sway in the wind, the vibrant green of the land stretching out before her. There's a peace here, in the rhythm of the earth, and she finds herself lost in the quiet beauty of it.

As they walk, Kshipra offers her ideas for improvements to the irrigation system saying, "that will improve timber quality". Rajan listens carefully nodding in approval. He seems to values her input, even on matters that might seem trivial to others.

"Let's do it," Rajan says his voice firm with conviction. "I trust you. You know the land well."

Kshipra feels a rush of warmth at his words. They're a team, and with every passing day, their bond grows stronger. As they walk back to the house, Rajan takes her hand in his, his grip feels firm yet gentle."You've changed everything for me, Kshipra," he says softly in the best way possible."

Kshipra squeezes his hand, her heart filled with love. "I feel the same way, Rajan. You've made me feel at home here, more than I ever thought possible."

One evening, Kshipra prepares dinner. Rajan has always loved her cooking, but tonight, she's making something special, his favorite fish curry. The scent of the spices fills the kitchen, and Kshipra can't help but smile as she remembers how her mother used to cook this same dish when she was younger. The act of preparing it brings her comfort, as if her mother's presence is with her in the kitchen.

Rajan walks in as she's stirring the pot, and a smile spreads across his face. "It smells amazing Kshipra," he says, leaning in to steal a taste from the spoon. "I can never get enough of this." Kshipra grins. "You're lucky I enjoy making it for you", and they both laugh.

He watches her for a moment with a soft gaze, "I'm the luckiest man in the world," he says, his voice sounds sincere. "Not just for your cooking, but for everything you've brought into our life."
They sit down to eat together, the fish curry tastes delicious and comforting. As they eat, Rajan reaches across the table and takes her hand, his fingers brushing against hers. "You're not just my wife," he says, his voice full of emotion. "You're my partner Kshipra, in everything and always remember this."

Kshipra feels the weight of his words settle in her heart.

"I'll always be here for you, Rajan," she repeats softly "always."

As time passes, Kshipra and Rajan's bond deepens. They work together on the estate, facing challenges and celebrating victories. They argue occasionally, but even in those moments, their respect for each other remains unshaken.

The days blend together, each one similar but unique in its own way. The mornings are always filled with purpose.

Kshipra has her own set of ideas, and Rajan respects that, letting her take charge in areas where her knowledge and passion shine. Their teamwork is effortless, but it's more than just shared work. It's a connection, an unspoken understanding that has formed between them.

As the months pass, the bond between Kshipra and Rajan grows even stronger. There are moments when they laugh together for no reason, when their eyes meet across a crowded room and they exchange a glance that speaks volumes. Their intimacy isn't just about physical closeness; it's the way they communicate, the way they've learned to understand each other without words. Madhu witnesses every bit and feels pride of both of them.

While Murli is unaware of how his love and care for Kshipra gradually reshapes to hatred and jealousy. It didn't happen overnight though. He feels the poking pain of losing her every moment, for days together he would just lie down on his bed covering his face, and all that love for her flows down through his tears for months together.

Sudha feels helpless to console him as she witnesses her brother in deep sorrow day in and day out and blames Kshipra for his condition, her anger over Kshipra burns on high flame with each moment of Murli's suffering. Just like a blacksmith airs the heat and molds the iron, Murli's weeping airs the anger in Sudha and molds it into a hatred asking for revenge.

Unaware of these seed of revenge, Kshipra is lost in her new life.

The sun rises gently over the fields. Kshipra is already out, her pallu tied firmly around her head, walking between the rows of her crops with a quiet purpose. The soil is damp underfoot, freshly mulched with compost she prepared over weeks. Neem extract sprays hang in the air, sharp and earthy. She kneels beside a tomato plant, inspecting the leaves for signs of disease, her fingers practiced and sure.

At the edge of her field a small group gather, three men and a woman from the neighboring village. They linger at first, hesitant, until she notices them and waves them over.

"You've used mustard cake this time?" one of the men asks, crouching beside her.

Kshipra nods "mixed it with cow dung and jiggery and fermented for a week. The roots take it well and the result is stronger plants, fewer pests."

They listen, ask questions, and soon begin taking notes on torn pages of old school notebooks. This has become a rhythm now. Visits like these, discussions under the neem tree, ideas exchanged over steel tumblers of buttermilk.

Later in the day, she gathers them in the courtyard and draws simple diagrams in the dirt; crop rotation cycles, water-saving trenches, natural pest repellents. The group expands each week; more curious faces, more quiet nods of understanding.

And so, an idea takes root. Kshipra proposes they form a small group. They'll help each other on sowing days, share seeds, test new methods across different soils. Each season, they'll track their yields and compare notes.

There's no formal name yet, just hands clasped together in agreement and laughter that comes easier with shared purpose.

In that moment, as she watches them head back with jute bags slung over shoulders, Kshipra feels something shift. The land gives more when worked with together hands. And she, she is no longer farming just for herself.

Over time, Kshipra find a steady rhythm in her life. Her

days are a blend of hard work on the estate and the satisfaction of watching Rajan's operations slowly expand.

Rajan needs frequent travel for liquidating more wood. At times it leaves Kshipra over-burdened managing the estates, her fields and house hold all alone.

One afternoon, Kshipra is out in the fields, overseeing her latest crop planting. The work is physically demanding, and the pressure to keep everything running smoothly weighs heavily on her shoulders. She checks on the workers, makes sure everything is on track, but inside, the responsibility feels overwhelming.

When she returns back home, the exhaustion is clear on her face. Madhu is in the kitchen, stirring a pot of tea, her movements slow and deliberate as though she's already sensed Kshipra's weariness.

Kshipra pauses at the door, unsure whether to go in or retreat to her room. But Madhu, without turning around, speaks quietly, "You look tired, beta. Come, sit down. I'll bring you some tea."

Kshipra sighs softly, the tension in her shoulders easing a little. She walks into the kitchen and sits at the table. Madhu brings her a steaming cup, setting it in front of her.

"Rajan is pushing the boundaries a bit more, isn't he?" Madhu asks, settling down across from her.

Kshipra nods, taking a slow sip of the tea and just passes a tiny smile "I want to do this, but sometimes it feels like too much. The land, the workers, the plants, the farms... it all feels so heavy some days."

Madhu watches her carefully, with a kind gaze "It's a lot for one person to carry," she says, her voice low but steady. "But you don't have to carry it alone, Kshipra. Rajan may be driving the business forward, but you have built a foundation strong. And don't forget, I'm here for you."

In that moment, Kshipra feels a deep sense of gratitude. She may have a mountain of responsibilities to carry, but with Madhu by her side, she doesn't feel as if she's carrying it alone.

Invisible cracks

Lately, she has started noticing a pattern; whenever she talks about her farms Rajan never seems entirely supportive. He listens, but there's always hesitation, an invisible wall between them. She knows that he is not happy about her opting to develop a farm and that he doesn't say it openly as Madhu is been supportive about it.

While at the dinner time, Kshipra clears her throat softly and speaks, keeping her voice light. "There's a summer exhibition and many variety of crops, seeds will be displayed, I want to join. It's just for two days." She pauses, watching Rajan and continuing "It's at Gandhinagar" It requires overnight journey."

Rajan stops mid-motion, his hand hovering over his plate. His face remains unreadable but Kshipra notices the slight tightening of his jaw. He isn't convinced.

Madhu picks up on the tension, looks between them. She tilts her head slightly before speaking, "that's not a problem at all. I am here. I'll take care of everything." She turns to Rajan, as if expecting him to drop his resistance, "for two days we can manage, just fine."

Encouraged, Kshipra adds, "I've been waiting for this oppourtunity for so long. Last time, I missed it but this time, I really want to go."

Rajan exhales, his fingers tapping lightly against the

table. His expression doesn't soften. She knows he doesn't like the idea, but he has no strong reason to object either.

Finally, without looking up, he mutters, "We'll see."

Madhu doesn't give him the chance to backtrack. She turns to Kshipra with a reassuring smile. "That settles it then. You can go, dear. We'll manage here just fine."

Kshipra feels a small wave of relief wash over her. Rajan hasn't said yes but more importantly, he hasn't said no. That, for now is enough.

Kshipra thoroughly enjoys the exhibition. She goes crazy looking at the varieties she picks many different seeds and saplings, visits stalls providing different irrigation alternatives as well. But that is not all, there are several bankers providing funds for farmers as well. This is new information for Kshipra.

It's an overnight journey back home for her. She boards the bus, feeling utterly drained. As the vehicle rattles through the dark, fatigue overtakes her. But soon, she realizes something is wrong; her body burns with fever, every joint aching with a dull, relentless throb. She passes the night in pain, curled against the window, shivering in silence.

By early morning, the bus pulls into the station. Kshipra gets down, her limbs trembling, head spinning. With great effort, she drags herself out of the terminal. She recollects Madhu mentioning that Rajan would pick her up and that she had carefully mentioned the date and time of her arrival, before leaving. In her mind, she had pictured him waiting. But there is no one.

She stands for a while, trying to steady herself, eyes scanning the nearly empty platform. A few sleepy-eyed rickshaw pullers linger in the soft light of dawn.

The air is already warm, but to her fevered skin it feels harsh and unwelcoming. Time stretches. People move past her but no one moves toward her.

It strikes her slowly that she is someone no one has waited for.

She wipes her brow, her hand trembling, and begins the slow walk to the nearby horse cart stand. Her bag drags behind her. Her steps are unsteady, each one pulled from a body that wants to collapse. She hires a tonga and gives the driver her address.

By the time she reaches home, her clothes cling with sweat and weariness. She knocks then leans against the doorframe barely able to hold herself upright. Minutes crawl by before the door creaks open.

Rajan appears, hair tousled, face groggy with sleep. He doesn't even look at her. He simply opens the door and turns away, walking back inside without a word.

She stares at his retreating figure. Her lips part, but she can't summon a voice. The doorway feels colder than the road outside. She steps in slowly, quietly, feeling like someone who doesn't quite belong.

Rajan's behavior becomes more rude, as the days pass.

This is not hidden from Madhu as slowly it becomes very casual in everyday routine and Madhu is not at all happy with this. Several times she notices Kshipra sobbing quietly and Madhu fails to understand the growing distance between them. She does not want to step in between both yet but fails to understand the change.

Madhu sits in her living room, thinking about how tired Kshipra and Rajan look. The charm in their relation looks lost some how. They are always busy with work and never have time for themselves, she feels. Madhu knows that they need a break. She wants to find a way for them to spend some time together without the pressure of work.

Rajan walks into the courtyard holding a clay cup. "You haven't watered these roses in two days," he says, crouching beside the plant.

Kshipra kneels next to him, brushing soil from her fingers. "I wanted to see if you'd notice."

He glances sideways, amused. "I always notice. You just never ask."

She smiles then lowers her gaze. "Some things are easier when you don't expect answers."

For a brief moment, the air between them stills; not out of discomfort, but recognition and a silent acknowledgement that something unspoken had been blooming just like the neglected roses between them.

Just then a postman arrives with a letter. Madhu opens it and sees a marriage invitation. She smiles to herself, excited about the opportunity it gives her.

Madhu calls Rajan and Kshipra into the living room. "Look, I have an idea," she says. "There is a wedding coming up, and it would be great if both of you go and enjoy some time together, I am unwell so I can't join."

Rajan looks at Kshipra and then at Madhu. "But, Ma," he says, "You're not feeling well. I can't leave you alone."

Madhu shakes her head. "Don't worry about me," she says softly. "I will stay at home and rest. You both need to go and have fun. It's important for you to relax."

Kshipra looks concerned. "But Ma, are you sure? You need rest. I can stay with you." Madhu smiles gently. "No, Kshipra I am fine. You and Rajan go. It's important that you spend time together."

Rajan still isn't sure. "I don't like leaving you alone when you're unwell, Ma." Madhu sighs, trying to be patient. "Rajan, I promise I'll be okay. You can go and enjoy the wedding. I'll take care of myself. Please don't argue. It's a small break for both of you and I can manage for 3-4days"

After a long pause Rajan finally agrees "Okay Ma, We will go. But we will come back as soon as possible."

Kshipra smiles and hugs Madhu. "We will go for you, but take care of yourself, but when is the wedding?"
Madhu pats on her forehead "Oh, look at me I didn't see the date myself" and she continues looking at the invitation followed by calendar hanging on the wall "its on 7th of this month, it's next Sunday. You both can leave on Thursday then you will be able to attend all the functions".

Rajan interrupts "No, we will leave on Saturday just for the wedding". Madhu again argues and they continue for next 10mins while Kshipra just watch them looking forward to some settlement. Madhu is determined and she seals the argument saying "You are leaving on Thursday and that is it."

As they leave Madhu settles down, feeling content and ready for some quiet time at home. Madhu wished their bond would strengthen again, but little did she know, that the destiny serves the script and we are not authorized to draft it what-so-ever.

As expected by Madhu, this plan doesn't serve any

purpose. On the contrary she notices more distance between both and this bothers her all the more. Days pass.

Madhu's cousin brother's daughter Preeti visits them for a job interview and gets selected. Madhu insists that she stays with them as it is not feasible to travel for 2 hours or more to reach her office and another 2 to come back.

Kshipra doesn't respond to this but Madhu notices unconvinced expressions on her face which she fails to understand as it doesn't suit Kshipra's helpful nature.

Madhu makes it a point to check up with her. While winding up in the kitchen that night Madhu touches on that topic "Kshipra is it ok if Preeti stays here? She looks at Kshipra's face as she does not just want to hear her reply but also wants to see her expression on this. Kshipra quietly nods "Ya, its fine Ma".

Madhu holds her hand and turns her to have a face-to-face conversation "What's the matter, you don't want her to stay with us?" Kshipra is not willing to express herself at all and just says "No, it's ok" After some pursuing Kshipra opens up.

"Did you proposed Rajan marry her?" Madhu laughs "Oh that is bothering you?" But both had denied the proposal for their reasons. Don't worry about that Preeti is not of Rajan's type. You know how she is outspoken and ambitious.

Kshipra instantly reacts "But, even I am ambitious Ma.

Maybe that is the reason Rajan is …" She holds back. But Madhu catches it "What? Rajan is what? Is there some issue between both of you? Kshipra feels sorry for expressing which actually just came out without intention. Madhu knows all but never had a talk with either of them on this topic. She pulls Khspira and takes her to the living room.

Lights are off and just a little bit of street light is pepping from the half-open window and a flowing curtain. Kshipra's eyelids close as she doesn't want her emotions to be displayed in front of Madhu but tears break the barrier as if they are determined to express today.

Kshipra sits quietly, her hands folded neatly in her lap as she leans toward Madhu, her voice soft, almost hesitant at first. The room feels heavy, the air thick with the unspoken tension. But her eyes; sharp and clear betray the weight of what she is about to reveal.

"Ma," Kshipra almost whisper, "there is something i didn't want to tell you. It's about Rajan and Preeti, something that happened a few months ago, while you sent us for that wedding."

She pauses, taking a deep breath as the memory rushes back, a shadow looming in her mind. Madhu doesn't say anything but watches her closely, sensing the seriousness of her tone. Kshipra gathers herself, knowing this won't be easy.

"It's just when the ceremony was winding up", Kshipra

continues, her fingers nervously tracing the edge of her sari. "I was talking to some relatives, you know, like we always do at these family gatherings. And then, I spot Rajan and Preeti in a corner, almost hidden from view."

Kshipra's voice falters for a moment, but she presses on. "At first, I think nothing of it. But then something doesn't sit right. They're standing so close, too close for cousins. Rajan has his hand on Preeti's arm, and she's leaning in, saying something to him. I can see her face so focused, like she's hanging onto his every word. And Rajan... he's laughing, but it's not like his usual laugh. His eyes... they're different, Ma, almost too interested."

She looks down for a second, the memory swirling in her mind. "I stand there for a moment, watching, trying to make sense of it. It's not just a casual conversation. It feels... intimate. They're whispering to each other, their heads close, but I can't hear what they're saying. The whole world around them seems to vanish. It's like nothing else matters except them."

Kshipra's voice shakes as she speaks the next words. "I didn't say anything right then. I couldn't bring myself to. But I knew... I knew something was wrong. And now, I can't stop thinking about it. I just don't know what to make of it anymore."

Kshipra looks at Madhu, her eyes searching for understanding, for guidance. The silence in the room is deafening, the weight of her words hanging between them, demanding attention.

Madhu is shocked to hear this, her eyes fill with tears and anger when Kshipra further mentions "Rajan is not aware that I witnessed this but Preeti, she hugged him tightly when she noticed me and looked at me as though she wanted to make her point that he belonged to her".

Kshipra's voice sounds suffocating. She rests herself on the chair behind her. Madhu bends down and sitting on her knees holds Kshipra's hands tight and the grip gets more intense as her anger rolls down her cheeks.

"He was only thirteen when his father died." She stares out into the distance. "It was a Sunday. He had gone early to the lower patch, you know the one just past the bend? He loved the land. Loved the smell of wet earth, the way it comes alive after rain."

She closes her eyes for a moment. "There was a loose stone on that slope. He slipped, hit his head. It was quick, far too quick."

Kshipra instinctively reaches out, placing her hand over Madhu's.

"After that," Madhu continues, her voice thinning with memory, "everything changed. It was just me and Rajan. And I wasn't allowed to fall apart, not for long. He wouldn't let me. He said the land needed us, said my crying wouldn't sow seeds."

Her eyes glisten, but she doesn't blink them away. "He was a child, but he carried himself like someone far older. He walked miles for seeds, lifted baskets bigger than him and studied through all of it. His evenings were with soil on his hands and books in his lap."

Madhu lets out a breath, "My brother, Priti's father and Priti were our lifelines then. They visited often. They were family already. And as Rajan and Priti grew, we began to think... perhaps they were meant for each other."

Kshipra listens, not speaking.

"But then," Madhu says, her voice softening, "but then they went to college, found their own skies. Their paths shifted and when I finally asked them, both of them, they said no; politely but firmly." A rueful smile touches her lips then fades.

Madhu looks at Kshipra again. "You must do what your heart tells you."

Kshipra swallows hard, emotion coiled in her chest. She doesn't yet know what to say. But in this moment, it is enough that they sit here together, two women tethered to the same wound in different ways, trying to understand what love, duty, and loss have made of the man they both care for.

Kshipra convinces her, not to confront Rajan unless she witnesses any such episode herself.

Madhu feels hurt and shameful in front of Kshipra for

his son's wrongdoing. Her eyes express so but Kshipra holds both her hands, holding her chin raising her face up expressing without saying a word that she should not feel guilty for Rajan's behavior.

With anger and tears-filled eyes, Madhu utters "If you wish to call off this marriage, you can do so and I assure you that no one will ask you any questions or try to stop you from taking this decision, I promise".

Kshipra responds by saying "no Ma that would be an easy option for me and him as well. He is supposed to be committed to me and he will".

Kshipra gets up and heads to her room, while Madhu takes the same chair. She sits there for long closing her eyes and letting her emotions flow. Her son cheating on his wife is not only difficult to accept but also difficult to understand for her. She recollects how as a kid he would take care of his tiny belongings and not allow anyone to touch his toys but now what was he doing with his wife? Not only hurting her but also allowing somebody else to hurt as well.

Once, Kshipra and Rajan were the perfect picture of a happy, jolly couple. Their laughter would fill the house, and dinner time was always a warm, shared ritual. They'd talk about their day, joke, and tease each other playfully. But now, things are different. The warmth in their home seems to have disappeared, replaced by a suffocating quietness that lingers, especially at dinner.

Most evenings, Rajan sits at the dinner table alone, his plate in front of him and hand moving through the food mechanically, like he's simply completing a task. There's no joy, no conversation. It's as if the ritual of eating has become a mere formality for him, a routine he has to follow, but with none of the enthusiasm or connection that once accompanied it. His eyes seem distant, lost somewhere beyond the food, as if his mind is elsewhere, and his silence only deepens the distance between him and Kshipra.

Kshipra too, has changed. The woman who used to talk animatedly about her day, who once filled the room with her energy, now finds herself staring blankly at her plate. Her appetite has waned, and her thoughts are consumed with the same troubling questions that haunt her at night. She feels the weight of the silence but doesn't know how to break it, especially with Rajan retreating further into himself. The dinners, once a place of connection, has become a reminder of the growing divide between them.

Kshipra feels Madhu's eyes on her. She senses her mother-in-law is noticing the change in her mood, even if nothing is said.

Madhu knows Kshipra well enough to recognize the silent struggle within her daughter-in-law. Kshipra's eyes are no longer as bright and her shoulders slightly slumped in a way that speaks volumes.

One evening, everything shifts all the more.

Rajan returns late from the town market, unusually quiet. Kshipra serves dinner, trying to read his expression, but he doesn't meet her eyes. After a few minutes of tense silence, he finally speaks.

"Tell me something, Kshipra," he says, setting down his glass. "Was there ever anything between you and Murli?"

Kshipra freezes. Her fingers tighten around the edge of her saree. "What are you saying?"

Rajan's voice rises, laced with frustration. "I saw the way he looked at you, even during our wedding. I remember him pulling me aside saying, she deserves happiness. Hope you give her what she needs. What was that supposed to mean?"

Kshipra's chest tightens. "Murli and I are childhood friends. That's it."

Rajan's eyes are sharp. "Then why did he say it like it was a warning?"

Kshipra feels heat rise in her face; anger, sadness, confusion, "maybe because he never understood boundaries. But don't put this on me, Rajan. If you trusted me, you wouldn't be asking this."

He doesn't reply. Instead, he gets up and walks out into the night air, leaving Kshipra standing alone in the kitchen, heart pounding.

Several questions arise. What did Murli say to him? Did he plant this seed of doubt? And why would Rajan believe it? Of all, why this now?

Her thoughts swirl until exhaustion finally takes over, but the seed of mistrust has been sown. Not doubt of love, but of how fragile love can be in the shadow of someone else's unresolved story.

Kshipra's thoughts connect this episode to the fact that Preeti didn't eventually stayed with them as proposed by Madhu. She feels this is what bothered Rajan. This thought disturbs her all the more.

Kshipra recollects all the happy moments with Rajan and questions herself, "was this thing always in his mind?"

Madhu can feel the unease in the air, the tension that has settled over the family. But it's not just Kshipra's distress that concerns her. The change in Rajan's behavior is just as unsettling. Where once he was warm and engaging, he now feels like a shadow of the man he used to be. His silence, his withdrawal, and his coldness are all things Madhu can't ignore.

Madhu understands Kshipra's congestion but she too feels a growing sense of helplessness. Both of them are caught in a strange, uncomfortable limbo, and neither seems capable of reaching out to the other. It's as if they're all waiting for something to change, but no one knows how or if it ever will. Somehow Madhu is sure that it's not only about Preeti, but something else as well, she definitely has the urge to understand that.

Madhu advises Kshipra to visit her parents place for a few days to help her feel more relaxed and at ease. Kshipra listens to the advice and resolves to plan a week-long visit to her parent's home.

Drifting Hearts

Kshipra's heart feels a mixture of relief and hesitation as she steps off the bus and walks toward her childhood home. The familiar sights and sounds of the street tug at her, offering a sense of comfort that she hasn't felt in weeks. She breathes in deeply, the air as she approaches the front gate.

Before she can even reach the door, she hears the familiar sound of footsteps from inside quick and eager. The door swings open, and there stands her mother Vasanti, with that unmistakable smile that Kshipra has missed more than she realizes. Vasanti's face lights up and eyes soften with warmth as she takes in her daughter.

"Kshipra, you're home!" Vasanti exclaims, her voice is full of the comforting affection Kshipra has been craving for. She steps forward, pulling Kshipra into a tight embrace, the kind that only a mother can offer. For a moment, Kshipra allows herself to melt into her mother's arms, feeling the weight of the world momentarily lift. It's a simple gesture, but it fills her with warmth she didn't know she needed.

Behind them, Kshipra hears her father Madhukar, shuffling into view, his glasses perched on the edge of his nose as he looks up from a book he had been reading. When his eyes land on Kshipra, his face breaks into a wide grin, the kind that has always made her feel like the center of his world.

"There she is, our Kshipra!" Madhukar says, his voice is filled with joy. His arms open wide, and without a second thought, Kshipra steps into his embrace, the sense of being cherished wrapping around her like a soft and soothing blanket.

"Look at you," he adds with a teasing tone, pulling back just enough to examine her face. "You've been working too hard. You've lost weight! And why didn't you inform about that you are coming. You must be taking care of yourself, huh?" He says it lightheartedly, but there's a deep tenderness behind his words, an unspoken concern that she hasn't fully let go of.

Kshipra smiles faintly, her exhaustion is visible now that she's home. But she doesn't mind. There's something about their presence that instantly puts her at ease, as though the outside world her troubled marriage, the silence between her and Rajan has faded into the background. Here, in her parent's home, she feels like herself again, even if it's just for a moment.

Vasanti holds her at arm's length, looking her over with affectionate scrutiny. "You're too thin dear. You need to rest and relax. Home should feel like home, after all."

Her voice is soothing and it calms the swirling unrest inside Kshipra. There's simplicity here, a steadiness in her parent's love that makes everything else seem just a little bit easier to bear.

As they guide her inside, Kshipra can't help but feel the tension she's been holding in her shoulders ease. Her parents' presence is a reminder that, no matter how complicated her life may be right now, there is always a place where she can be cared for, a place where she's still someone's little girl. And for tonight, that's enough. Her eyes search for Ajay though may not be at home at, she knows. Realizing what Kshipra was looking for Vasanti says with a smile "your brother has come yesterday, he must be at farms with Sudha and Murli." She looks at Madhukar, "send someone and inform him that I am here." Madhukar nods and walks out.

It's evening, and Kshipra sits alone in the corner of the verandah, her body relaxed yet her mind heavy. The world outside seems to slow down with the arrival of twilight.

But Kshipra's gaze isn't drawn to the beauty of the fading light; it's fixed elsewhere across the way, towards Murali's house.

She watches absently as the evening unfolds, her thoughts tangled in the mess of her own heart. Then, something shifts. Out of the corner of her eye, she sees Murali, standing on his terrace. His presence is calm and steady, a stark contrast to the whirlwind of emotions Kshipra is experiencing. His eyes meet hers, just for a fleeting moment.

The brief exchange lingers in the air, as if time itself holds its breath. For a moment, Kshipra feels a small, almost imperceptible shift in her chest a soft comfort, like someone acknowledging her existence, her presence, in a way no one else has in a long time. It's a relief, a distraction from the constant whirlpool of worries that cloud her mind, particularly the unspoken tension between her and Rajan. She hasn't realized how much she's missed this feeling the sense that someone sees her, even from afar. A friend's comfort is what she needs of all at this very moment.

But just as quickly as the moment begins, the purity of that connection falters. Memories, painful and recent, seep in clouding the simplicity of what had once been a close friendship. The warmth of their old bond feels distant now, overshadowed by the heaviness of Murli's confession. What had been a quiet, innocent comfort between them is now tainted, burdened by the weight of unspoken feelings and the complexities they've brought into her world. Her heart stirs with the echoes of the past, but it quickly shifts, burdened by what has irrevocably changed. "Kshipra feels like asking Murli where Ajay is, but she resists."

Kshipra's eyes wander, seeking somewhere else to rest, somewhere other than Murali's gaze, as if to shake off the flood of emotions that the brief connection has stirred. The quiet comfort is fleeting, and she finds herself, once again, alone with her thoughts, left to wrestle with the tangled mess of her feelings for Rajan, her uncertain future, and the growing distance between them.

Little did she know, this part of her world too had turned grey.

As dinner time approaches, Kshipra waits nervously for Ajay to return home so they can eat together. She imagines a dinner like the ones they used to have, with Ajay, Kshipra, and their parents all sitting together, just like earlier days. She anticipates, since Murli was back and Sudha was not seen , probably Ajay and Suddha are together but still she expects Ajay to return home early as she was here.

Minutes pass, it grows increasingly late, and Ajay still hasn't returned. Kshipra's anticipation turns to worry and disappointment. The absence of Ajay, combined with her doubt of his detachment, weighs heavily on her, deepening the emotional distance she feels in their relationship. What was meant to be a comforting and familiar dinner now feels unfinished and tense.

Kshipra has dinner with her parents, trying to make the best of the situation despite Ajay's absence. After dinner, Kshipra retreats to her bedroom, overwhelmed by a mix of sadness and frustration.

She lies awake, not very happy about how Ajay is prioritizing others over her. She understands that Ajay might be spending time with his fiancée, but that doesn't lessen the sting of her disappointment. Kshipra had hoped that during her short visit, Ajay would make an effort to spend more time with her, considering she was only there for a few days. This lack of attention from Ajay makes her feel undervalued and neglected, amplifying the emotional distance she has been sensing for sometime. Her mind races with thoughts, and sleep slips away as she struggles with a mix of longing and discontent.

It's not that Ajay wanted to stay away; he was unaware that Sudha was deliberately keeping him from his sister. Sudha harbors resentment because Kshipra, in her view, did not acknowledge her brother's love and married someone else. This perceived slight fuels Sudha's desire for revenge, leading her to keep Ajay occupied and away from Kshipra.

Ajay returns very late that night, while Kshipra is fast asleep. Although exhausted, Kshipra notices when Ajay enters the room, but she holds back, not wanting to make him feel guilty for his late arrival. She remains quietly in bed, pretending to be asleep.

After finishing his dinner, Ajay quietly enters Kshipra's room and sits down beside her bed. He gazes at her face for a long time, holding her hand gently. In this silent moment, it's clear that Ajay too misses his sister deeply. Despite the changes in his life and the distance that has grown between them, his affection for Kshipra remains strong. This silent vigil beside her bed reflects his inner turmoil and the love he still holds for his sister, even though circumstances have changed. Kshipra feels a mix of emotions, comforted by his presence but also saddened by the complexities that now define their relationship.

The next morning, as Ajay wakes up, he is greeted by the enticing fragrance of his favorite foods wafting from the kitchen. He immediately realizes what's happening: Kshipra is cooking all his beloved dishes. Excited and eager to taste the delicious food he jumps out of bed and runs to the kitchen.

Kshipra is there, busy with her preparations, when she sees Ajay running towards her, her face lights up with joy. They share a warm and happy moment, laughing and talking as they enjoy breakfast together. These are the moments Kshipra has been yearning for simple, joyful times with her brother and her parents, a respite from the stress.

The kitchen is filled with the sounds of sizzling food, clinking utensils, and the sibling's laughter. It feels like old times, and for a while, Kshipra's worries melt away. She treasures these moments, feeling a sense of fulfillment and happiness that she hasn't felt in a long time. This is exactly what she hoped to find when she decided to visit her parent's home; a sanctuary where she could reconnect with her family and find solace in their love and companionship.

Just as Ajay and Kshipra are enjoying their happy moments in the kitchen, Sudha drops in. The atmosphere changes immediately as Ajay's body language shifts upon seeing her. Sensing the change, Kshipra decides to give them some space. She mentions that she'll come back in a few minutes and leaves the kitchen, allowing them to continue their conversation.

As Kshipra steps out of the kitchen, the soft click of the door closing behind her lingers in the air. She turns to Ajay, who is still absorbed in stirring the pot on the stove.

"Do you think we should invite Kshipra for dinner tonight?" Sudha asks, her voice is casual but carrying an undercurrent of hope. Ajay pauses, his hand hovering over the ladle as he considers her words. He lowers it slowly, his brow furrowing. "I mean, it's fine to invite her, but.." He hesitates, glancing over at Sudha. "I just don't want either Kshipra or Murali to feel uncomfortable. Things are a little different now, you know?"

Sudha tilts her head slightly, studying him. "I understand your concern, but I'm sure they'll be fine. It's been so long since we've all had a meal together. It'll be nice, just like old times."

Ajay sighs softly, glancing toward the door where Kshipra had disappeared. "I know, but we can't ignore the tension. It's there, whether we acknowledge it or not."

Sudha's expression softens "Ajay, we can't let that stop us from trying to bring the family together again. It's important for everyone, isn't it?. I really think it'll help. Besides, it's just dinner".

Ajay looks at Sudha, his mouth tightening in reluctance. "I suppose you're right," he mutters, finally giving in. "Okay, let's invite her. But we'll keep it casual, no pressure."

Sudha smiles warmly with a spark of satisfaction in her eyes. "I'll go ask her then." She pauses at the door, glancing back at Ajay. "I'm sure it'll be good for everyone, you'll see."

Ajay exhales slowly, his fingers still drumming lightly on the counter. As Sudha is about to leaves the kitchen and Ajay stands lost in thought as part of him is still uncertain, but another part of him feels a quiet sense of hope, as though this small gesture might begin to heal something that had been broken for far too long. Just then Kshipra steps back into the kitchen, her presence sudden and slightly unexpected. She hesitates for a moment in the doorway, her eyes meeting Sudha's.

Sudha is quick to sense an opportunity, smiles warmly, "Kshipra," she begins with an inviting tone, "why don't you come over for dinner tonight? We'd love to have you."

Kshipra's heart skips a beat. The invitation feels almost too kind, but the mention of dinner suddenly makes her stomach twist. The last thing she wants right now is to face Murali, his presence lingering in her thoughts like an unwelcome shadow.

Sudha, not acknowledging the slight tension in Kshipra's stance continues, "It'll be like old times, just a casual meal."

Kshipra's mind races her thoughts a blur of conflicting emotions. She opens her mouth to politely decline but feels a wave of pressure building. Sudha is watching her expectantly, her expression look warm and sincere, and Kshipra doesn't want to disappoint her. She glances at Ajay, who is now at the stove, casually stirring the curry and waiting for her answer.

"I... I don't know, Sudha," Kshipra says, her voice wavers slightly, betraying her discomfort. "It's just that i want to spend time in my room, you see" and Kshipra pauses. Her words hang in the air, her reluctance clear. Sudha, however, misinterprets the pause, mistaking it for hesitation rather than the unease. "Oh, don't worry about a thing. It'll be nice. Just like before," Sudha reassures her, stepping closer, insistent is very clear in her voice.

"Okay... I'll join you for dinner," Kshipra finally says. She forces a smile, though it doesn't quite reach her eyes. "Thanks for the invitation."

In the evening, Kshipra heads to Sudha's place for dinner. Sudha's parents welcome her lovingly, but there's a noticeable tension in the air. Murali tries to act extra friendly and normal, though it's clear to Kshipra that he is not entirely at ease. She too masks her discomfort, trying to be gracious and engage in the conversation.

During dinner, they chat about various topics, reminiscing about their childhood and sharing stories. Despite the underlying tension, the dinner progresses smoothly. Kshipra manages to navigate the awkwardness, maintaining her composure throughout the evening.

After dinner, Kshipra and Ajay return home together. The evening, though strained at times, offered a mix of nostalgia and complex emotions. Kshipra reflects on the evening, appreciating the efforts made by everyone to make her feel welcome.

The next morning at breakfast, Kshipra notices her mother, Vasanthi, looking at her expectantly as she wants Kshipra to convince Ajay to return home and take responsibility of the family business, particularly the fields that Madhukar has built from scratch. Vasanthi hopes, Ajay should work closely with his father, learn the intricacies involved and eventually manage it independently.

Kshipra feels hesitant to approach Ajay about this. Unlike in the past, when she would freely offer her advice, she now finds it challenging due to the changed dynamics between them. Despite her reluctance, she knows she has to fulfill her mother's request. Gathering her courage, she looks at Ajay and starts the conversation.

"So, how is your business going?" she asks.

Ajay replies, "It's good. I'm trying to improve it, though."

Kshipra seizes the moment. "Why don't you come back? We have expanded the fields and purchased more land. It would be great if you could help manage it. "Vasanti backs it saying "how long will you stay away from us, this house need you all the more now."

Ajay, aware that his business isn't doing as well as he hoped, understands the practicality of returning home. Despite trying to project confidence, he realizes there's little choice but to agree. "I'm doing fine with my business, but since you all are insisting, and it might be better for the family, I'll come back. I'll try to wind things up within a month and settle here."

At this point, Kshipra glances at her parents, Madhukar and Vasanthi, and makes another proposal. "Now that Ajay is coming back, I think it's time for him and Sudha to get married."

Ajay's face lights up with happiness at the suggestion. The family agrees, and they decide to talk to Sudha's parents and set a date for the wedding before Kshipra returns to her home. The decision brings a wave of excitement and anticipation, filling the household with a renewed sense of purpose and unity. This moment signifies a positive turn in their family dynamics, promising a brighter future as they come together to support one another.

Kshipra had hoped that during this visit, she might reconnect with Sudha and rekindle their old friendship. However, though Sudha invited Kshipra for a dinner she never made time for their friendship as such, leaving Kshipra to realize that the closeness they once shared had been left behind. For Kshipra she can leave Shobha as a friend with an understanding that while some relationships evolve and grow, others may naturally drift apart. But, Kshipra cannot allow Sudha go away like this when she is going to be Ajay's wife.

As she prepares to leave, Kshipra cherishes the happy moments she shared with her family during this visit and holds onto the hope that time and circumstances might someday bring her and Sudha closer again.

Kshipra stands on the verandah with her luggage, ready to depart. From the windows of their respective rooms, Murali and Sudha watch her, but neither makes a move to come down and see her off. Kshipra had hoped for a farewell from them, especially from Sudha, when she invited Kshipra for dinner and it looked like Sudha wanted things back to normal but it looks otherwise for now..

Ajay, aware of the situation, also feels disappointed that Sudha doesn't come to bid Kshipra farewell, he picks up Kshipra's luggage and prepares to leave.

Kshipra takes a moment to hug Madhukar and Vasanthi. Her mother holds her tightly, tears streaming down her face and cries a bit, overwhelmed by the emotions of parting with her daughter once again. Kshipra comforts her mother, holding back her own tears to stay strong for her.

After these heartfelt goodbyes, Kshipra finally leaves with Ajay, carrying with her a mix of emotions. Sadness for the unspoken words and missed connections, but also gratitude for the moments she did share with her family during her visit.

Kshipra is aware that her mother-in-law, Madhu, must have had a conversation with Rajan about not allowing Preeti to come and stay with them. She isn't sure exactly how Madhu conveyed the message, whether directly or indirectly but she knows that Madhu is a strong and persuasive woman who will insist on what she believes is right. Kshipra is uncertain about Rajan's response to this discussion.

Reaching home after a tiring journey still gives Kshipra a feeling of being relaxed as she unpacks her bags and sets her things right in her room. Kshipra steps out of the bedroom, she finds Madhu waiting with tea and some snacks. They sit down across from each other at the dining table. Kshipra, with a bright smile begins to speak with excitement forgetting all about Preeti. Kshipra knows her mother-in-law has sorted this issue, but how? She is not willing to ask.

"Ma, I am so eager to tell you this!"

Madhu looks up with piqued curiosity and guesses, "Okay, so Ajay is finally getting married, right?"

Kshipra raises her eyebrows, surprised by the guess, "really? You think so?" Madhu laughs and says, "I'm just guessing!"

Both of them chuckle. Kshipra leans in, her eyes shining with enthusiasm. "Ma, yes, he is getting married, and also we've convinced him to come back! And guess what? He's agreed!"
Madhu's face lights up with joy as she knows what this means for Kshipra "Oh, that's amazing! I'm so happy to hear this. I've been looking forward to the wedding! Now, you get to be the big sister and help with all the arrangements and enjoy the celebrations!"

Kshipra nods excitedly. "Yes, I can't wait!"

Madhu, with a loving smile, suggests, "Let's go shopping for the wedding. I'll buy you some new jewelry for the occasion. And I'll also get something nice for Sudha as a gift."

Kshipra smiles warmly, feeling grateful for her mother-in-law's support. "That sounds wonderful, Ma. Thank you so much."

Madhu pats her hand gently "anything for you Kshipra. We'll make this wedding perfect together!"

Madhu asks, "When is the marriage?"

Kshipra replies, "Next month, on the 13th. It's a Sunday."

Madhu nods, noting the date. Kshipra adds, "Though I have been there now, I will need to go at least four to five days early to help my mother with all the preparations for the wedding."

Madhu, ever the supportive mother-in-law, agrees and says, "That sounds like a good plan. We will make sure everything is ready here so you can focus on the wedding preparations. It's going to be a wonderful celebration."

The conversation brings a sense of warmth and anticipation to the household as they look forward to the joyous occasion ahead.

Madhu knows how much Kshipra is struggling with the stress of her marriage. To lift her spirits, she proposes an idea one morning as they sit in the living room. "Kshipra, I know things have been tough lately, but I have an idea to cheer you up," Madhu says with a warm smile.

Kshipra looks at her mother-in-law curiously. "What is it, Ma?"

"Let's get involved in the preparations for Ajay's wedding! How about shopping for saris?" Madhu suggests enthusiastically.

Kshipra's face brightens. "That sounds wonderful. I haven't thought about that at all. Thank you, Ma."

A few days later, they go to a sari shop.

Madhu holds up a beautiful sari. "Look at this one, Kshipra. It would look stunning on you. And this one for your mother, it's perfect!"

Kshipra nods, admiring the selections. "Yes Ma, these are beautiful. Thank you for helping with this. It means a lot to me and my family." Madhu pats Kshipra's hand affectionately. "Of course dear, your family is my family too. Let's pick out something lovely for your sister-in-law as well."

Their next stop is a men's clothing store. Madhu hands a kurta to Kshipra. "What do you think about this for your father?" Kshipra inspects the kurta and smiles. "It's perfect. He will love it."

"And we should find something nice for Ajay. He deserves a special gift," Madhu smiles warmly saying so. Kshipra hugs Madhu tightly, "Thank you, Ma. This means so much to me." Madhu returns the hug affectionately saying "anything for you, dear!

As Kshipra gets ready and packs her belongings, she tells Madhu that she'll be leaving today and that Madhu and Rajan should come at least one day before the marriage for the Haldi function. Kshipra expresses her excitement, eagerly anticipating their arrival. With a happy smile, she bids farewell and heads out.

Back at her parent's place, Kshipra is brimming with excitement as she dives into the preparations for her brother's wedding. She busily prepares a variety of sweets, adding to the festive atmosphere. The house is filled with the joyful buzz of wedding preparations, creating a lively atmosphere.

Kshipra couldn't shake off the feeling of discomfort every time she noticed Murali staring at her. It had become a frequent occurrence and she knew she had to address it.

While Murali visits their house to convey Radha's message to Vasanti, Kshipra decides it's time to speak up. "Can I talk to you for a moment, Murali?" Kshipra's voice trembles with hesitation as she approaches him. Murali turns towards her with curious expression "Sure Kshipra, What's up?"

Taking a deep breath, Kshipra gathers her courage. "It's

just that I've noticed something, and I feel I need to address it."

Murali's brow furrows in concern. "What is it?"

"It's about how you stare at me sometimes. I don't like it," Kshipra confesses with unease.

Murali's eyes widen in surprise then soften with understanding. "Oh, I'm sorry, Kshipra. I didn't realize I was making you uncomfortable."

Kshipra nods, grateful for his acknowledgment. "it is been happening quite often lately and I just want to let you know how it makes me feel."

Murali sighs, a hint of remorse in his voice. "I understand. But this is something I've been doing since we were kids. It's like a habit, you know? Whenever I see this house and catch a glimpse of you through the window, I can't help but look."

Kshipra's heart softens at Murali's explanation. "I get that Murali. But things have changed since we were kids. Our friendship isn't the same anymore."

Murali nods in understanding. "I see what you mean. I'll try to be more mindful of my behavior from now on."

A relieved smile graces Kshipra's lips. "Thank you, Murali. I appreciate it. I don't want anything to further spoil the essence of our friendship."

Murali returns her smile with gratitude. "Ofcourse Kshipra. I value our friendship too much for that, though..." he pauses and leaves.

As Murali leaves, Kshipra feels a weight lift off her shoulders. She's glad they were able to have an honest conversation about the issue. It's a reminder of the strength of their bond and the importance of communication in any relationship.

Early this morning while Kshipra is arranging things in the living room she overhears Madhu's voice talking to Vasanthi. They embrace warmly, and Vasanti instructs Ajay to take their luggage inside and place in Kshipra's room. Kshipra turns around with a bright smile upon hearing that Rajan and Madhu have arrived. She rushes outside and attempts to touch Madhu's feet, but Madhu lifts her up and hugs her tightly, their close bond is evident to everyone present. Vasanthi and Madhukar observe proudly, admiring the strong relationship between their daughter and her mother-in-law.

"My dear look around, you've done such a wonderful job preparing for the ceremony," Madhu says, holding Kshipra close.

"Thank you, Ma. I'm so glad you're here," Kshipra replies gratefully, feeling a surge of warmth and love.

As Kshipra basks in the warmth of the moment, Rajan enters without acknowledging her, causing a ripple of concern among the family members.

The evening arrives, and the house is filled with the vibrant hues of yellow, orange and red as guests gather for the Haldi ceremony.

Kshipra too, adorned in traditional attire, radiates beauty as she prepares for the event. She and Rajan are the first to apply Haldi to Ajay. Kshipra's eyes fill with emotion.

"You look stunning Kshipra," Rajan whispers, a tender smile playing on his lips.

Kshipra smiles saying "This moment means so much to me," Kshipra replies tearfully, feeling overwhelmed by the significance of the occasion.

The Haldi ceremony proceeds with joyous celebrations, accompanied by lively music and dancing.

Kshipra arrives at Sudha's place with the Haldi, continuing the festivities.

"Kshipra, thank you for coming, It means a lot," Sudha says, forcing a smile as she greets her friend.

"Of course Sudha, I wouldn't miss it for the world," Kshipra replies politely, though she can't shake off the uneasy feeling in her heart.

The sun rises on Ajay and Sudha's wedding day, the air is filled with excitement and anticipation. The house is adorned with colorful decorations, and the fragrance of flowers fills the air. Kshipra, dressed in a resplendent saree, assists Sudha in getting ready and sometimes peep in Ajay's room to checkup on him, while Radha and Vasanthi oversee the final preparations.

Radha's eyes glisten with pride as she looks at her daughter. "You look absolutely radiant, Sudha. I can't believe my little girl is getting married." Sudha smiles warmly at her mother.

Ajay is looking dashing in his wedding attire and is surrounded by his friends and family, preparing for the auspicious ceremonies ahead.

"Today's the day I become a married man. It's surreal," Ajay admits with a hint of nervousness in his voice. "Don't worry, you've got this," one of his friends reassures him, tapping him on the back.

The wedding rituals commence with the Ganesh Puja, invoking the blessings of Lord Ganesh for a successful and harmonious marriage. As the pandit chants mantras, the atmosphere is filled with devotion and solemnity.

"Panditji, please bless us and guide us through this

sacred union," Sudha prays with closed eyes, in reverence.

Following the rituals, Amidst the chanting of Vedic hymns and the showering of blessings from family and friends, Ajay and Sudha exchange garlands.

Kanyadaan ceremony takes place, where Sudha's parents formally give her away to Ajay, symbolizing their acceptance of him as their son-in-law.

"Today, we entrust our daughter to you, Ajay. May you find love, happiness and prosperity in your marriage," Radha says emotionally.

Ajay touches Vasanthi's feet and then Radha's feet saying respectfully, "I promise to cherish and protect Sudha for the rest of my life."

Confirming their acceptance as husband and wife now they are ready to make the seven sacred commitments to each other as they take rounds around the sacred fire together holding hands. They look at each other both remembering their journey from holding hands and running all over the village and fields till this moment of holding hand for that lifelong commitment.

With this first step the couple promises to support and respect each other in their religious, ethical and moral duties. They agree to uphold truth and righteousness in their lives together.

Second vow emphasizes the importance of wealth and prosperity. The couple commits to working together to ensure the well-being and financial stability of the family.

With the third vow they pledges to share love, affection, and emotional fulfillment, ensuring a harmonious and loving relationship throughout their lives.

Fourth vow focuses on the promise to raise virtuous children and nurture the family, ensuring a legacy of love, care and education.

At the fifth vow they promise to support each other in all aspects of life, sharing both happiness and sorrow, and to stand by each other in times of difficulty.

Kshipra looks at Rajan with filled eyes and achy heart. She recollects her wedding day and the promises made by them to each other.

Kshipra recollects, Panditji saying while Kshipra and Rajan take the seventh vow.

Seventh vow marks the couple's togetherness in all stages and they promise to stay together in all circumstances, through every phase of life, and in all forms of love and loyalty, forever. And at that very moment she suffocates as the unpleasant words of Rajan uttered several times gather in her thoughts. Rajan's voice feels sharp, dismissive, indifferent even now and echoes louder than the mantras, "You always expect too much." "Why must everything be about you, always?" Words he had tossed carelessly, but which stayed with her like thorns under skin.

She gulps the feeling and come to the present moment while the couple completes the vows.

Panditji smiles warmly at the newlyweds. "May your union be blessed with love, understanding and eternal happiness."

As the newlyweds step into a new chapter of their lives together, the atmosphere is filled with joy and celebration, marking the beginning of their beautiful journey ahead. Vasanti and Kshipra welcome the couple with warm love and blessings.

That night, as Kshipra, Rajan, and Madhu leave, Kshipra couldn't shake a lingering feeling of sadness. She is not able to comeover the moment before their departure, how Ajay and Sudha had simply smiled and waved goodbye. It felt strange, almost as if they didn't care enough to ask her to reconsider staying back for couple of days. The absence of Ajay's usual insistence weighes heavily on Kshipra's heart making the journey ahead feel unpleasant for her.

Unsaid Goodbye

After all the marriage festivities are over, Ajay takes over the working of the fields as Kshipra has asked him to come back. He winds up his business, which has been suffering financial losses, and begins working in the field with his father.

In the early morning light, Ajay and Madhukar walk through the fields. The air is fresh, and the earth feels cool beneath their feet.

"Ajay, this is where we plant the Jawar," Madhukar explains pointing to a section of the field. "We need to start early to ensure a good yield."

Ajay nods, but his gaze is distant. "I understand baba."

Madhukar watches his son closely, noticing the lack of enthusiasm in his voice. "You know, this work requires dedication and passion. It's not just about following instructions."

"I know, baba," Ajay replies, trying to muster some enthusiasm. "I'm here to learn."

Madhukar sighs, sensing the struggle in his son's heart. "Ajay, I can see this isn't where your heart lies. Your mind seems elsewhere."

Ajay stops and looks at his father. "It's just... I had different dreams, baba. Working in the fields was never part of my plan."

Madhukar places a hand on Ajay's shoulder. "Dreams change, son. Sometimes we have to adapt. But if your heart isn't in it, the work will suffer. We can't afford that."

Ajay nods slowly. "I understand baba. I'll try my best. It's just hard to shift my focus."

Madhukar squeezes his shoulder reassuringly. "I know it's difficult. But we are family, and we support each other. We'll find a way through this together."

Ajay gives a faint smile, appreciating his father's understanding. "Thanks, baba, I'll give it my all."

As they continue working, Madhukar remains worried, but he hopes that, in time Ajay will adapt and perhaps even grow to appreciate the life of a farmer.

Days pass and Madhukar start keeping unwell. Willingly or unwillingly Ajay gets loaded with all the responsibilities of fields all alone which he is hardly able to manage. Vasanti and Madhukar expect Sudha to contribute in whichever possible way but they very well know Sudha has never worked in fields willingly, hence they don't directly suggest this. Yields start reducing, falling and Ajay starts hiding this from his parents fearing the consequences. This leads to even selling part of their farm to sustain. This stage really breaks Madhukar and Vasanti.

Madhukar feels the urge to share this with Kshipra but Ajay and Sudha are against this.

Sudha frequently complains about Ajay's decision to return to the village. "The business we had in the city was good enough," she grumbles. "We could have improved our situation, tried something else. Coming back to take care of the farm was a terrible decision."

She often blames Kshipra for this, and Vasanthi and Madhukar feel really bad about this. Though Ajay and Sudha don't openly criticize Kshipra in front of them, Vasanti frequently overhear their conversations.

One evening, Ajay and Sudha sit in their room, discussing their situation.

"We wouldn't be in this financial mess if we had stayed in the city," Sudha says, her voice edged with frustration. "Kshipra insisted we come back. Now look where we are."

Ajay sighs, running a hand through his hair. "Sudha, we've been over this. The business was failing. We were losing money every month."

"But we could have tried something else," Sudha insists.

"Instead, we're stuck here, and it's all because Kshipra convinced you to return."

Ajay looks away, a hint of guilt in his eyes. "She's my sister, Sudha. She was helping."

"Helping, by dragging us into this mess?" Sudha's voice rises. "If she wants to help, she should come and support us financially. It's her responsibility after misleading you."

Ajay clenches his jaw but says nothing.

In another part of the house, Vasanthi and Madhukar discuss their concerns.

"I don't like the way Sudha talks about Kshipra," Vasanthi says, with a suppressed voice low. "She's too harsh."

Madhukar nods, his expression troubled. "I agree. Kshipra was only trying to help. It's unfair to blame her for everything."

"They need to find a way to work together," Vasanthi continues. "This constant blame isn't helping anyone."

Madhukar sighs deeply. "I worry about Ajay. He's caught in the middle of all this. He needs support, not more pressure."

The tension in the household grows, with Ajay feeling

increasingly torn between his wife's frustrations and his love for his sister. The ongoing blame from Sudha and the strained relationships weigh heavily on him, making the financial struggles even more challenging to bear.

As days pass at Kshipra's house, Madhu's health too begins to decline, and her movement becomes restricted. She rarely leaves her bedroom now, and Kshipra often takes her for walks and to the doctor, forcibly.

With Madhu unwell, the household responsibilities that she once managed with ease now fall heavily on Kshipra's shoulders. What was once a manageable routine suddenly becomes overwhelming, many a times. Kshipra finds herself juggling cooking, cleaning, and organizing while trying to keep up with her farms, managing estate as well when Rajan travels. The stress start to take its toll and her tasks at work began to slip, and at home, things began to pile up.

As the days passed, Kshipra realize that she couldn't keep up with everything on her own. She needs help. After much thought, she decides to hire a maid to assist with the housework. She decides to speak about it to Madhu first.

"Ma, I think we need some help around the house," Kshipra suggests gently one evening, helping Madhu settle into bed.

Madhu nods weakly. "If you think it's necessary, Kshipra, I trust your judgment."

However, Rajan is less supportive. "When my mother could handle all the household work for so many years, why can't you?" he questions, with sharp tone.

Kshipra feels the frustration rising but tries to remain calm. "Rajan, I also have my work with the farmers and the organization. They rely on me, and I want to continue supporting them."

Rajan shakes his head. "We don't need a maid. You just need to manage your time better."

"Manage my time better?" Kshipra's voice trembles with suppressed frustration. "I'm already taking care of Ma and the entire house. With a maid, I can still fulfill my responsibilities here and also work with the farmers."

"That's an excuse," Rajan retorts. "You're just trying to avoid your duties at home."

Kshipra's patience snaps. "It's not an excuse, Rajan! I have a responsibility to the farmers as well. They depend on me. And why is it wrong to seek help? It doesn't mean I'm shirking my duties."

Madhu, overhearing the argument from her bed, calls out weakly, "Rajan, let Kshipra get some help. She is doing more than enough."

Rajan looks conflicted but remains firm. "I just don't understand why you can't handle it like Ma did."

"Because I am not Ma," Kshipra says with her voice soft but firm. "And times have changed. I want to make a difference with my work. It's important to me."

The tension simmers between them, with Rajan unwilling to yield and Kshipra determined to stand her ground. The disputes grow more frequent, each small argument threatening to erupt into a bigger fight.

One evening, after another exhausting day, Kshipra finally confronts Rajan again. "Rajan, this isn't just about the housework. It's about me wanting to contribute to something bigger. We can afford a maid. Why can't you see that this would help everyone, including Ma?"

Rajan looks at her, the frustration evident in his eyes. "I just don't want us to rely on outsiders for something we can do ourselves."

"We're not failing by getting help," Kshipra insists. "We're ensuring that we can continue to do what we love and care about. Please, Rajan, try to understand."

Rajan sighs, the fight leaving his body. "alright, let's try it your way. But I expect you to still manage the household."

The argument ends, but the tension lingers, as both try to navigate their responsibilities and expectations, hoping to find a balance that will bring peace to their home.

Days pass and months pass, Madhu's health deteriorates further and so does Kshipra and Rajan's relationship.

Almost a year and a half after Ajay and Sudha's marriage, Sudha is about to give birth to their child. With Madhu's permission, Kshipra decides to visit her parent's place, knowing Sudha will need her during this important time.

When Kshipra arrives, she notices even more change in Ajay's behavior. This difference has only widened and she has noticed it each time she visited. This time she decides to just focus on Sudha and baby for now and not to think much about anything else.

"Sudha, how are you feeling?" Kshipra asks, gently placing a hand on her shoulder.

"I'm okay, Kshipra. Just a bit nervous," Sudha admits, her voice trembling slightly.

Kshipra smiles warmly. "Don't worry. I'm here for you. I'll take care of everything."
When the time comes for Sudha to deliver, Kshipra takes her to the hospital, staying by her side through it all. She handles all the arrangements, making sure Sudha

is comfortable and well taken care of.

"Thank you, Kshipra," Sudha says, settling into her hospital bed. "You've been such a help."
"It's my duty and my joy," Kshipra replies, squeezing her hand. "I'm here for you."

That same night, Sudha delivers a beautiful baby girl. Kshipra stays awake, watching over the child while Ajay comforts Sudha.

Even after many years, Kshipra still remembers the night Radha told her she had a baby brother. She doesn't recall exactly how Ajay looked back then, but she feels that he would have been the same. As she gazes at the newborn, her motherly feelings stir once again.

While Sudha sleeps peacefully, Ajay comes and sits next to Kshipra. She gently hands the baby girl to him as he reaches out to take her in his arms. Kshipra watches him closely, feeling overwhelmed by his expressions as he gazes down at his daughter.

"I can't be happier for anything else in the world," Ajay says, with deep emotion.

Kshipra sighs softly and nods in silent acceptance. He continues, "You know, our Panditji told me once that my life would be influenced and blessed by the womens in my life. Ma, Sudha, and now my daughter... I'm truly blessed."
Kshipra's heart skips a beat as he finishes the sentence.

It isn't the fact that Ajay recognizes the importance of them in his life that overwhelms her but it's the painful truth that she isn't on this list.

She, who raised him as her own child when she was still so young, she who was not just his sibling but also his closest friend, she who depended on him more than anyone else in the world at times while he would always looked at her as his support system for all the major decisions in his life.

The thought makes Kshipra feel suffocated, and tears begin to gather in her eyes. She doesn't want Ajay to see her struggle. With a tiny smile she stands up and turns walking quickly toward the restroom to give herself a moment to let her emotions out.

That whole night, Kshipra lies beside Vasanti, holding her hand. All the memories of her time with Ajay, from childhood until now, play in front of her eyes. She knows it's time for her to leave not just this home, but Ajay's personal space as well. But she can't leave with these feelings unresolved. So, she decides to visit the hospital in the morning again before leaving.

The next day, she returns, determined to support Sudha despite the cold reception.

"Sudha, do you need anything?" Kshipra asks, trying to hide her hurt.

"No, Kshipra we're fine," Sudha replies, avoiding eye contact.

The dismissal stings, but Kshipra persists. "I just want to help. This is Ajay's child, and I care deeply for both of you."

Ajay finally speaks his tone cold. "Kshipra, we know you care. But we can manage. Please, go home its too much crowd here otherwise, some or the other people keep on visiting as well."

Kshipra is already ready to leave while Ajay continues "Sudha's mother and I can handle things here."

Kshipra's smile falters, but she nods. "I'm leaving, Ajay. I just had to see the baby once before I go."

"We appreciate that, but you've done enough," Sudha says gently. "Go home. Your mother-in-law needs you too."

Kshipra understands that they want her to return to her house, but she also knows that she could have spent more time with them. She had hoped to be there until Sudha and the baby were ready to come home, so she could spend time with them at her parents' place. But now, she realizes that is far of a possibility.

Kshipra returns home to Madhu and Rajan and gets back to her routine.

Kshipra sits besides Madhu in her bed, she confides in Madhu. "Ma, I don't understand. I want to help, but they keep pushing me away."

Madhu sighs, her expression become sympathetic. "Sometimes, people don't realize the value of the help and love and care offered and moreover love which comes from our own people. You always do your best, Kshipra."

Kshipra nods, trying to hold back tears. "I just wanted to be there for them and for me as well"

Madhu reaches out and holds Kshipra's hand. "You're a good person, Kshipra. They'll see that in time. For now, rather always try and focus on yourself as well."

Kshipra takes a deep breath and nods. "I am trying Ma, It's just hard to feel so unwanted by all whom you deeply love." Kshipra hesitates as this comes out from her. Madhu knows she is talking about, who all.

As the days go by, Kshipra continues to juggle her responsibilities, her heart heavy with a sense of neglect from those she loves. Her relationships with her Rajan, Ajay, and Sudha become increasingly strained.

Tensions rise at home, and every interaction with Rajan feels laden with unresolved conflict.

There are occasions when Kshipra visits her parents place and the colds reception from her loved ones burns her heart.

Murali watches Kshipra's struggles closely and sometimes deliberately. His feelings toward her, once love, have twisted into something darker. He finds a strange sense of satisfaction in her suffering, a sense of calm in her visible distress.

The naming ceremony for Ajay and Sudha's child arrives, offering a distraction.

Kshipra reaches her parent's place a day before the occasion.

Madhukar and Vasanti sit sipping their morning tea. A soft breeze stirs the hem of Vasanti's sari as she gazes at the fields in the distance. Inside the kitchen, Kshipra stirs the dal on the stove, the rhythmic clang of the ladle steadying her thoughts.

From the direction of her brother Ajay's room, muffled voices reach her ears, rising and falling like waves. At first, she ignores them, focusing instead on garnishing the dal. But then, her name punctures the air.

"Because of Kshipra, we're in this mess!" Sudha's voice trembles with suppressed anger.

Kshipra pauses, her heart skipping a beat. She steps closer to the doorway, wiping her hands on the edge of her sari. The door to Ajay's room is ajar. She hesitates for a moment then knocks lightly.

"Can I come in?" she asks, her voice sounds calm but firm.

Ajay looks up from the bed, startled while Sudha's face is a mask of irritation.

"Come in, since you're already listening!" Sudha snaps, lifting her chin defiantly.

Kshipra steps inside her steady gaze meeting Sudha's fiery one, "What's the matter?" she asks softly.

The door creaks open as Kshipra steps into the room. Before she can speak, Sudha's voice sharpens. "Oh, look who finally decides to listen instead of control." Her tone is biting, the accusation deliberate. "Do you ever stop deciding things for the rest of us, Kshipra?"

Sudha doesn't wait for Ajay to respond. "What's the matter?" she echoes mockingly. "The matter is you! Because of you, we're drowning in debt. And now, if you have even an ounce of responsibility, you'll give us the land in your name so we can sell it anyways it should belong to us. Ajay can restart his trading business with that money and save this family!"

Kshipra's lips part slightly, but she says nothing yet. Her gaze shifts to Ajay, silently asking for his opinion.

Ajay's expression darkens, "Sudha is not entirely wrong," he says, his voice feels low but cutting. "I was doing well with my trading business, but you were the one who convinced me to wind it up and come back to the farms. And look where that's brought me!"
Kshipra's breath catches, but she steadies herself, "I didn't ask you to wind it up without reason Ajay," she

says. "Murali told me…"

"Murali" Ajay interrupts his tone sounds bitter. "Ofcourse, Murali explained things to you, and you decided what was best for me."

"I didn't decide Ajay," Kshipra counters gently. "I suggested because I knew the losses were piling up and I couldn't bear to see you sink further."

"That's easy for you to say," Sudha interjects with raised voice. "You don't have a child to raise, we do. And now, you sit on land that could save us, but you won't part with it, will you?"

"Enough Sudha!," Madhukar's voice booms from the doorway, startling them all.

Madhukar and Vasanti step into the room, their faces a mixture of anger and disappointment. "Have you forgotten what Kshipra has done for this family?" Madhukar demands glaring at Ajay "She has been your rock since the day you started your trading business and much before that. She didn't force you to return to the farm she guided you like a sister should!"

Sudha, still holding her ground, picks up her child from the cradle. "This isn't about who did what in the past. This is about our present and our future. If she really cares, she'll help us now."
Kshipra steps forward, her voice is calm and unwavering, "Sudha, if I give you the land and it will solve your problems, I'll do it. It all belongs to Ajay and

you. I don't want to see you struggle."

"No!" Madhukar interjects, "That land is yours, Kshipra. You earned it with your own hard work. It isn't something I handed to you, and I will not allow you to give it up for anyone not even your brother."

Kshipra's gaze lowers, Madhukar understands her silence, he almost shouts "Kshipra, its registered in your name right?"

He believed she agreed back then when Madhukar had clearly instructed that this was her earning and she should only own it.

But years later, when this fight breaks out she looks at him and finally says, softly looking at Madhukar, "I didn't argue but I still registered it in mother's name, everything I bought, even afterward." She tries to justify her action "see now they need it and you all are together so Ajay can use it in a way which suits them, I mean you all".

There is a long silence between them.

Madhukar takes a deep sigh before saying, "Ajay needs to sort it out by himself Kshipra, hope you understand." He slightly looks at the direction where Ajay is and continues "and you too Ajay."

Sudha shakes her head in frustration. "This is exactly the problem! You all treat her like she's above the rest of us." She cradles her baby tightly and storms out, heading next door to her mother's house.

Ajay stands frozen, his emotions a storm within him. "You see what's happening, Kshipra? My family is falling apart. My wife has left, my child…" His voice breaks, and he turns away. "It's all because of you."

Kshipra blinks back the sting of tears but refuses to let them fall. "Ajay," she says quietly, "I've always tried to help you, not hurt you. If you believe I'm the reason for your unhappiness, I'll step back. But please remember family isn't about blaming each other. It's about standing together."

Ajay doesn't respond and his silence feels like a chasm between them. Kshipra turns to her parents, who look at her with pained expressions. "It's okay," she says, mustering a small smile. "Everything will work out. It always does."

As Kshipra walks back to the kitchen, the weight of the evening settles heavily on her shoulders.

They all are yet to digest the unpleasant episode. Its evening and Ajay is not yet back. Kshipra tries to catch the glimpse of Sudha throughout the day but face the neglect whenever their eyes meet.

Kshipra feels suffocated and though Vasanti stops her as it is already dark, Kshipra steps out of the house for sometime.

Her feet walk towards the riverside. She sits on her regular place. Her face looks calm and her body absolutely steady. The turmoil inside her doesn't allow this calm and she blasts into uncontrollable tears. She cries a loud until she is almost unconscious talking all that she feels but cannot express.

In that isolation Kshipra vents out all that she is been going through. All that happened, this morning and back home with Rajan as well. Feeling safe that she expressed all this in isolation, she looks at the river and feels that the river absorbed all her sorrow, she feels a bit relieved as she glances back to the river while returning.

The Quite Savior

Next morning many people from the village gather, and the house buzzes with activity. Kshipra moves through the crowd, her face a mask of polite cheerfulness, trying to keep up appearances despite the turmoil inside.

Amid the crowd, Kshipra spots a familiar face "Usha?" she calls out. Her voice is filled with surprise and joy.

Usha turns, her face lighting up "Usha! It's been so long!" The two women face each others from a distance and their laughter mingles with the noise around them.

"It's been ages," Kshipra says, stepping forward to look at her old friend. "How have you been?"

"I've been good, busy with life," Usha replies. "And you? How are things with you?"

Kshipra hesitates, not wanting to burden Usha. "I'm also good," she says with a small smile. "It's just... life, you know?"

Usha's eyes soften with understanding. "I get it. But I'm here now, and I'm not going anywhere. Let's catch up again sometimes."

Kshipra feels the warmth she hasn't experienced in a long time. "I'd like that, Usha. I've missed having a friend to talk to."

As the ceremony continues, Kshipra notices Murali standing at a distance, his gaze fixed on her as usual. His presence feels like a poking shadow, and she quickly looks away, focusing back on Usha.

They reminisce about their school days. Kshipra is grateful for the distraction and smiles. "Yes, I remember. We had so much fun back then."

For a while, Kshipra feels a sense of normalcy, a brief respite from her struggles.

Later in the ceremony, Kshipra observes Usha moving through the crowd, observing few familiar faces of her old friends. Kshipra realises that Usha notices the palpable tension between them as she sits alone in a corner.

Usha approaches her again. "Kshipra, it's been so long," she says warmly, sitting beside her.

Kshipra's face brightens slightly. "Usha, it's good to see you. How have you been?"

"I'm well," Usha replies, then lowers her voice. "But you don't seem happy, Is everything alright?"

Kshipra sighs,. "Ya all good just that Rajan didn't come, and nothing else" Kshipra utters glancing at Sudha.

Usha nods, feel strange discomfort amongst the close friends and it's hard to see especially when she has seen them so closely, years back though. She looks at

Kshipra saying "things don't look similar to me"

Kshipra sighs again. "Yes, things changed. But let's not talk about me. How are you?"

"I'm fine, but I can't help but worry about you," Usha says gently. "If you ever need to talk again, I'm here.

Usha understands her pain and that how Kshipra is feeling neglected and left out by her loved ones.

Usha, having watched Kshipra carefully since childhood, notices a stark difference. The once beautiful, vibrant, cheerful woman now appears worn down. The beauty is still there, but the warmth, the spark, and the positivity seems fade.

Usha tries to assure "You will never be left out alone Kshipra because you never leave anyone alone" Kshipra looks at Usha with a question mark on her face.

Usha continues, "You know Kshipra, no one made me friend but you! You were the only one back in school days; who would talk to me, spend some time with me, practically acknowledged my being."

Usha recalls the school days and reminds Kshipra with the intense feelings.

Usha turns to Kshipra with a soft glint in her eyes; half nostalgia, half gratitude. "You remember seventh standard?" she begins quietly.

Kshipra looks at her, tilting her head, "Hmm, what about it?"

"That week I didn't come to school, a full week. Everyone kept asking; teachers, classmates. Even the PT sir said, 'Where's the girl who runs faster than the boys?'" Usha smiles faintly.

Kshipra chuckles, "Yes, I remember. I came looking for you." Usha nods slowly, "no one knew what was happening. But you, you came all the way to my house. You stood outside, asking my mother to let you see me."

"You weren't even allowed to talk to me properly," Kshipra recalls, her voice tightening with old anger.

"They had decided I wouldn't go to school anymore," Usha says. "That I should start helping with housework, maybe learn tailoring. They said that's enough education for a girl, they even hide my school bag and my uniform."

"And I told them they were wrong," Kshipra says, sitting up straighter. "I tried to convince your father. I remember he looked at me like I was from another planet."

"He didn't budge," Usha says. "But you didn't stop. You went straight to our class teacher the next day. You told her everything."

"And then the teachers came to your house," Kshipra

adds, a smile touching her lips now. "The headmistress even spoke to your father."

Usha's eyes shimmer. "They changed their minds because of you. If you hadn't spoken up, if you hadn't cared, I would have dropped out then and there. Everyone else moved on, but not you."

Kshipra looks away, touched. "I didn't think I was doing anything special." "But you did," Usha says firmly. "That one week shaped the rest of my life. I never forgot it, Kshipra. You believed in my right to study when even my own family didn't."

Kshipra finally meets her gaze, "Maybe… maybe I was just doing what a friend is supposed to do." Usha smiles and says softly, "No. You were doing what only you could do."

While silence stretches between them, gentle and full, Usha recollects how she would watch the four of them, Kshipra, Rajan, Ajay, and Sudha always laughing, playing, and being inseparable. There was a sense of freedom and joy in the air as they jumped and ran together, their bonds unshakable. Usha would stand on the side lines with a smile on her face, but there was always a tinge of envy in her heart. She had always admired their closeness, their effortless happiness and wanted to be part of them but she never found that space there.

Back then, Usha had been a part of the group at times though but never quite in the centre. She always felt like an outsider looking in, though she was happy for them, seeing their connection as something special. Now, as she sees Kshipra in this condition, she understands that the dynamic is no longer the same. The bond they once shared is strained, and the warmth that once defined their friendship is nowhere to be found.

Usha helps Kshipra calm down and give her time to accept what the reality is, only then she will be able to move ahead in life, "I will not say that forget everything and live your life because I know you can't. Just that give yourself some time and i am sure you will make things right in a way they should be".

Kshipra feels the moral support from Usha.

As they speak, Usha notices Sudha talking with some guests. She reachout to her and joins the group standing a little away, as Kshipra watch Sudha smiles tightly. "Busy with the baby, you know. It's a lot to handle."

"I can imagine," one of them replies, noticing the strain. "You seem a bit stressed."

Sudha's smile falters. "It's just... a lot. But we're managing."

Usha nods sympathetically just being an observer. Just then, she notices that Sudha seems to be intentionally steering away from Kshipra, her gaze briefly meeting Kshipra's before quickly shifting to another group of people. Sudha moves closer to another friend, her body subtly leaning in, as if seeking a kind of closeness, even though the rest of the group is still gathered nearby.

Sudha glances around again, as if confirming that Kshipra isn't watching them too closely. "Yes, it's... nice to see everyone. But, you know, things are a bit different these days," Sudha says, her tone quiet but pointed.

One of the friends raises an eyebrow, sensing that Sudha is speaking in coded terms. "Different how?" she asks, intrigued.

Sudha hesitates, her eyes flicking over to Kshipra before she speaks in a low voice. "It's just... a lot of pressure with the baby, and... there's so much going on in the family. I just don't know how to handle everything sometimes." Her voice trails off, and she leans in even closer to the friend, as if to distance herself from the unspoken tension with Kshipra.

Her friend nods, "I understand. It must be overwhelming. But you're handling it all well, Sudha." She pauses before adding, "I'm sure you'll find your balance again."

Sudha smiles faintly but doesn't seem entirely convinced. "I hope so," she replies softly.

Another friend picking up on Sudha's discomfort decides to change the subject. "So how's the little one? Is she keeping you up at night?"

Sudha brightens slightly at the mention of her child.

"Oh, she's wonderful."

At that moment, Usha notices Murali standing alone across the room, watching the proceedings with a detached air.

Usha spends the rest of the ceremony observing the others. She notices the strained interactions, how Ajay barely acknowledges Kshipra, how Sudha seems on edge, and how Murali's gaze never softens.

As the ceremony winds down, Usha approaches Kshipra once more before leaving, "Kshipra, please remember, I'm here for you, If you need anything."

Kshipra nods, her smile is tired but grateful. "Thank you, Usha. It means a lot."

Usha leaves the ceremony with a heavy heart, more determined than ever to be there for her friends, despite the changes in their dynamics.

Usha looks at Kshipra for long before she walks out; as if she is not able to disconnect from Kshipra at all. She feels a pang in her chest. In the midst of the awkwardness, she can't help but wish for things to go back to how they were, when everything seemed simpler and more genuine.

Usha walks passing the same lanes and the same river side and gets restless and she couldn't help but remember days back then. She closes her eyes with a deep sign and her memory plays an episode for her.

The late afternoon sun spreads parting warmth across the riverside. The air is filled with the sound of running water, laughter, and the occasional splash as four friends Kshipra, Ajay, Murali, and Sudha play along the bank. Their school bags lie forgotten on a rock nearby, their carefree joy replacing the weight of the day's lessons.

Usha, walking back from school, pauses on the path that runs parallel to the river. She clutches her satchel and watches from a distance, her eyes fixed on the group. The friend's backs are turned to her, but she can see their animated movements, hear their voices carried by the breeze.

Kshipra stands in the middle of it all, her laughter distinct, as she splashes water toward Murali, who tries to dodge but slips slightly, drawing even more laughter from Sudha. Ajay is skipping stones further downstream, pretending not to notice but clearly enjoying the playful chaos.

Usha feels a pang of longing. She knows these friends from school, but she has never been part of their close-knit circle. Still, she can't help but stop to watch, drawn by their camaraderie.

As the shadows lengthen, the friends gather their things. Murali swings his bag over his shoulder and motions to Ajay, who finally leaves his spot by the water. The group heads toward the path that Usha stands on, running ahead and jostling each other. As usual Ajay holding tip of Kshipra's hair tied in pleat. Kshipra moves slightly ahead and her hairs slip from Ajay's hands. It bothers him so much, he quickly manages to catch her pace and hold it back. His face clearly shows hoe secure he felt to be connected to his sister.

Usha watches all this from a distance trying to avoid disturbing them.

They pass her without a glance at her except Kshipra. Kshipra slows her pace and looks back. Her eyes brighten when she sees Usha.

"Usha!" she calls out, walking over with an easy smile.

The others pause briefly but then continue ahead, Murali and Sudha exchanging a glance as they leave Kshipra behind.

"How are you?" Kshipra asks as she approaches Usha.

Usha hesitates, her fingers tightening on her satchel strap. "I'm fine… How are you?"

"I'm good," Kshipra replies, her voice warm. "You're heading home?"

"Yes." Usha glances at the retreating backs of the others. "I saw you all near the river. You always seem to have so much fun there."

Kshipra tilts her head thoughtfully. "We do, you know I like this river bank the most. You should join us sometime. Would you like to sit for a while now? if you're not in a hurry, of course."

Usha blinks in surprise "really? But... won't they mind?"

"They'll survive, don't worry" Kshipra says with a grin. She turns toward the others "Ajay! You all go ahead. I'll catch up."

Ajay stops and frowns, looking at her. "No, Kshipra. Come on now. Let's go together."

"I'll come soon," she replies firmly.

Ajay sighs, clearly displeased, but walks back to a rock and sits down, picking up stones and tossing them into the river. Murali and Sudha hesitate for a moment before moving on, their laughter fading into the distance.

Kshipra turns back to Usha. "Comeon let's sit by the water for a bit."

They walk back to the riverbank, where Kshipra sits down and pulls off her shoes, dipping her feet into the cool water. Usha follows hesitantly, smiling as the water touches her toes.

"It feels nice, doesn't it?" Kshipra says, looking at Usha.

Usha nods, a small smile playing on her lips. "I too like it here. It's peaceful."

They sit in comfortable silence for a while, the water swirling gently around their feet. Then Kshipra spots a cluster of flat stones near the edge. She says, standing up, "let's climb those."

Usha hesitates but takes Kshipra's outstretched hand. Together, they step from stone to stone, balancing carefully and laughing whenever they wobble.

From his spot on the bank, Ajay watches them, his expression softening. Though he doesn't say a word, he picks up fewer stones, his eyes following their movements.

After some time, Kshipra and Usha return to the riverbank. The sky is painted with hues of orange and pink as the sun dips lower.

"I should go now," Usha says quietly, brushing the dampness from her feet.

"Me too,"Kshipra replies, She turns toward Ajay. "Let's go!"

Ajay stands, dusting off his hands. The three of them walk back toward the path, Kshipra chatting lightly with Usha while Ajay walks a few steps behind.

As Usha nears her home, she waves goodbye, her heart feeling light. She glances back at Kshipra, who smiles and waves back before walking on with Ajay again holding tip of her plait.

Usha couldn't help but laugh at Ajay looking at this.

Usha's thoughts linger on the moment. "She always notices me," she thinks "even when no one else does. She makes me feel like I belong."

Usha talks to herself "not even my parents liked me due to my dark complexion and all the classmates, how they teased and behaved. But in all this she was the only one who talked to me, befriended me. We may have not spent a lot of time together but whenever we did it soothed my heart always", wiping her tears Usha continues "How can I leave her alone when she needs someone the most? It is just a phase for her and it shall pass. Till that time I will always be there for her, she promises herself".

Usha makes it a point to visit Kshipra's parent's place again. The events of the previous night have left her uneasy.

Usha enters Kshipra's room preparing to leave the next morning. Kshipra looks up and is surprised to see Usha again.

"Usha, I didn't expect you", Kshipra exclaims.

"I wanted to see you again" she murmurs to herself "I am feeling so restless" Usha continues with a smile. "Can we talk for a while?"

Kshipra nods, closing her suitcase. "Of course, Let us sit."

They sit on the edge of the bed and Usha takes a deep

breath, "Kshipra, I am really worried about you. You seem so different from the girl I remember from school. What's been going on?" Usha's gaze sweeps around, Kshipra understands what she is looking for. Kshipra informs, "they have gone to the temple early morning."

Usha diverts her saying "leave that, see Kshipra its ok if you are not comfortable to share but you know very well what you mean to me. You had all three of them to be your closest but for me you were and are only one I feel closely connected to. I noticed everything during the function and it's not just the curiosity to understand the problem between you guys but I am seriously moved to see you like this. Where is that charm, that liveliness?

Kshipra faces hard to see Usha into her eyes, her gaze is down. Both are in tears, Kshipra is inconsolable for quite some time but all the more taking care that her sobbing is not heard by her parents.

Kshipra sighs, her shoulders slumping. "It's been tough, Usha, my relationship with Rajan is strained, and things with Ajay and Sudha aren't any better. I feel like I'm being pulled in every direction."

Usha listens intently. "I can see that, is there anything I can do to help? Anything"

Kshipra shakes her head slowly. "I appreciate it, Usha. But these are issues that have been building up for years. I'm not sure how to fix them."

Usha places a comforting hand on Kshipra's shoulder, "may be we can figure out a way together."

Kshipra looks at Usha, her eyes filled with gratitude. "Thank you, it's been a long time since I felt like someone really cared."

"I do care," Usha says earnestly. "You've always been someone I admired, Kshipra. I hate seeing you like this. Maybe we can start by tackling one problem at a time?"

Kshipra nods, a small smile forming on her lips.

Kshipra continue talking, with Usha listening patiently and offering support. Kshipra opens up about her frustrations with Rajan's lack of understanding, her worries about her parents, and the strain between her and Ajay and Sudha.

After a moment of silence, she suggests, "You know, I'm planning to visit my grandma for a couple of days. It's a remote village, very serene. Why don't you join me? It could be a nice change for you. Meet me at the bus stand at 10pm tomorrow."

Kshipra shakes her head. "No, no, it won't be possible. I am leaving tomorrow. "That's the change you need Kshipra, I will wait for you", Usha insists.

The next morning Vasanthi enters the room, carrying a tray with snacks and tea. Vasanti sets the tray down with a smile. "If you are planning to visit with your friend, you go Kshipra I can speak with Rajan later. I'm sure he'll understand. Just go for a couple of days; it'll be good for you." Kshipra is surprised to hear this from Vasanti as she has not yet mentioned any such plan to her.

Vasanti reads Kshipra's surprised face and smiles saying "I dropped by your room last night to leave some water for you and heard you blabbering, Usha, I can't come with you, repeatedly."

Vasanti listens to Kshipra as she briefs about visiting Usha's grandma's place.

Kshipra hesitates, looking at her mother "but what if something happens at farms while I'm away?"

Vasanthi reassures her. "Rajan will manage dear. Sometimes, a change of scenery is all you need to feel better. Just go and relax."

Kshipra is left with no reason to deny.

For the matter of fact she too wants to go but felt that guilt to leave behind all issues and live for herself.

The Destined Journey

The next day, Kshipra and Usha set off for the remote village. Usha chats about her childhood memories with her grandmother trying to lift Kshipra's spirits.

As the bus rolls along the winding roads, Usha sits beside Kshipra, her mind buzzing with concern. She knows that Kshipra needs more than just a change of scenery; she needs healing, both physically and emotionally. And there's no better place for that than her grandma, Lakshmi's place.

 Usha tries to engage Kshipra in conversation, hoping to draw her out of her thoughts, but Kshipra remains silent, staring out of the window with vacant eyes.

As they stop for breakfast in the morning at a roadside dhaba, Usha notices Kshipra picking at her food, her appetite seemingly non-existent. Concerned, Usha tries to lighten the mood by pointing out the scenic views around but Kshipra remains unobservant.

They board the bus again and Usha makes yet another attempt to divert Kshipra from her thoughts, gesturing towards the rolling countryside she says, "Look at those lush green fields, Kshipra, Isn't it beautiful?"

Kshipra offers a half-hearted nod, but her gaze remains fixed on the passing landscape, lost in her own thoughts. Usha sighs inwardly. For now, all she can do is be there for her friend, offering support and companionship on the journey ahead.

The sun begins to set, the bus pulls into the quaint village where Usha's grandma resides. The air is filled with the scent of earth and the sounds of nature, and Kshipra feels a sense of calm wash over her as they step off the bus.

The village, bathed in the soft, dim natural light of dusk, still exudes a quiet charm. The silhouettes of its thatched roofs and winding paths create a serene, timeless atmosphere. The faint glow from distant windows hints at the warmth of home, while the surrounding fields stretch out, fading gently into the shadows.

The trees, their leaves rustling in the evening breeze, add a touch of life to the tranquil scene. Despite the darkness, the village's simple beauty continues to shine, a peaceful haven untouched by the rush of time.

Usha leads Kshipra towards Lakshmi's house, a cosy abode nestled amidst lush greenery. The house, though humble with its mud and wood structure, exudes a sense of warmth and tranquility.

As they enter, Kshipra notices Lakshmi, a sprightly octogenarian with a twinkle in her eye, welcoming them with open arms.

"Come dear," Lakshmi's voice is filled with warmth. "Come, sit down and relax."

They settle on the wooden bed as Lakshmi serves them refreshing glasses of juice.

Lakshmi approach Kshipra to handover a glass of juice and takes a back feeling Kshipra's sorrowful aura. She manages to cover up her expressions and looks in to Kshipra's eyes with a search.

Their eyes meet briefly; Kshipra acknowledges Lakshmi's guiding energy unknowingly while Lakshmi with her wisdom acknowledges Kshipra's surrender, to be. Usha breaks the connection for now as she utters,

"Lakshmi," Usha begins with a gentle yet concerned tone, "She is my friend Kshipra and I bought her here for a change as she's been going through a tough time. She needs your wisdom and guidance."

Lakshmi nods sagely, her eyes crinkling with understanding, "Ofcourse, my child. I'm here to help in any way I can."

Kshipra is surprised to hear 'wisdom', 'guidance' and 'help', for her understanding is that, they came here just for a change.

Lakshmi sits beside Kshipra, her eyes portraying a mixture of pain and attempted composure. Lakshmi can't help but notice the innocence in her smile, a frail facade masking deeper turmoil. Sensing Kshipra's unease, Lakshmi moves closer and gently takes her hand, feeling the subtle tremors of instability that emanate from her.

Without exchanging words, they share a silent communion, their eyes speaking volumes in the quietude of the moment. Kshipra's eyes, laden with unspoken sorrow and anguish, convey a narrative of their own, and Lakshmi's heart swells with compassion as she discerns the depth of Kshipra's suffering.

Usha, addressing her grandmother as Lakshmi, shares a unique bond with her. Choosing to use her name instead of the traditional "grandmother" fosters a sense of intimacy and closeness between them, allowing for open communication and understanding.

Three of them sit in the dim light of the evening when a small boy comes running toward Lakshmi, enveloping her in his tiny hug. Both of them laugh as he asks, "Where are my berries?" Lakshmi unties a knot in her pallu and hands him the berries, placing them in his little palm. He is eager to leave and dashes off with the same speed, but Lakshmi catches his hand, pulling him back. "Wait, did you come only for the berries?" she asks.

The young boy gives a small smile, acknowledging his mistake, and extends his other hand toward Lakshmi. "Please give some aloevera leaf for dadi, so she can run after me again," he says.

Lakshmi gets up, picks one aloevera leaf kept aside, and both of them laugh aloud as she hands it to him. He then runs off, full of excitement.

Kshipra and Usha has been quietly watching. They look

at Lakshmi with curiosity. Lakshmi sits between Usha and Kshipra and begins explaining, "If you apply a mixture of turmeric and slaked lime on your heels and cover them with an aloevera leaf after slitting it, the pain will heal overnight."

"Oh, is it? My mother-in-law has the same problem. Hope I knew this remedy before, but I will use it on her once back home.

Later that evening, Lakshmi sits by Kshipra side, her hand resting on Kshipra's forehead. With a gentle touch, she attempts to discern the subtle energies that envelop Kshipra's being. The aura that surrounds Kshipra is heavy with the weight of sorrow and pain, and Lakshmi's empathetic heart reaches out to her in silent solidarity.

The morning sun casts its warm glow over the serene village as Lakshmi serves breakfast in humble mud utensils, each dish prepared and presented with care.

As Lakshmi turns to walk out of the room, Kshipra stirs, her eyes seeking the comfort of familiarity. She hesitates, looking around. "Where is Usha?" she asks softly.

Lakshmi stops, she turns back to Kshipra. "Usha is around, my dear," she replies with a knowing smile. "She needs some space to rest. She'll be here, don't worry."

Lakshmi's eyes sparkle with a quiet wisdom. She looks

at Kshipra with calm, knowing eyes, "My dear, life is like a river, carrying many things along, some clear and bright, others heavy and dark. The currents you feel today may not have started with you. Often, they flow from distant places, carrying the stories of those who came before you. Their joys, sorrows, choices and even their regrets ripple through time and shape the paths we walk.

"Every family is like a tree. The roots stretch deep, hidden beneath the surface, connecting us to the soil of the past. Sometimes that soil nourishes us, other times, it may carry pain. These wounds may start as tiny cracks, unnoticed at first, but they grow over generations, passed down until they reach us."

"But listen carefully, Kshipra. No matter how twisted or tangled the roots may seem, the tree still reaches for the light. All it takes is one moment, one decision, one soul brave enough to say, "this ends with me." That soul can heal not only itself but also the roots below and the branches above."

"We often feel trapped in cycles we don't understand. Why does this pain feel so familiar? Why do the struggles of those before us echo in our lives? It's because these patterns are woven into us. But patterns are not prisons. They are threads, and you have the power to weave something new.

"Every challenge you face, every heartbreak you endure, is not a punishment. It's a calling, a calling to look deeper, to understand, and to let go. Life doesn't seek to burden you; it seeks to free you. But that freedom comes when you are willing to face the shadows and bring them into the light."

"Kshipra, you must also understand, the family you are born into, the people you meet, even the bonds that brings you pain are not random. Often, these connections are chosen by the soul before it enters this life. You choose them with purpose, to learn something, to heal something, or to fulfil certain goals. Sometimes the purpose is clear; other times, it takes years to reveal itself."

"You are not just living your story, Kshipra. You are rewriting the stories of those who came before you and shaping the stories of those who will come after. This is not a burden; it is a gift. It means that within you lies the power to break chains that have held for generations. You are here not by chance but by choice, your soul's choice to heal and rise, and not just for you but for all of them."

"Healing doesn't mean erasing the past. It means holding it gently, understanding its weight, and setting it down so you can move forward freely. As you do, you inspire others to do the same."

"You may feel small now, but the work you do within yourself send ripples far beyond what you can see. You are not just a drop in the ocean, Kshipra. You are the ocean in a single drop."

Lakshmi's voice softens further, "and remember, you

are not alone, you are deeply supported, whether you see it or not. Trust the process, child. Trust that everything you need is already within you, waiting to be discovered."

Kshipra is stunned to hear all this and attempts absorbing it for long.

Post having light dinner, Lakshmi gently holds Kshipra's hand and guides her toward the bed. Her touch is tender, her movements deliberate, each step carrying a silent reassurance. Once Kshipra lies down, Lakshmi pulls the sheet over her, tucking it carefully around her shoulders. She sits at the edge of the bed, her calm voice barely above a whisper.

"Don't worry, my dear. There is no hurry. You don't have to tell me anything now. Whenever you feel it, whenever the words come naturally, whenever you feel the urge to let them flow like a song, you can share them with me. And if you don't want to, that's perfectly fine too. This space is yours, and I am here, with no expectations, only patience."

She pause, her gaze is steady but soft. "I will only say this, to understand the reality of what we face today, we sometimes need to visit yesterday. The pain you feel, the heaviness in your heart, the panics, these are symptoms, not the cause. We are not here to treat the surface, Kshipra. We need to gently uncover where the wound truly lies. And for that, we must look into the past, not to stay there, but to heal it, to free you."

Lakshmi adjusts the lamp, dimming its glow to a warm, comforting hue. She places her hand lightly on Kshipra's forehead for a brief moment before rising. "Rest now," she murmurs. "Everything will unfold in its time, when you feel the rightful urge we can visit your past life."

Kshipra nods, feeling a strange sense of comfort at Lakshmi's words. Her eyes flutter shut, and the room falls into a peaceful quiet.

The moon rise high in the sky, casting a pale, serene light through the window. It's midnight and the stillness of the night is broken only by the soft rustling of the trees outside. Lakshmi, awake and feeling something stir deep within her, opens her eyes. She is startled to see Kshipra sitting at the edge of the bed; her face is a blank canvas, devoid of expression.

Lakshmi's heart quickens with concern. She sits up, unsure if Kshipra is even conscious. She watches for a moment, but Kshipra doesn't react, her gaze fixed somewhere far beyond the room. Lakshmi moves gently to her side and places her hands on Kshipra's shoulders, giving her a soft but firm shake. "Kshipra," she says, her voice calm but loud "Come back to me, child."

Kshipra blinks, as if waking from a deep, distant place. Her eyes are empty, glazed with a deep sorrow. Then, as if the floodgates of her heart have been opened, she speaks in a broken whisper, her voice trembling with pain.

"I love them all, Lakshmi… but why do they test me every time? Ajay… he's only a few years younger than me, but I raised him like my own child. I was just a child myself, but I had this feeling… this deep, motherly love for him, even then." Her breath hitches. "How could they say I spoiled their life? How could Rajan doubt me?"

Tears start to well up in her eyes, and before Lakshmi can respond, Kshipra's face crumples in agony. She begins to cry, quiet at first, but then the sobs grow louder, more uncontrollable, as if all the weight she's carried for so long is finally being released.

Lakshmi doesn't speak. She simply lets her cry, holding space for her pain. Her hands remain steady on Kshipra's shoulders, offering silent comfort as Kshipra continues to pour out her heart.

"I was just a girl, Lakshmi. How could they not see that I always cared? Why did they have to blame me for everything? For everything that went wrong in their lives? They never saw how much I supported… how much I tried to protect them… how much I loved them, why was I left in a situation where I couldn't set things right?"

With each word, Kshipra's tears seem endless. She weaves the story of every moment that has haunted her, each memory, each hurt, spilling out with raw intensity. Her voice cracks with the weight of each past grievance, her strained relationship with Rajan, the burdens she felt she had to carry, the feeling of being misunderstood, the feeling of being unwanted by those she cared about most.

As Kshipra continues her venting, Usha quietly enters the room. She stands at the threshold, unsure of how to help, her eyes filled with concern. She reaches her hands out instinctively, but Lakshmi raises her hand in a soft gesture, signaling for her to wait.

Usha halts, her shoulders heavy with helplessness. She stands by, watching as Kshipra's cries grow louder, her body shaking with the force of her emotions. The room gets thick with grief.

Kshipra's sobs eventually subside, but the emptiness in her eyes remains. She seems utterly exhausted, physically and emotionally drained. The words, though they have spilled out in waves, still seem to cling to her chest. And then, without warning, she becomes limp in Lakshmi's arms.

Lakshmi gently catches her, guiding her head to rest on her lap. She strokes her hair softly, her touch tender and soothing. Kshipra's breath is shallow, and Lakshmi knows that her exhaustion has overcome her.

Usha, still standing quietly by the bed, watches the scene unfold. She sits on the edge of the bed, her heart aching for her friend. But Lakshmi's calming presence fills the room with a steadying force. She places her hand gently on Kshipra's head, letting her fingers run through the tangled strands of her long hair, offering comfort and support.

As time passes, Kshipra stirs slightly, her breath evening out, and Lakshmi remains by her side, watching over her with unwavering care. The night stretches on in silence, with only the soft sound of Lakshmi's hand moving through Kshipra's hair, guiding her back to consciousness, one gentle stroke at a time.

Usha watches them both, unable to hold back the tears that have formed in her eyes. She doesn't speak, but her heart is filled with love for Kshipra the kind of love that doesn't need words.

As Usha sits on the edge of the bed, her brows furrowed in confusion and concern, she finally breaks the silence. "Lakshmi," she begins hesitantly, her voice barely above a whisper, "there are so many people in the world who face broken relationships or financial troubles. But I've never seen anyone go through this kind of pain, this depth of suffering. Why Kshipra? Why is it so much worse for her? If they are not good to her, shouldn't she just leave them? If the money isn't enough, why not start fresh somewhere else? Why is she clinging to all this hurt?"

Lakshmi looks at Usha and the look doesn't seem pleasant "Leave? Leave just like you did?" Then Lakshmi closes her eyes slowly and tiny tear drops hand on the edge of her both eye lids. Usha's face drops.

Lakshmi looks up, "Usha," she begins, her eyes reflecting the wisdom of lifetimes, "pain isn't measured the same way for everyone. For some, a mustard seed is just that a small, insignificant thing, easy to cast aside.

But for others, that same mustard seed can feel as large as the tallest mountain you can imagine, an insurmountable obstacle. It is not the size of the trouble itself, but the weight it carries in their soul that makes it heavy."

Usha listens, her eyes fixed on Lakshmi, but her expression still carries questions.

"A cut on your hand," Lakshmi continues, "can sting and bleed, but it will heal quickly. A cut on your heart, though... that is different. It festers, it lingers, and it can take years, even lifetimes, to mend. Kshipra's pain is not just hers. She carries the weight of generations. Her soul has chosen, whether consciously or not, to suffer so she can heal not just herself but the lineage she comes from. This is her path, her purpose. Some souls are born to mend the threads of the past, to weave a future where the cycle of pain is broken. Kshipra is one of those souls."

Usha's breathe catches at the gravity of Lakshmi's words. She looks at Kshipra, her friend, lying unconscious yet restless, and then back at Lakshmi. "Will you be able to guide her through all of this? Will she ever be... normal again? Will she return to the Kshipra she used to be? Will the old days come back for her?"

Lakshmi's face softens, and a small, sad smile graces her lips. She shakes her head gently. "No Usha, the old days will never come back, they never does. Days gone are like water spilled, they cannot be gathered again. Even as she heals, it will not bring her back to who she was. But that is not the goal." She pauses, her gaze distant as if looking at something far beyond the present moment.

"When all this is over," Lakshmi says, "when the wounds have closed and the lineage has been healed, Kshipra will not be the same. She will be someone else; someone stronger, someone freer. The past will not return, but something new will arrive. Something different, something unexpected, may be something better. And it will be hers to embrace, hers to shape. It may be difficult, yes, but it will also be transformative."

Usha looks down, processing the weight of Lakshmi's words. She sighs deeply, her shoulders heavy with both hope and trepidation. "I just want her to be happy," she whispers.

Lakshmi looks at Usha with warmth. "She will be, Usha. But happiness, true happiness, is not about going back. It is about finding light in the present and creating it for the future. And that is the journey Kshipra is meant to walk."

The room falls silent, accept for the faint sound of Kshipra's breathing. Usha sits quietly, absorbing Lakshmi's wisdom as the night stretches on, and the moon watches over them all.

The morning sun filters through the leaves reaching on the garden as Lakshmi works with practiced hands, her fingers gently loosening the soil around a bed of flowering plants. The faint scent of jasmine lingers in the air, and the rhythmic sound of her trowel against the earth fills the tranquil space.

Kshipra approaches hesitantly, her footsteps slow and uncertain. She stops a few feet away, her hands clasped in front of her, and offers a tentative smile. There's a touch of guilt in her expression, as if the weight of last night still lingers. "Lakshmi," she begins softly, "I… I'm sorry if I disturbed you and Usha last night. I don't remember everything, but I know I must have been difficult. I'm really sorry for troubling you both and Usha is.."

Lakshmi breaks her in between "Usha will be practicing deep meditation. Don't worry she is around and will join you once its time for you to go back home. Since you were tired and asleep, she didn't wake you to inform.

Lakshmi looks up, her face breaking into a warm, understanding smile. She dusts her hands on her sari and walks over to Kshipra. "Everything happens for a reason," she says gently, her voice as soothing as the morning breeze. "And everything happens at the right time."

As she speaks, Lakshmi bends down and picks up a tiny flower that had fallen onto the grass. She holds it out to Kshipra, who takes it with a mixture of surprise and curiosity. Lakshmi's eyes soften as she continues, "Sometimes, we need to look deeper to find where the wound lies. And to do that, we must be willing to go back, to understand."

Lakshmi places a comforting hand on Kshipra's shoulder and guides her to the raised verandah encircling the old banyan tree at the edge of the garden. They sit down, the tree's thick roots forming natural backrests, its shade offering a cocoon of peace.

"Kshipra," Lakshmi begins, her tone reflective, "you are carrying so much pain, not just from this life, but perhaps from before. Childhood memories, past experiences… even a promise or contract you may have made in another lifetime. Sometimes, we live with certain patterns or entanglements because of these unresolved ties these patterns repeat until we understand and heal them."

Kshipra listens intently, her brows furrowing slightly as she processes Lakshmi's words. "Are you saying," she asks hesitantly, "that I might be suffering because of something I don't even remember, something from my past life?"

Lakshmi nods reassuring "exactly, if you are ready and willing, we can explore this through a past-life regression session. It's a way to journey into the past and uncover the origins of your struggles, but," she adds, her voice firm yet kind, "it is not about instant results. You may or may not find all the answers in one session. The goal is to understand the link between your past and present and to see the thread that connects them. Once you find the wound, then we can begin the process of healing."

Kshipra looks thoughtful, her fingers lightly tracing the

petals of the tiny flower Lakshmi had given her. "If I find the wound," she says, "what then? What's the outcome of all this?"

Lakshmi smiles softly. "The outcome is clarity, understanding. You'll know why you're feeling this way, why these things are happening. That knowledge can be transformative. Healing is a journey, Kshipra. Sometimes it begins with a single moment of realization. Other times, it takes multiple steps, different approaches. But it all starts with your willingness to explore."

Kshipra's gaze meets Lakshmi's, her eyes filled with a mixture of apprehension and determination. "I want to know," she says firmly. "I want to see my past life. When is it possible?"

Lakshmi's smile widens. "If you are comfortable, we can begin this evening," she replies. "But remember, this is just the beginning. Tonight, we will take the first step to uncover where the wound comes from. It may take one session, or it may take many. We will go at your pace, as you feel ready."

Kshipra nods, her resolve looks strengthening. "I'm ready to begin," she says.

Lakshmi gently squeezes her hand. "Then let's prepare for this evening," she says. "It will be a journey not just to the past, but to understanding yourself."

The two women sit quietly for a moment, the banyan

tree standing tall above them, as if silently bearing witness to the start of an important journey.

The morning hums with a quiet energy, carrying with it the promise of discovery and healing.

Post sunset Kshipra walks to the room as directed by one of Lakshmi's deciple.

Kshipra hesitates for a moment before stepping into the dimly lit room. The soft glow of a red lantern on the ground casts flickering shadows on the walls, giving the space an otherworldly calm. Lakshmi stands beside the lantern, her presence steady and grounding.

"Come, lie down here," Lakshmi says gently, patting a thin mat spread on the floor. Kshipra obeys, feeling the coolness of the mat against her back. Lakshmi kneels besides her as the lantern's glow catches the serene determination in her eyes.

Lakshmi utters "Set an intention Kshipra for who do you wish to connect with in your past life, set a clear and firm intension.

Rajan's face flashes beneath Kshipra's closed eye lids and all the memories of Rajan gather in her thoughts at a time.

"This isn't a fantasy, Kshipra," Lakshmi begins calmly but sounds authoritative. "What you're about to experience is simply a shift in awareness. You'll be conscious throughout, aware of every sensation if an ant bites you, you'll feel it. If I speak, you'll hear me. But at the same time, you'll access memories hidden deep within you. You may see visuals, or you may simply sense them or feel them or just know them and this is perfectly normal."

Kshipra nods, her pulse starts quickening.

"Close your eyes," Lakshmi instructs. "Breathe deeply... slow down your breath."

Kshipra obeys, her breaths gradually becoming steady, almost rhythmic. Lakshmi's voice softens, taking on a soothing cadence.

"Imagine a staircase in front of you, ten steps leading downward. With each step, you go deeper into a state of calm, closer to the memories waiting to surface."

Kshipra's mind paints the image vividly a staircase stretching downward, each step worn smooth by countless journeys.

"Ten" Lakshmi whispers. "Step down. Feel your feet touch the surface."Kshipra's body relaxes further.

"Nine... eight... seven…" Lakshmi's words guide her, each step pulling her deeper into herself.

By the time Lakshmi reaches one, Kshipra feels as though she is floating, her body weightless, her mind open. "You are in a garden now," Lakshmi continues. "It's vibrant, full of life; flowers blooming, insects buzzing, a soft breeze brushing against your skin."

The scene unfolds effortlessly in Kshipra's mind. She almost feels the cool air and hears the rustle of leaves.

"Walk through the garden," Lakshmi instructs. "Let the breeze guide you. Ahead, there's a stream. See the water flowing gently."

Kshipra imagines the stream's crystal-clear water gliding over smooth pebbles. She steps closer, feeling the spray of water against her skin as though she is truly there.

"Now, cross the stream using the wooden over bridge. The breeze will lead you further."

Kshipra feels herself moving forward, crossing into an unknown realm, walking over the bridge feeling the cool air brushing over her skin and leaving her with the soothing feel. But then, the light in her mind begins to dim.

"Ahead of you is darkness," Lakshmi's voice comes again, steady and unyielding. "Do not fear it. This is where your past begins."

The darkness envelops her like a cocoon, not cold or threatening, but profound. In that void, Kshipra senses a presence of a guide, unseen yet palpable, radiating strength and support.

Lakshmi's voice becomes a lifeline, threading through the stillness. "Trust the journey. What lies ahead is your truth, your story. Let it unfold."

Kshipra surrenders, stepping further into the unknown, her heart pounding softly in anticipation of what she might discover.

Images flickered, shadows of another time, another life.

This is the very session already glimpsed at the beginning, where it had all surfaced for the first time.

Kshipra is back to her present moment. She is lying on a bed and her face is full of sweat and her heartbeats high. Lakshmi places her palm on Kshipra's forehead. Gradually Kshipra's breaths slow down to its regular pace. She opens her eyes, wipes her sweat looks at Lakshmi who gives a convincing smile to her.

Kshipra gets up from the bed, her body still trembling from the emotions stirred during the session. Her eyes are red and swollen and the tears aren't stopping. She looks at Lakshmi, who is seated nearby with her calm and reassuring presence.

"Is this the reason Rajan is treating me this way?" Kshipra's voice quivers as more tears fall. "He thinks I didn't love him... that I didn't accept his love because he was poor. How do I explain it to him now?"

Lakshmi places a gentle hand on her shoulder.

 "Kshipra, you have already tried to convey it to his soul. These things take time. Let us see how it unfolds. For now, give it space."

But Kshipra shakes her head, the anguish rising again. "What about Ajay? I want to see what I did to deserve his hate in this life. I want to understand!" Her voice cracks as she begins crying uncontrollably, the weight of her emotions feels overwhelming.

Lakshmi sits patiently, letting Kshipra release her pain before speaking. "We have to take one step at a time," she says gently. "You've uncovered so much today. It's a process, Kshipra. These revelations need time to settle."

Kshipra looks up, her voice breaking, "but Rajan... at least now I know why he's treating me this way. What do I do? How can I help him understand?"

Lakshmi nods, her eyes steady. "Now that you're aware, you can take small steps to help him. Your actions in this life can also guide his understanding. Be patient, and allow things to unfold naturally."

"For Ajay," Lakshmi says, "let a couple of days pass. Then, we can have another session where you set your intention to meet him in your past life. For now, just rest. Focus on healing what you've uncovered today."

Kshipra nods weakly, her sobs reduced to shallow breaths. Lakshmi's words linger in the air, grounding her.

"Take one step at a time," Lakshmi repeats gently. "Let the healing begin here and now. The rest will come in its own time."

Kshipra closes her eyes, her body trembling but slowly relaxing as she allows Lakshmi's words to sink in. The room is quiet except for her soft breaths, signaling the start of another step in her journey.

For next 2-3 days Kshipra doesn't interact much with anyone. Lakshmi too gives her the required space.

This evening Kshipra comes to Lakshmi with concern "It's been more than a week, I need to go back". Lakshmi softly responds, "Yes, you should." Kshipra continues "But, I won't be able to unless I know …." Lakshmi cuts her saying "I understand Kshipra, you want to have another session". They both look into each other's eyes, Kshipra's eyes spill calling for hope while Lakshmi's eyes willing to part the same.

Next morning the process is repeated, Lakshmi's voice guiding Kshipra taking her deep down the past crossing the bridge between the lives. Kshipra intends to meet Ajay's soul this time and Kshipra is once again trying to find the right door to her past reality. She hesitates to put the foot forward but this time she does it more confidently to enter the right door.

Kshipra steps through the right door, her heart brimming with a mixture of curiosity and trepidation. The air around her feels dense and surreal, as though she has entered another dimension. Lakshmi gently prompts, "What do you see, Kshipra?"

"It's very cloudy... hazy," Kshipra replies, her voice tinged with uncertainty. "I can't see anything clearly."

Lakshmi encourages her with a calm yet firm tone, "Concentrate, breathe deeply and focus, the vision will get clearer as you focus."

Kshipra closes her eyes momentarily, grounding herself with slow, deliberate deep breaths. As she concentrates, the swirling haze begins to lift. "I see... a small girl," she says softly. "She's crying. Her clothes are dirty, and her face is smeared with mud and tears."

Lakshmi asks gently, "Where is she?"

"She's walking toward a well," Kshipra continues. "There are four or five ladies fetching water. She stands there, looking so lost."

Lakshmi probes further, "And then?"

"Another lady emerges from behind a wall," Kshipra says, her voice feels trembling with emotion. "She raises her hand and approaches the girl."

"Can you identify this lady?" Lakshmi asks.

Kshipra shakes her head. "No... I can't tell who she is. But she's taking water from the well and cleaning the girl, wiping her face and hands. She's speaking to her, asking something... but the girl just keeps crying."

Lakshmi waits patiently then asks, "What happens next?"
"The lady holds the girl's hand and takes her to her house," Kshipra replies.

"Can you identify the house or the lady now?" Lakshmi inquires again.

Kshipra pauses, and then her voice grow softer, almost as she's realizing it for the first time. "That girl... that girl is me. And the lady... she's my mother in this life."

Lakshmi nods, acknowledging Kshipra's recognition. "What else do you see?"

Kshipra's voice takes on a wistful tone. "There's a boy and a girl playing in the courtyard of the house. It's a simple, humble home. The boy looks at me and asks his mother, who is she?'"

"And who is that boy?" Lakshmi asks.

"That boy..." Kshipra hesitates, and then her voice strengthens "he's Ajay, my brother in this life." Lakshmi asks"and the girl?"

"I'm not sure yet," Kshipra says, shaking her head.

"What happens next?" Lakshmi asks, guiding her gently.

Kshipra keeps breathing slows as she visualizes the scene. "I'm cooking... trying to fit into this family. But the boy, my brother doesn't accept me. He doesn't see me as a sister."

Lakshmi remains silent, letting Kshipra explore the emotions and visions at her own pace.

Kshipra continues searching the memories, trying to uncover more. But after a while, she says softly, "That's it. That's all I see."

Lakshmi's voice is calm yet firm as she guides Kshipra deeper into the memory. "Okay, Kshipra try to focus, what do you see next? After a few years, are you still with them?"

Kshipra nods, her expression looks tense. "Yes," she whispers "I am still with them, but I'm helping the freedom fighters now. Because of that, the family is facing many problems."

"What kind of problems?" Lakshmi asks gently.

"The boy… he's grown up now," Kshipra begins, her voice is wavering. "His hatred for me keeps growing. The British come to their house frequently, searching for me. They raid the house, destroy everything, and he can't take it anymore. He doesn't want me to stay with them. But the couple, the mother and father, they protect me. They refuse to send me away."

Kshipra sobs while continuing, "Each evening, there's news of another killing, and I'm scared every day until everyone return home, I feel if they all will be back or no? Each day looks scary as if some bad news will arrive anytime."

Kshipra feels an ache cross her heart as she recollects her panic attacks she gets when anyone is expected back home and delayed, fearing the worst.

She continues "That night he sent two soldiers, as they approached my parents hide me under the mattress and tied a cloth over my mouth. Raju was warned, not to disclose where i am. They beat my father until he was bleeding heavily. While I could not shout, my heart, my mind, my soul screamed louder and I decided.." and then Kshipra screams a loud, as though trying to release the pain she carried from then.

Lakshmi's eyes gets shut and tears flow, she swallows her feelings and asks after allowing Kshipra's emotions to settle, "and then?" "Then I run away, so that the Britishers don't bother them," Kshipra says, her voice breaking. "I can't watch them suffer anymore.

Kshipra is emotionally drained by now as if she herself doesn't want to see further. She feels the need to close it' just for now.

"Okay," Lakshmi says, her voice is steady and encouraging. "Now move forward. Where are you next?" Kshipra hesitates, "I… I can't see anything," she whispers.

"Focus," Lakshmi urges. "Go ahead, many many years ahead. Where are you?" did you die young?

After a long pause, Kshipra's voice trembles as she speaks. "I see a bed… I'm lying on it. I can feel the wrinkles on my face, deep wrinkles. I'm very, very old. I am alone."

"Alone?" Lakshmi asks gently. "Yes," Kshipra says with

tears in her eyes. "There's no one to take care of me, no one. I'm lying there just waiting. I hear some chants but i am not able to recollect what that is…that's it."

Lakshmi gives her a moment of silence then says softly, "You've carried this pain for so long. It's time to let it go."

Lakshmi brings Kshipra back to her present. Kshipra weeps silently for long lying on that bed. She doesn't even know what is making her cry so much. Lakshmi holds her hand all this while till she is calm.

Kshipra's body begins to relax, her breathing steadies. The memory lingers, but a faint sense of release starts to emerge.

Before Kshipra leaves Lakshmi advises Kshipra to delve into her family history as well, exploring the experiences of her mother and grandmother to uncover any recurring themes. "By understanding these patterns," Lakshmi continues, "you can as well begin to untangle the knots that bind you."

Kshipra feels confused "So whatever I am going through is due to this past life so if it's clear than why dwell into the ancestors"

Lakshmi continues further "You have quite an insight of your past life and all this is linked if you have a pattern in the family that brings you exactly at this place where you are today.

Everything is linked together. It's like if you are destined to reach some place, all the paths or rather whichever path you take, your path will reach there and unless you break your ancestral pattern we will not be able to give closure to your sufferings and your lineage's sufferings and more than that to your 'soul's purpose'.

While your past life pushed you, these ancestral patterns grabbed you and this makes you stuck in here and in this situation. So, it's important to address on both the fronts."

Unweaving the Tapestry

As the sun sets on the final day of her stay, Kshipra reflects on her time in the village, grateful for the insight she has received yet mindful of the challenges that lie ahead. With Lakshmi's guidance and Usha's unwavering support, she knows she has the strength to face whatever comes her way. And as she prepares to return home, a newfound sense of hope blossoms within her, lighting the path to a brighter tomorrow.

As the first light of dawn breaks Usha comes to Kshipra's room and Kshipra prepares to leave. Their hearts are heavy with unanswered questions. But as they bid farewell to Lakshmi, a sense of hope blossoms within them.

Though Kshipra's journey may be long and arduous, they know that with Lakshmi's guidance and their unwavering support, she will find her way back to herself in due time.

As Kshipra and Usha embark on their journey back home, the echoes of Lakshmi's words reverberate in Kshipra's mind like a haunting melody. "Break the trap" Lakshmi's voice urges, "free your past and future generations from this pattern."

Kshipra's thoughts drift back to her mother's words, spoken with a bitterness that still lingers in her memory. "Even my sisters are the same, they too don't like me."

The juxtaposition of Lakshmi's wisdom and her mother's bitterness creates a tumultuous storm within Kshipra's soul. As the landscape passes by outside the window, she feels trapped between the echoes of her past and the uncertainty of her future.

In the quiet confines, Kshipra turns to Usha, her voice trembling with emotion. "Do you think it's possible?" she asks, her eyes searching for reassurance. "Can we really break free from these patterns of our past?"

Usha nods, her expression filled with determination. "Yes, Kshipra," she replies with an unwavering voice. "We have the power to rewrite our story, to create a new legacy for ourselves and for generations to come. Few get the chance to do it and few really miss doing it!"

With each passing moment, Kshipra feels a newfound sense of resolve take root within her. She may not have all the answers yet, but she knows that she has the strength to face whatever challenges lie ahead.

And as the journey continues, she vows to confront the shadows of her past head-on, to break free from the patterns that have held her captive for so long. For in the depths of her soul, she knows that true liberation lies in the power to rewrite her own story.

Kshipra is unable to figure out how she can manage to meet her cousins and try to find the pattern if any. But, as the days pass she gets desperate to meet them and all day this thought bothers her.

Just then she gets a invite for her cousin's wedding, which would be the last marriage of the generation. Kshipra feels relived as most of her maternal cousins would attend it for sure.

Kshipra is not willing to leave Madhu and go for the marriage amidst Madhu's poor health. But, she knows that she won't get a better chance to meet her cousins. She plans to visit just for a day.

The wedding is in full swing, a grand celebration of love and tradition. The air is filled with the rich scent of marigolds, the sound of laughter and music weaving through the crowd, and the warmth of lights flickering in every corner.

Kshipra watches the bride and groom exchange garlands, their faces glowing with a mix of excitement and nervousness. It's a beautiful moment, full of promise, but a strange heaviness settles in Kshipra's heart, one that she can't seem to shake.

She looks around at her family; her uncles, aunts, cousins, all gathered under one roof after what feels many years. It should feel warm, comforting, like a reunion full of shared memories and laughter. Instead, there's something else, a tension, barely perceptible but undeniable, lurking beneath the surface. The smiles are a little too forced and the greetings a bit too polite. The familiarity of their faces, once a source of comfort, now feels strangely distant.

Kshipra's gaze drifts from one person to the next,

sensing an invisible divide, a gap that was never visible before. It's as if the years apart have subtly but irreparably changed something.

She decides to sit down at one of the dinner tables, trying to shake off the feeling. The food is delicious, as always; rich, fragrant, and comforting. Yet, as she eats, her mind remains restless. The chatter around her grows louder, but her thoughts only grow heavier.

Kshipra's attention shifts when she notices her two elder cousins, Rohit and Neel, sitting at opposite ends of the courtyard, not acknowledging each other's presence. It strikes her as odd. She remembers them as inseparable when they were younger. They were always together, whether it was playing in the narrow lanes, sharing books, or sneaking into the kitchen for sweets. They were partners in mischief, in laughter, in everything.

Curious, she leans over to her aunt, who's sitting beside her, and asks softly, "Why aren't Rohit and Neel talking to each other?"

Her aunt sighs, stirring her rice absentmindedly as she looks over at the brothers. "Things changed, Kshipra. You know how life is. When they were younger, they had nothing to fight over. But as they grew up, things became... complicated."

Kshipra's brow furrows and she listens intently as her aunt explains. Rohit, being the elder of the two, had always been the responsible one, excelling in his studies and eventually landing a lucrative job in the city. Neel, on the other hand, had big dreams but struggled to find his footing.

"At first, Rohit helped him a lot," her aunt continues. "He paid his bills, supported his business ideas but, over a period Neel started feeling lesser. He felt like he was living in Rohit's shadow, like everyone compared him to his successful brother."

Kshipra frowns, her eyes flicking back to the brothers. "But that's not Rohit's fault, right?"

Her aunt shakes her head, her face softening. "No, it's not. But you know how pride works. Neel began resenting Rohit. He felt like Rohit looked down on him, even though Rohit never did. Eventually, they stopped talking completely. And see now, even at a family wedding, they sit on opposite sides like strangers."

Kshipra glances over at them again. Rohit is absorbed in his thoughts indifferent to everything around him, while Neel sits with a group of younger cousins, forcing laughter that doesn't quite reach his eyes.

Kshipra wonders how much pain both of them are carrying, how many unspoken words and unresolved emotions lie between them, hidden behind their pride. She has a different angel to view at this now!

Later that evening, Kshipra moves away from the noise of the wedding party and finds herself sitting with her cousin Meera. Meera's little daughter is running around joyfully, playing with the other children, but Meera herself looks distracted, as though her mind is far away.

"You look tired," Kshipra says gently, concerned by the heaviness in her cousin's eyes.
Meera exhales sharply, as though the question itself weighs on her. "It's not tiredness, Kshipra. It's something else."

Kshipra watches her closely, sensing that there's more she's not saying. After a brief silence, Meera speaks again, her voice quieter this time. "Did you notice that Varun isn't here?"

Kshipra nods. She remembers how Varun used to be fiercely protective of Meera when they were younger and visited Kshipra's house during summer vacations. Kshipra knew that he was the one who always walked her home from school, made sure no one troubled her, and looked out for her in ways only a brother can.

Meera forces a smile, "He doesn't talk to me anymore. He hasn't visited my home in years."

Kshipra is taken aback. "Why? What happened?"
Meera's gaze drifts to her daughter, who's now laughing with her friends. "It started after my marriage. Varun never liked my husband. He thought he wasn't good enough for me. He felt I deserved someone better."

Kshipra's eyes widen with disbelief. "But wasn't he happy for you?"

"At first, I thought he was," Meera whispers. "But over time, he began to distance himself. When I invited him for festivals, he made excuses. When my daughter was born, he came once but barely even held her. Then one day he just stopped calling altogether."

Kshipra feels a pang of sadness for her cousin. "Did you try to fix things?"

Meera's voice cracks as she answers, "Many times. But he won't listen. He says he has nothing against me, but he doesn't want to be part of my life anymore. And it hurts, Kshipra, It really hurts."

Kshipra doesn't know how to respond. She feels the weight of Meera's words settle over her like a heavy cloud, unsure of how to ease her cousin's pain.

Kshipra's eyes sweep across the room, taking in the sight of her entire family gathered together, yet something is different now. The warmth, the closeness she once felt, is replaced with a quiet tension, an invisible fracture running through the people she's always loved.

She catches sight of Ajay from across the room, serving food to the guests, his face looks calm and focused. But as she watches him, her heart clenches painfully. Her eyes burn with tears, and she whispers to herself, this cannot be our fate. I can't let this happen. I won't let whatever this pattern is, tear us apart. Whatever the reason behind all this hurt, I will find it. And I will fix it.

Her gaze drifts again, moving over her cousins, each one a snapshot of a childhood once filled with joy and innocence. Their faces so familiar, so carefree flash in her mind, one after another, until they blur together. It's as if their younger selves are still there, waiting for her to remember what they all once had. Kshipra shuts her eyes, fighting the surge of emotion threatening to overwhelm her. She stops the tears before they can fall, unwilling to let them go to waste. There has to be a way to fix this, to bring them back together she won't give up on them. She can't.

As the wedding celebrations continue around her, Kshipra withdraws into herself, her thoughts tangled in the stories she's just heard. She had always believed in the strength of family had always thought that no matter what happened, siblings would stand by each other. But now, sitting in the midst of the festivities, she sees a different reality.

Rohit and Neel, Meera and Varun, Just like herself and Ajay, the families that had once been bound by love and shared history, now fractured by pride, misunderstandings, and unresolved pain. It's like the fabric of their connections is slowly unraveling, piece by piece, and no one is willing to reach out and stitch it back together.

Kshipra wonders, does love truly fade so easily? Or does it get buried under the weight of expectations, disappointments, and wounded pride? Could it all slip away, just like that?

Later that night, as the bride bids farewell to her family, stepping into a new life with her husband, Kshipra feels a deep ache in her chest. The people she loves, the ones she thought would always be there, could they one day walk away? Could she too, one day find herself standing on the outside, looking in, wondering what went wrong? The thought terrifies her.

But, that was not destined to happen at this moment.

Armed with newfound insight and understanding Kshipra decides to return to Lakshmi's village, her heart feels heavy with the weight of her discoveries.

But even as Kshipra grapples with the implications of her discovery, she feels a glimmer of hope ignite within her. With Lakshmi's guidance, she knows that she has the power to break free from the chains of her past and forge a new path forward.

Serve of the undesired

Back home as the sun sets, Kshipra's looks towards the horizon with hope and optimism, ready to confront whatever challenges lie ahead with courage and grace.

Kshipra sits alone in her room, surrounded by the quiet of the night while her mind is filled with tumultuous thoughts and emotions. She reflects on the journey she has embarked upon, the revelations she has uncovered, and the weight of the ancestral patterns that have shaped her family's history.

"I never imagined it would be like this," she whispers to herself, her voice is barely above a whisper. "All these years, I thought I was alone in my struggles, but now I see that it runs much deeper than I ever realized."

Her soul feels heavy with the burden of past generations, the echoes of their conflicts and discord reverberating through her very being. But amidst the darkness, she clings to a glimmer of hope, a flicker of light that shines through the shadows.

"Lakshmi," she murmurs, the name rolling off her tongue like a prayer. "There's something about her, something that draws me to her. She holds the key to unlocking the mysteries of my past, to finding peace and healing for my soul, healing my loved ones."

With resolve burning in her heart, Kshipra makes a decision. She will return to Lakshmi's village, to seek guidance and solace in the wise old healer's presence once more. For she knows that she cannot continue to carry the weight of her family's burdens alone, that she needs the support and wisdom of someone who understands the depths of her struggle.

Just when Kshipra thinks of planning another visit to Lakshmi, Madhu's health further deteriorates!

Kshipra gets engaged in taking care of Madhu as she needs assistance round the clock now. There is no option but to rely on Rajan for her farms as well.

As the days pass, a subtle unease starts to creep into Kshipra's mind. She tries to push it away, telling herself everything is fine, but there's something she can't shake. Rajan's once-constant check-ins on the farm become less frequent. The crops, once thriving now show signs of neglect, leaves curling, patches of dryness and the soil no longer rich and damp.

One morning, Kshipra walks out to the fields and stops short. A stretch that had been green last week now lies dry and cracked underfoot. She kneels down, scoops a fistful of soil, it crumbles in her palm like dust. A chill runs through her. This isn't just poor weather or temporary mismanagement, its decay.

She stands abruptly, brushing dirt from her hands. Rajan had said everything was under control. But this, this is something else. Her breath quickens as she turns and walks briskly back toward the house. Something is wrong. And Kshipra is done pretending its not.

When Kshipra raises her concerns, Rajan assures her with a smile, too quick and too forced "It's just a temporary setback," he says, brushing off her worries. "We'll take care of it."

But as time goes on, the problem only worsens. The yield drops, and the plants begin to wither. Kshipra feels her heart sink. Could she have missed something? She tries to push the thought away, but the nagging feeling only grows. Rajan had promised to manage the farm, and yet, she is left to watch it falter under his watch.

Her mind races grappling with doubts and unanswered questions. But she's determined to trust Rajan, to give him the benefit of the doubt. Perhaps this is just a rough patch. Still, something feels off.

One evening, while walking near the teak estate, Kshipra overhears a conversation that stops her in her tracks. Rajan and Vishal, the estate manager, are talking in hushed tones. She hides behind a thick bush, straining to hear their words.

Rajan's voice is low, tinged with frustration. "I don't have a choice. The returns on the teak have been poor the past couple of seasons. The weather's been unpredictable, and maintenance costs are through the roof. I'm selling off some of the weaker parts of the estate and one Kshipra uses for her farming. It's the only way to minimize the damage."

Kshipra's breathe catches. The teak estate, their symbol of prosperity and her farms is being sold, and she wasn't even told.

She shifts slightly, her hand brushing the bark of the tree behind her. Rajan's next words slice through the dusk.

"Let's keep this between us for now. She doesn't need to know until it's settled."

Kshipra feels her knees weaken. He's selling their future without even asking her. Her trust begins to unravel, thread by thread, the silence of the forest around her now echoing her own

 "Rajan," Vishal says, concern evident in his voice, "are you sure about this? Selling parts of the estate? The market downturn has already hurt us."

Kshipra's blood runs cold. She leans against the tree, the weight of the revelation sinking in. Rajan has kept this from her, the financial struggles and the losses. Why hadn't he confided in her? Why hadn't he been honest about the difficulties?

The betrayal hits her like a blow to the gut. She feels the anger rise, hot and sharp, but it's mixed with a deep sadness. The teak estate, once their pride is being dismantled, and she wasn't even given a choice.

The next day, the knot in her stomach tightens. Rajan seems distant, preoccupied, and when she tries to discuss the farm, he brushes her off, offering vague reassurances. "Everything's under control," he says, but she can see the strain in his eyes, the cracks in his façade.

That night, Kshipra confronts Rajan. She can't hold it in any longer. "Why didn't you tell me, Rajan? About the losses, about the estate?" she demands, her voice shaking with frustration and hurt.

Rajan freezes, his eyes betraying a flicker of guilt, but he quickly masks it. "I didn't want to burden you," he says, his voice sounds defensive. "You've had enough to deal with. I thought I could handle it."

"And the farm?", Kshipra shoots back, her voice rising. "You promised me you'd take care of it. While I've been working myself to the bone, you've let it fall apart. And now, you've sold parts of the estate without even telling me or Ma?"

Rajan sighs, running a hand through his hair. "I thought I was doing what was best. But I see now… I see what you're saying."

Kshipra shakes her head, her disappointment is palpable. "You've let everything slip away, Rajan. The farm, the estate, our future and you never even told me." She watches him, waiting for a response, but the silence between them speaks volumes. Rajan has made his decisions, and Kshipra now knows the truth. The foundation they had built their lives on is crumbling, and it is his negligence that has brought them to this breaking point.

Estate is compromised and fields are almost gone.

Days continue…

Kshipra stands in the dimly lit kitchen, chopping vegetables for the evening meal. Her hands move mechanically, but her thoughts are far away, lost in the words Lakshmi had spoken to her earlier. She tries to shake them off, but they cling to her mind, patterns she can now see clearly but doesn't know how to release.

The smell of cumin sizzling in hot oil fills the air as she stirs the dal, but even the warmth of the kitchen can't ease the tension inside her.

"Kshipra" Rajan's voice cuts through the quiet, sharp and impatient. She hurries to the bedroom where Madhu, lies on the bed. Madhu's frail body rises and falls with shallow breaths, her face once full of life now drawn with exhaustion.

"It's cold again," Rajan snaps, holding a glass of milk that has lost its warmth. His eyes, red from lack of sleep, are filled with frustration, though his worry for his mother is undeniable.

"I'll bring another glass of milk," Kshipra says softly, taking the glass from his hands.

She's been caring for Madhu with all the strength she has. She helps her eat, massages her sore joints, stays up late into the night adjusting pillows and offering water. But it never feels like enough not for any other reason but because she cared for Madhu. Kshipra feels hurt as still Rajan always finds fault.

The evening stretches on, and Kshipra finds herself sitting by Madhu's side, adjusting her pillows once again, offering another sip of water. Madhu looks up at her with tired eyes, her voice barely a whisper. "You're a good girl, Kshipra. Don't let anyone tell you otherwise."

But her words are drowned out by Rajan's constant complaints. He paces the room, his frustration bubbling over. "You're always distracted. If you'd just focus, she'd be better. Look at her." His tone is harsh, and it cuts through Kshipra like a knife. She bites her lip, swallowing the urge to defend herself. It wouldn't make any difference. No matter what she does, it will never be enough. More than anything else what bothers Kshipra is that Madhu witnesses all this while her health is so very low.

Without exchanging a single word, both Madhu and Kshipra silently acknowledge the truth about Rajan's behavior. There's an unspoken understanding between them, an awareness that the reality of their situation is far from the facade Rajan constantly tries to maintain. Though neither of them says it aloud, they both know the cracks in the image he's built, and in that shared silence, there's a quiet recognition of the complexities beneath the surface.

The next morning, the house feels eerily quiet, the usual sounds of the day somehow appear muted. Kshipra enters Madhu's room, her heart already heavy with a sense of dread. The sight before her stops her in her tracks.

Madhu lies motionless on the bed, her body unnaturally still, as if frozen in time. Her once warm, comforting presence now seems distant and lifeless. The glass of water that Kshipra had left beside her remains untouched. The surface of the water looks still and undisturbed.

A cold chill runs down Kshipra's spine, her breath catching in her throat. She steps closer while her hand trembles as she gently shakes Madhu's frail shoulder. "Ma?" she whispers with her voice soft and fragile, as though speaking too loudly might shatter the quiet.

But there's no response. The room feels heavier, the silence grows thicker. Her heart races as fear creeps in, but she already knows. Something is terribly wrong.

Her heart races as she calls Rajan, and within minutes, they're both standing in the room with the doctor. The diagnosis is a heavy blow, the confirmation of Kshipra's worst fear.

Madhu is gone, gone forever!
Rajan crumples to the bed, his grief overwhelming him. He clutches his mother's lifeless hand, his tears flowing freely. Kshipra stands frozen, unable to move, her mind in a fog. No one knows what Kshipra has lost other than a mother-in-law.

The days that follow, blur together in a haze of rituals, visitors, and condolences. Each day feels like a repetition of the last, a procession of faces offering empty words of sympathy, their voices muffled in Kshipra's ears. The house, once full of life, now feels cold and heavy with the weight of loss. Kshipra moves through it all like a ghost, her every step mechanical, every action done out of habit rather than thought, each task feels more hollow than the last.

Her own grief, the ache deep in her chest, is buried under the crushing weight of all that she has to do. It's as if there is no room for her sorrow, not here, not in Rajan's house. His grief consumes everything, his sharp words and bitter silence leaving no space for her to mourn.

She pushes her pain down, deeper and deeper, her heart aching with each passing day. In the quiet moments, when the house is still, her sorrow rises like a tidal wave, but she swallows it down, tucking it away where no one can see. She is invisible in her own pain, her sorrow unnoticed by anyone, including herself.

Rajan's grief soon turns to anger, and he directs it all toward her. "It's your fault," he says one evening, his voice trembling with rage. "You were too busy day dreaming. If you'd been paying attention, Ma would still be here."

The house still carries the weight of mourning, yet Kshipra finds herself juggling responsibilities far beyond her own grief. Relatives visit for condolence for days.

Preeti and her father linger even after the other relatives have left, subtly disturbing the fragile balance between Kshipra and Rajan.

She moves about the kitchen, exhaustion pressing down on her shoulders as she prepares dinner. The air feels unusually heavy, and it takes her a moment to realize why Preeti is nowhere to be seen. A strange unease coils inside her, its grip tightening with every passing second.

Wiping her hands on the pallu of her saree, she steps into the hallway, her eyes scanning the dimly lit space. That's when she hears Preeti's voice, soft but distinct coming from behind the half-closed door of her bedroom. A chill runs down her spine. Her heart pounds in her ears, but her hands remain steady as she pushes the door wide open, the hinges letting out a sharp, protesting screech. The sound startles them.

Rajan and Preeti freeze, their entwined bodies now separated by shock. But Kshipra doesn't spare them a single glance. Without a word, without a single tear, she turns on her heels and walks away.

In the kitchen, her breath comes in short, ragged bursts. Her hands tremble as she clutches the edge of the counter, her nails digging into the wood. She wants to scream, to break something but all she can do is let the storm rage inside her.

Minutes pass before she composes herself. She walks back to the bedroom. Preeti is gone. Only Rajan remains, standing by the window, his back to her, gazing into the darkness outside.

Kshipra steps forward, grabs his arm, and turns him to face her. She wants to say something, anything. But no words come. Her lips quiver, her throat burns, yet all she can do is stare at him, her eyes flooding with the weight of a thousand unshed tears.

Rajan's face holds no guilt. No remorse. Nothing!

The silence between them feels suffocating.

Kshipra turns away, stepping into the hall where Preeti now sits on the couch with her blank face, "better you leave tomorrow morning," Kshipra says in low but firm voice.

Preeti doesn't argue. She simply lowers her gaze and raises her eyebrows.

By morning, they are gone. That evening, Kshipra confronts Rajan.

He sits in the living room, lazily, as if the previous night never happened. She stands before him, fists clenched at her sides. "Why?" she asks, her voice hoarse with restrained fury.
He doesn't even look up "why, what?" "Why did you do this to me?" Kshipra almost shouts with frustration.

Now, he lifts his gaze, his expression unreadable. "You think you're a perfect wife, Kshipra? You think you've done your duty?"

Her breath hitches. "I've given everything to this marriage." Rajan scoffs, "everything? You couldn't even take care of my mother properly and then you were too busy mourning instead of being there for me."

The accusation hits her like a slap. But he isn't listening. He stands up, towering over her. "You were supposed to keep this family together. Instead, you failed. And now you want to act like the victim?"

His voice grows louder, edged with venom. "Do you know how frustrating it is to come home to a wife who is always lost in her own world?

Kshipra feels the sting of his words. She freezes, the accusation hitting her more than a physical blow.

"How can you say that?" Her voice is barely a whisper, shaking with disbelief and hurt "You and Ma were my world Rajan."

"You were always distracted, your farms, your farmer's community and all. You didn't care enough," Rajan continues, his anger pouring out in harsh words. You have just become a mental case.

Tears fill Kshipra's eyes, but she says nothing. She sits on the edge of the bed, the tears coming silently now. I did everything I could, she thinks. But it will never be enough for him.
"She wasn't just your mother, Rajan! She was mine too!" and it's not about Ma, for now. Do not drift the topic.

For everything in the world you just want to blame me? Even for your sinful act..?

Kshipra's hands tremble, but she refuses to back down. "And that gives you the right to betray me?"

"Maybe you pushed me to it and remember that i have not forgoten about what is between you and Murli!" he snaps.

The words strike like lightning, burning through every last shred of patience she has. "You disgust me," she whispers.

In a flash, his hand lashes out. The slap lands hard across her face, sending her stumbling backward. Before she can regain her balance, he grabs a chair and hurls it across the room.

She barely has time to react before it crashes into her side, knocking her to the ground. Her vision gets blur, her breath comes in gasps, and then darkness spread all around her. She lies there for a long time, not in her senses.

Somewhere in the middle of the night, consciousness returns, slow and painful. The cold floor presses against her cheek. A dull ache spreads through her body, every breath sending sharp pain through her ribs.

For a moment she lies still, the events replaying in her mind like a cruel nightmare. But it isn't a nightmare. It's real. And something inside her changes forever.

Leaving the Broken

Later that night, Kshipra sits at the small desk in their bedroom, the only light coming from the dim lamp beside her. Her hands shake as she picks up a pen and writes a letter, her words carefully chosen but trembling with emotion.

"Rajan, I am not a mental case and I cannot stay in this house under constant blame. I need time to heal, to find myself. I need some money for my journey and i am taking just that. This is for my peace of mind."

She folds the letter with care and places it on the bedside table. Before the next morning, she packs her bag, just a few clothes and a notebook. It feels like a lifetime ago that she packed this bag for a different journey, a journey that led her to Rajan, to this house, to Madhu. But now, the road ahead feels different. She isn't sure what awaits her, but she knows she can't stay here any longer.

She doesn't look back as she closes the door behind her. The world outside feels vast, uncertain and for the first time in a long while, she breathes deeply, as if stepping into a new chapter of her life.

As she walks away she feels a strange pull towards the house as if it is not allowing her to go. Her feet feel so heavy; she is barely able to walk. She feels she is leaving Madhu behind. She still walks as tears flood.

All the earlier memories flash trying to get washed away with her tears.

Kshipra boards the bus, her mind keep racing far ahead of the vehicle, as if her thoughts are moving faster than the wheels turning beneath her. Memories of Ajay and Sudha flicker through her mind like a series of brief, sharp flashes, moments of laughter, shared secrets, and the bittersweet feeling of friendship lost.

Each image cuts deeper into her heart, and by the time she arrives at her stop, she feels a strange heaviness in her legs. They refuse to take her to the house she once called home, choosing instead to lead her to the riverbank.

Here, among the waters, are all the memories she holds dear, the place where the four friends once found solace in each other's company. The river seems to mirror her turmoil, reflecting the storm brewing within her. She reaches the bank, and the weight of everything she has been carrying overwhelms her.

Her knees buckle, and she collapses, breaking down in tears, feeling as though the arms of her mother, are the only thing that could provide any comfort, any protection from the chaos inside her.

The night falls around her, darkness creeps in, but Kshipra remains unaware of the world shifting around her. All that matters is the aching emptiness inside, the pain she can no longer hold inside.

Just as she sits lost in her sorrow, she hears a voice and soft, concerned. "Kshipra, what are you doing here at this hour?" It's Usha, and when she sees Kshipra's condition, she understands without needing to be told. There are no words needed; the pain is clear. Usha walks up gently, her heart heavy with concern, and says, "Come, I'll take you home."

Kshipra, barely able to lift her head, stares at Usha with eyes clouded by pain. Her voice is barely a whisper, but the words cut through the air like a dagger. "Which home? No one wants me. No one cares about me. I don't want to go anywhere."

Usha's heart breaks at the sight of her friend, and a tear escapes her eye, but she quickly wipes it away. She moves closer, letting Kshipra rest her head on her shoulder. Kshipra sobs uncontrollably, and Usha simply holds her, the quiet act of support speaking louder than anything she could say.

As the minutes stretch into hours, Kshipra's voice trembles as she starts to speak, her words a mixture of pain and resignation. "I understand now… about the rivalry between my siblings, the way we've all been caught in this pattern. But knowing that doesn't make it hurt any less."

Her sobs rack her body as she continues, "Nothing worked for me. Nothing ever works for me. I can see the past, I understand what happened, but how will they ever understand? Who will tell them the truth?" Her voice cracks, and just as her words trail off, exhaustion takes over. Kshipra almost falls unconscious in Usha's arms, her body limp but her heart still heavy with unsaid words.

Usha knows that in Kshipra's fragile state, she cannot be left to wander, not now. She doesn't hesitate. Gently, she lifts her friend in her arms, her face set with determination. Kshipra murmurs weakly in her unconscious state, her words incoherent, but Usha listens quietly, absorbing every whispered sorrow.

Together, they make their way to the bus stand heading towards Lakshmi. At this hour they have to wait till its time for the first bus of the day. As the hours stretch on, and as the bus haults just before the dawn Usha walks, her mind focused only on getting Kshipra the help she needs, offering comfort and a silent promise to stand by her no matter what.

Meanwhile, in her humble home in the village, Lakshmi sits in quiet contemplation, her weathered hands folded in her lap. She can sense Kshipra's turmoil, her inner turmoil and pain, and she knows that the time has come for their paths to cross once more.

"She carries the weight of generations past," Lakshmi murmurs to herself, her voice filled with compassion. "But she also carries the seed of transformation within her. I will welcome her with open arms, and together, we will walk the path towards her healing and renewal."

Mild sun rays bother Kshipra's eyes, causing them to flutter open. As she wakes, she feels something different, a shift within her. She sits up, her gaze scans the room, and recognizes the place; she stayed here a few months ago. She quietly asks herself, "How did I come here? Or am I dreaming?" Just then, Lakshmi enters with a cup of herbal tea, offering it to her. "Take this, you will feel better," she says gently.

Kshipra hesitates offering a small hesitant smile, then takes the cup and sips. "Was Usha with me? I feel so but I don't recollect traveling here," she murmurs, her voice appears tinged with confusion.

Lakshmi sits on the edge of the bed with calm and reassuring expression. "You weren't in your senses, dear. Usha dropped you off and left immediately as she couldn't stay back."

Kshipra's eyes close for a moment, guilt flickering across her face. "I'm troubling her too much. Yes, of course, her family will worry about her. She had to go."

Lakshmi sighs deeply then encourages Kshipra to rest a bit longer. "You should lie down, dear, just a little more time."

But Kshipra isn't ready to rest. She reaches out, holding onto Lakshmi's wrist as she turns to leave. Lakshmi stops and looks back at her. "Give yourself some time, dear. We'll talk over lunch."

Lakshmi sits quietly, her eyes locked with Kshipra's. She seems to wait, her calm presence an invitation for Kshipra to speak. There is a silence that stretches between them, but it is not uncomfortable. It feels like the air itself is holding space for the revelation Kshipra is about to share.

Finally, Kshipra takes a deep breath, breaking the silence. "Lakshmi, I…" She falters, her voice trembling as she tries to find the right words. "I've found something. Something strange, something I didn't expect."

Lakshmi raises an eyebrow slightly, signaling her to continue. Kshipra presses her palms to her lap, as if steadying herself before speaking.

"As I traced my family's roots, I discovered a pattern, a pattern of conflict. It's between siblings. Every generation there seems to be an unresolved tension between brothers and sisters; Rivalries, betrayals, misunderstandings. I didn't understand it at first. I thought it was just isolated incidents, but it's the same story, repeated again and again."

Lakshmi leans forward slightly, her interest is piqued. Her eyes remain soft, yet knowing. "Tell me more," she says in a voice that holds both gentleness and authority.

Kshipra nods, her mind swirling as she recalls the stories she uncovered. "I found it in my great-grandparents' generation, in the letters they left behind.

It wasn't just about wealth or inheritance, though that was part of it. There was something deeper, something more; disconnect, a fracture in the family bond. My great-uncle and great-aunt, siblings who were once close had a falling out over a difference in belief. One followed a spiritual path that the other disapproved of. Their bond, once strong, was shattered."

Kshipra pauses, gathering her thoughts. "I thought it was just a personal dispute.

My grandmother and her brother, they were torn apart by a secret. It was never spoken of, but it was clear there was something unsaid between them. And it carried on with my parents, too. My mother and my aunts are always distant, always at odds, despite their shared childhood. They never really healed that rift."

Kshipra exhales, feeling heaviness in her chest as she reflects on the pattern. "And now, here I am. Now, I see how this pattern lives in me too. I've always avoided conflict, mistaking it for peace. But maybe its fear passed down."

Lakshmi's expression is steady, but there is a spark of recognition in her eyes. She doesn't interrupt, but her presence encourages Kshipra to continue.

"I've always been the peacekeeper, the mediator. I've avoided confrontations, tried to smooth things over. But now that I see this pattern, I can't ignore it anymore. It's as if it's a curse, this inability to heal the divisions between us. It's like the energy of conflict has been passed down, an unresolved knot in the family. And I don't know how to break it."

Kshipra's voice wavers as she finishes speaking, and for the first time, she feels truly vulnerable. She looks at Lakshmi, waiting for a response, unsure of what to expect.

Lakshmi sits quietly for a long moment, as if digesting what Kshipra has said. Her fingers lightly trace the edges of her shawl, a subtle movement that shows she is deeply considering the weight of Kshipra's words. The room feels pregnant with silence, as if everything in the space is listening to the revelation.

When Lakshmi finally speaks, her voice is calm, but there is an undeniable strength in it. "What you've uncovered Kshipra, is not a curse. It is a pattern, a karmic thread woven into the fabric of your family's lineage. It's been passed down from one generation to the next because it has not been addressed. The unresolved tensions, the unhealed wounds, are energies that continue to echo through time."

Kshipra's brow furrows in confusion. "But how do I break it? How do I undo something so deep, so ingrained?"

Lakshmi's gaze softens, and she leans forward, her eyes locking with Kshipra's. "The first step is to acknowledge it. You've done that. You've seen the pattern, and you've seen how it affects you, how it affects your relationships. This awareness is the key. But simply knowing the pattern exists is not enough. You must make a conscious choice to stop repeating it. You must break the cycle, not just for yourself, but for those who came before you and those who will come after you."

Kshipra listens intently, trying to absorb the gravity of Lakshmi's words.

"The next step," Lakshmi continues, "is to confront the energy that has been passed down. Not with force or resistance, but with understanding.

Look at the root of the conflict. Why does it arise in every generation? What is it teaching you? conflicts between the siblings, what is its core? Is it a fear of being seen, of being heard? Is it a fear of being loved, of being accepted for who they truly are?"

Kshipra feels the weight of the question "I've never thought about it like that," she admits, the revelation taking root in her consciousness. "I've always seen it as something external, as if it was a fight over something physical; resources, beliefs. But now, it feels like something deeper, a fear of loss maybe or a fear of not being enough."

Lakshmi nods slowly, her expression understanding. "Exactly, the patterns you see between siblings are mirrors of the internal struggles each individual faces within themselves. It's a struggle to understand one's own worth, to define oneself, to feel seen and valued. When these struggles go unaddressed, they manifest as conflict."

Kshipra feels a deep sense of clarity, but it is still

overwhelming. She's never viewed her family's issues in this way before. They've always seemed like personal failings, like weaknesses that should be avoided or ignored. But now, Lakshmi's words are unraveling the tightly wound threads of fear and self-doubt that have defined her family for generations.

"So, how do I heal this?" Kshipra asks, her voice is barely above a whisper.

Lakshmi's smile is warm, though there is a sense of finality in her words "by healing yourself first. The energy of your family is deeply connected to yours, but that energy cannot heal unless you begin with your own. You must learn to heal the wounds of the past, to forgive yourself, and your ancestors.

Forgiveness is not just for the other person, it's for your own soul too. Let go of the fear that has defined the relationships in your family. Let go of the belief that conflict is inevitable. You have the power to break the cycle."

Kshipra sits still, her mind reeling with the weight of Lakshmi's guidance. She feels a wave of emotion rise within her; a mixture of sorrow for the pain her family has carried, and hope that perhaps she can be the one to change the course of their history.

"I will do it," Kshipra says, her voice firm with newfound resolve. "I will break this pattern. I will not let it define me, or my relationships."

Lakshmi places a hand on Kshipra's hand and her touch feels light but grounding, "You are already on the path, Kshipra. Remember, the process of healing is not linear. It will take time, and it will require you to be patient with yourself. But know this, you have the strength, and you are not alone."

Kshipra nods, feeling a sense of peace settle within her. The path ahead may be challenging, but with Lakshmi's wisdom, she knows she has the tools to confront the family's legacy. And in that moment, she realizes that she has already taken the step.

Kshipra sits by the river her gaze is distant and lost in the endless expanse of water before her. Her heart feels heavy, like it's been wrapped in chains, weighed down by everything she's unable to express. The pain of her unspoken words to Ajay and Rajan gnaws at her every moment, and the ache in her soul feels endless. She's trapped in a silence no one can understand.

Lakshmi arrives, and stands behind Kshipra for a moment, observing her, before sitting down beside her. Lakshmi speaks softly, as if knowing the depth of Kshipra's pain without words "You carry too much, Kshipra. I see it, feel it. Your soul is burdened by more than you can bear. And yet, you are not lost. You can still find peace, still heal."

Kshipra's voice trembles, thick with grief "I don't know how. The words I need to say… to Ajay, to Rajan… they're stuck inside me. But I could speak to their souls and tried to convey, though I reached them. I don't know how to make them understand."

Lakshmi looks at her with a deep, knowing gaze. "You cannot convey to them until your soul is healed. Until you heal yourself, your words will remain trapped within you, lost in your grief. But there is a way. There is someone who can help you, someone who can guide you back to yourself."

Kshipra turns her head, her eyes searching Lakshmi's face. She feels the thread of hope beginning to weave itself in her chest, but she is also wary, not sure of what Lakshmi means "Who? Who can help me?"
Lakshmi's expression softens as she looks into Kshipra's eyes, "His name is Shantanu."

Kshipra blinks, confusion written across her face and her mind spins with questions. She looks at Lakshmi, silently asking for more, "Shantanu? Who is he? What does he do?"

Lakshmi exhales slowly, as though carefully choosing her words, "Shantanu is a healer, Kshipra. Not of the body, but of the soul. He has the power to help you find peace within yourself. To help you untangle the grief that weighs you down. But he is no ordinary healer. He does not offer his help to just anyone. He waits for those who are ready to face pain, to confront it and heal from it. And right now, you are ready. You just need to trust him."

Kshipra's heart flutters in uncertainty, a spark of hope mingled with fear. She's never heard of such a person, and the idea of going to someone so unknown fills her with doubt "but how do I find him? What if I'm not ready? What if I can't do what he asks?"

Lakshmi reaches out and places a hand gently on Kshipra's, her voice warm, comforting, "I will take you to him, he is not far from here. And when you meet him, you will know his presence, his energy, which resonates with souls. He will help you see what you cannot yet see in yourself. But you must be open, Kshipra. You must let go of the fear that holds you back." Kshipra lowers her gaze, thinking about the journey ahead. The idea of facing her pain head-on, confronting the raw, picking the broken parts of self, terrifies her. But deep down she knows Lakshmi is right. She can't keep running from this. She can't keep carrying this weight forever.

Kshipra looks up at Lakshmi, her voice small but resolute "I'll go. I'll find him. I don't know how, but I will, for them and for myself."

Lakshmi smiles, "We will leave for his Aashram, tomorrow morning." And the next morning they set for the journey to Shantanu's aashram.

Kshipra follows Lakshmi as her heart keeps pounding with a blend of anticipation and quiet fear. She has come so far, and yet the journey ahead feels like an uncharted path, shrouded in mystery. As they walk through the winding streets of the town, the noise and bustle of the city begin to fade, replaced by a serene quietness that seems to envelop them. The air grows cooler, and the scent of earth and greenery fills her senses.

With each step, she feels the weight of the moment settling in. She is about to take a monumental step in her spiritual journey. It feels like crossing a threshold into something far greater than she has ever known. She feels both afraid and exhilarated.

Walking the unknown path

As Lakshmi leads and Kshipra follows her, for the first time, Kshipra truly sees Lakshmi. Her grace, her essence, all about her looks different.

"She is walking this road for me" Kshipra talks to herself and also realizes that she must have walked down such journeys for many. "But what brings her on these paths" Kshipra wonders.

As they walk deep into the jungle the air smells of herbs and flowers Kshipra had never witnessed before. It feels pleasant and so appealing that Kshipra wants to sit and feel it for some more time. She sits on one rock embedded at the bottom of one huge tree watching Lakshmi still walking further and calls for her, "Lakshmi, can we sit for a while?" Lakshmi turns around, looks at Kshipra with a smile. She carefully takes out a bottle from her small cotton bag and gently sprinkles water over her face, befor she sits opposite to Kshipra.

After a while, Kshipra asks softly, "Why don't you live with them?" Lakshmi's eyebrows raise as Kshipra continues, "I mean, with Usha and with your son? I have never seen you while I visited Usha's house a couple of times."

Lakshmi doesn't respond at once. She sips the last of the water, sets the brass pot down, her eyes drift toward the peepal tree at a distance, its thick roots curling into the earth like veins of memory.

"I used to," she says, "When Usha's grandfather was still alive. The house felt full then. His voice, his laughter, but when he died everything went quiet inside me. I breathed, but I didn't live. I was not able to eat, sleep. I walked around like a shadow of myself."

 "Then I meet her, Mata Shivani. People feared her, called her strange. But when I meet her, she was like, still water. You look into it, and you start to see yourself clearly, for the first time. She didn't give me words. She gave me space, and silence. In that, I began to heal."

"My son hated it. He said I'm being pulled into darkness, into some black magic. But it isn't magic; its truth; eternal and simple, bigger than birth, bigger than death. They will never understand. One night, he fought, loud and cruel. And I left."

Lakshmi takes a deep sigh and continues "I followed Mata Shivani and came here to her Aashram, this Aashram. She parted her knowledge, her practices and rituals to me before she liberated."

Lakshmi looks at Kshipra and smiles "and you must have not seen me but I have heard about you from Usha, she never stoped talking about you. You are her first friend, her only light in a world that kept shutting her out. She wanted to stay with me Kshipra, always. She begged to her parents, again and again. But they didn't allow it. They say she has to grow up the way they choose, not how her heart needs. She followed her parent's wish. She unwillingly got married. They all knew it was for the dawry, they married her to the terminally ill man for all his family wanted was the money and his heir."

"She tolerated it all but she came here now, not for herself but for you. She would break any barear for you, be it built by her parents, or..."

Kshipra stares at her, as if the world has suddenly tilted sideways. Her lips part, but no words come. When she finally speaks, her voice trembles.

"I didn't know all this about Usha and that I mattered that much to her."

Her eyes fill, not with tears alone, but with wonder, a kind of stunned gratitude, "I thought I was just someone who sat beside her. I never knew I..."

Lakshmi speaks with a sigh "That's the thing, child. We rarely know the weight of our kindness in someone else's story."

Kshipra looks at Lakshmi with a slight smile then back at the path leading toward the inner sanctum of Shantanu's Ashram, a deep silence holds her now like something sacred has just moved through her.

They reach the edge of the town, where the structures grow sparse, and the landscape opens up into a sweeping panorama of trees, rolling hills, and vast expanses of natural beauty. Kshipra looks around in awe.

The environment seems untouched by time, as though the world has stopped in this sacred space. The sounds of birds singing and the whisper of wind through the leaves form a gentle symphony.

In the distance, the ashram appears a pristine, white structure that almost seems to float on the earth. As they walk closer Kshira notice its white walls contrast with the deep green of the trees, and its architecture looks simple yet harmonious, as if it were always meant to be part of the landscape. There are open courtyards filled with plants and wildflowers, their vibrant colors bursting against the soft, pale walls. A sense of peace radiates from it, a stillness that pulls Kshipra further in, offering her an embrace of calm and reassurance.

Lakshmi walks beside her with graceful steps.

As Kshipra and Lakshmi approach the ashram, the air feels with the serene hum of spiritual energy. Shantanu stands waiting for them. His presence feels magnetic, as if he embodies both the earth's grounding strength and the sky's limitless serenity.

Kshipra's breathe catches in her throat the moment she sees him. Standing tall and confident, his broad shoulders reflect a life of discipline, and yet there's an undeniable softness in his aura that immediately puts her at ease. His white attire, simple yet imbued with purity, flows around him with grace, while his long white hair and beard seem to radiate light. His piercing blue eyes look calm yet intense holding the depth of untold wisdom and Kshipra feels as though they could peer into the very depths of her soul.

Lakshmi smiles warmly, her eyes meeting Shantanu's and they exchange a glance, a silent acknowledgment of their deep connection. There is no need for words between them; the bond they share is palpable and profound, built over years.

"Welcome, Lakshmi," Shantanu's deep voice breaks the quiet, as he turns to greet her. "And you, Kshipra," he adds, his gaze now meeting hers with a knowing warmth. "I've heard much about you."

The sound of her name in his voice stirs something deep within Kshipra, a mixture of comfort and vulnerability. She feels her nerves melt away, replaced by a sense of belonging, as though she's exactly where she's meant to be. His presence is both reassuring and powerful, as if he can see her completely without judgment, only with deep compassion.

Shantanu steps aside, motioning for them to enter. Kshipra walks in, taking in the tranquil surroundings. The air inside is thick with a calming energy. Each breath she takes fills her with peace. The walls are adorned with intricate symbols. Their meanings are foreign to her but strangely comforting. The soft, ethereal sound of chanting floats through the air, mixing with the delicate clinking of bells and the scent of incense that lingers like a sacred offering.

The scent strikes her deeply; frangipani and burnt sandalwood. Her body stills. She's smelled this before, long ago…. It feels like home and warning, both at once.

The ashram feels alive with energy, as if the very building itself is vibrating with the presence of countless seekers and healers who have passed through its doors before.

They move through an expansive courtyard, where disciples work in quiet harmony. Some grind herbs, their movements appear deliberate and slow, while others are seated in meditation in the different section, eyes closed while their energy merging with the natural surroundings. There's a palpable sense of unity here, as if all who are present are bound by a shared purpose, each one contributing to the flow of energy that pulses through the ashram. Kshipra feels that same flow moving through her, her nerves settling into something akin to peace.

Shantanu leads them to a secluded room at the back of the ashram, where the energy feels even more still and sacred. Kshipra crosses the threshold, and as she does, she feels a wave of calm wash over her. It's as if the very air in this room holds the answers to all the questions she's been carrying in her heart. Time seems to slow, the present moment stretching out into eternity. In the center of the room lies a simple mat, surrounded by flickering candles and incense that casts a soft glow across the space. The room feels timeless, as if it exists both in the physical world and beyond it.

Shantanu turns to Kshipra, "Are you ready for what lies ahead?" he asks carrying the weight of ancient wisdom in his voice.

Kshipra's heart beats faster, she feels her nervousness rise, but she also knows this is why she has come. She has come seeking answers, to understand the pain of Rajan. To understand the pain of Ajay and others in her generation who are trapped in the same ancestral patterns. She knows that breaking free from this cycle will not be easy, but she is determined. There is no turning back now.

"I'm ready," Kshipra says, her voice steady despite the fluttering of nerves within her.

Shantanu's expression softens, and he nods, a look of approval and understanding passing through his eyes. "Very well, we shall begin as the sun rises tomorrow."

It's time for Lakshmi to leave, handing over Kshipra to this divine place. She looks at Kshipra and spots the restlessness on her face for parting from her.

Lakshmi steps forward and places a hand on Kshipra's shoulder, offering a quiet comfort. "Remember," she says softly reassuring, "you are never alone in this. We are here with you, and the divine will guide you."

As Lakshmi leaves Kshipra keep gazing at her till she is out of sight.

Kshipra is unable to sleep tonight. Though she has

come so far on this journey, tonight she feels a profound shift within her, in every sense. The stillness of her surroundings is so absolute that it unsettles her, while inside, her mind and heart are storming with unrest. Her soul seems torn, teetering on the edge of two worlds, neither here nor there. She stands up and walks around the room, her fingers brushing against the smooth, cold walls. The white walls reflect the faint moonlight pouring in through the window, making everything seem brighter, almost too bright. She runs her hands over the soft fabric of the curtains, feeling their coolness, their texture, as though grounding herself in this strange calm. The room, all in shades of white, feels like a blank canvas, sterile and empty, to be filled with so much unsaid. She takes a deep breath, her fingers tracing the edges of furniture, the contours of the stillness around her.

Then, she finally lies down, closing her eyes, but peace doesn't come easily. Her mind races the quiet almost deafening. Yet, as she glimpses the moon outside, it's silver light sooths her frayed thoughts, she drifts into a restless sleep, just before dawn's first light.

Morning arrives and Kshipra steps out of her room. She walks slowly, almost as if the stillness of the night hasn't yet left her, her steps quiet on the cool floor. The air is fresh, and there's a calmness that seems to hum with the promise of a new day. She makes her way towards the prayer hall, where the others are gathering, drawn by the same call.

As she enters, the warmth of the room wraps around

her. The soft, resonant sound of the singing bells fills the space, creating a peaceful atmosphere that wish to settles deep within her. The gentle ringing vibrates in the air, a perfect harmony with the chants of "OM" rising in unison, reverberating through the room. Kshipra takes her seat among the others, the weight of the night slowly lifting from her shoulders as the sacred sound envelops her, soothing her restless mind. She closes her eyes for a moment, allowing the energy of the chant to wash over her, grounding her in the present, in this moment of quiet connection.

Having lunch with all others present there is another experience for Kshipra. Shantanu's disciple takes her to yet another room, where Shantanu is sitting calmly with closed eyes. Disciple directs her to sit on another mat already placed.

Feeling their presence, Shantanu opens his eyes slowly. He looks at Kshipra gently saying "This is where we begin your healing from tomorrow, just at the dawn. For next seven days we cleanse, open and activate your chakras". Kshipra's lips try to convey a smile while she actually feels a pull in her stomach.

The next morning, as the first light of day breaks over the horizon, Kshipra arrives for her divine healing practice. Shantanu and his long-time disciple are already waiting in the peaceful, candle-lit room, the air filled with the calming scent of incense. The atmosphere is thick with mystery and respect. Shantanu gestures for Kshipra to sit, and with a wise, respectful tone, he begins to speak.

"Divine light healing," he explains, "is a way of awakening and balancing the energy centers within you, your chakras. Each chakra is like a door that connects your body to your spirit. When these centers are balanced, divine energy flows freely, helping you heal from within."

Shantanu moves to the center of the room and sits in a meditative posture. He begins to explain each chakra, guiding Kshipra to feel each one awaken as he speaks. He starts with the root chakra, located at the base of the spine, grounding her to the earth. "We start here," he says gently, "because only when we are grounded, can we rise higher."

They begin with simple breathing exercises, helping Kshipra feel the stability of the root chakra. Shantanu asks her to imagine a red light rising from the earth, flowing up through her body, giving her strength and support.

Each day, Shantanu guides her through awakening one chakra at a time. When they reach the sacral chakra, Kshipra feels a gentle wave of energy washing over her, connecting her to her emotions and creativity. The orange light she visualizes makes her feel more alive, more connected to her inner self.

Next, they move upward to the solar plexus chakra. As she pictures a golden light glowing there, Kshipra feels a warm, powerful energy spreading through her. This light represents her personal strength, helping her feel more confident and determined.

When they reach the heart chakra, Shantanu's voice softens. "The heart is where love lives," he says. "It's where we feel compassion, for ourselves and others." He helps Kshipra imagine a soft green light blossoming inside her chest, growing with every breath. She feels this light wrap around her, bringing healing to past hurts.

As the days pass, they continue up through the chakras. Kshipra envisions the blue light of the throat chakra, which helps her speak her truth, and the deep indigo light of the third eye, which opens her intuition.

Finally, they reach the crown chakra at the top of her head, where she connects to the divine. Shantanu describes it as a gateway to the universe, a place where she can connect with pure consciousness. He guides her to imagine a violet light descending from above, filling her completely with peace and grace.

Once all her chakras are open and balanced, Shantanu tells Kshipra, "Now we will begin the actual divine light healing."

He invites her to sit comfortably, resting his hands near her head, just close enough for her to feel the warmth of his energy.

Shantanu asks Kshipra to visualize a golden light coming down from the sky and entering through her crown chakra. "This is divine light," he says. "It is a light of healing, wisdom, and love." Kshipra feels the warm light filling her from head to toe, like sunlight flowing into her soul.

The light moves from her crown chakra to her third eye, clearing her mind and helping her see clearly. It then flows to her throat, allowing her to let go of any fears or doubts that have kept her from speaking her truth. The golden light continues to her heart, filling her with warmth and releasing any sadness or grief.

The light moves further down, past the solar plexus and sacral chakras, until it reaches the root chakra. As the light flows through each chakra, Kshipra feels deeper and deeper healing, like layers of pain and fear melting away.

At the end of each session, Shantanu places his hands over her heart, sealing the divine energy within her. "Healing is a journey, Kshipra," he says softly. "It begins with letting go and ends with acceptance. You are healing not just for yourself, but for your ancestors and those who will come after you."

Each day, Kshipra leaves the healing room feeling lighter, more at peace. The divine light fills her completely, healing wounds and giving her spirit the rest it needs.

For each chakra, the process is the same. The divine light enters through the crown, moves through the entire body, and then flows down through the root chakra. From there the light moves deep into the earth, grounding her to the core of Mother Earth. She feels a celestial connection from the universe above, passing through her, and into the earth below. Each chakra is balanced by this flow, harmonizing her energy and allowing healing to happen from the inside out.

Shantanu advises Kshipra to practice divine light healing daily for the next few days. By now, her consciousness has reached a different level altogether.

This morning, after her routine, Kshipra sits for her meditation. As she closes her eyes, Lakshmi's voice resonates in her mind, "There must be some reality which Ajay and Rajan's souls carry, but you are not aware of it. That is why you couldn't convey to their souls what is needed for them to heal."

Kshipra's breathe halts and she opens her eyes, feeling suffocated. She takes a few deep breaths and allows the thought to settle, promising herself that it will be addressed. It's time for her to talk to Shantanu about her soul's request to see the unseen.

Shantanu, though in meditation with another group of healers, senses the request and hums in acknowledgment. He knows this moment is coming.

Shantanu gets up from his seat and walks toward Kshipra, his eyes catching her gaze, filled with curiosity. They stop in front of each other. Before Kshipra can speak, Shantanu places his hand on her shoulder, guiding her to sit on the verandah under an adjacent tree. He speaks softly, "I understand your curiosity, but it's not going to be easy. Not everyone is capable of this, and not all will achieve it. If you feel you can, then you can."

Kshipra looks down then gazes at Shantanu with a determined expression, "If I don't see the real reasons, then there is no point in coming this far in search of the truth. I feel this life is meant to make them understand certain things, and if I don't do that, then my life is a waste."

Shantanu interrupts, "No life is a waste. By saying so, you question the universe's ability to assign roles. Every being is here to perform their prescribed role. If you are meant to break the patterns, you will. But if you are not meant to do so in this life, no matter what you do, you will not be able to achieve it. But your soul progresses on its path regardless. No one's life is meant solely to teach or impart knowledge to others unless they have gained wisdom. Each soul has its own way of understanding life lessons. It's for your soul to understand your journey and lessons, while their souls will have their own teachings."

Shantanu continues in his soft tone, "What you can do is remove the fog from their vision. For that, you need to know what is unknown to you."

Shantanu pauses then adds, "Your chakras are perfectly balanced now, and you must maintain this state, so continue with your meditation.

To know the facts from Ajay and Rajan's perspective, you need a deeper meditation and an opening of your third eye. The new moon is in two days, and we will begin the ritual to open your third eye. The meditation will continue each morning until the full moon, when you will be able to see what you never knew before."

Kshipra sighs deeply, feeling overwhelmed. She asks softly, "Will I be able to heal their souls then and convey the truth they need to know?"

Shantanu gets up, places his hand on Kshipra's head, and nods, his slight smile conveying a quiet certainty. Kshipra is ready to face the unseen reality of her past life, but she has no idea how it will unfold through her mind, body, and soul.

Its time before the dawn of a new moon 'the time of divine consciousness' and Kshipra's soul is ready to face the ultimate reality.

The Sacred Energy

As Kshipra pours the cold water over her head and it runs down her Shantanu's voice resonates, "we shall begin at 3.30am daily till the full moon. At this hour your mind is naturally calm and the energy in the atmosphere is highly pure aiding in deeper meditation and easier to connect with intuition and consciousness. This is why it's called 'creators hour'." And as Kshipra walks to the meditation room Shantanu's voice continue "If you surrender to the practice, if your meditation is unbroken, the sight will come. By the time the full moon rises, your third eye will open and you will see not with your eyes but with the vision that never fades".

Kshipra stands at the threshold, her breath shallowing and fingers hovering over the wooden door. A strange stillness wraps around her, as if the very air inside the room pulse with something ancient, something unseen.

Her heartbeat feels steady, yet there is a weight not of fear, but of knowing the fear. She is about to step into something irreversible. Beyond this door, time would cease to exist. With a slow, deliberate motion, she pushes the door open and steps forward. Now, there is only this; her breath, the silence, and the path that would lead her to the unknown and unseen reality.

Shantanu stands in there waiting for her. He looks stronger and taller in that light. His face glows with his wisdom as always. Kshipra moves forward and sit on a place as he directs.

Shantanu moves around Kshipra slowly, preparing the space for the ritual. He begins to chant in a low, melodic voice that seems to vibrate in the air, each syllable resonating with an ancient energy. The sound fills the room, slowly pulling Kshipra deeper into herself. It's as if the very essence of the universe is speaking through him, guiding her to a place she has never been before.

Kshipra feels her breath slow, the air around her growing thick with energy. Her mind quiets as the sound of Shantanu's chanting becomes the only thing she can hear. The vibrations seem to reverberate in her chest, in her bones and slowly the boundaries between her physical body and the space around her begin to blur.

Shantanu guides "Close your eyes and breathe."

Kshipra obeys, lowering her gaze, feeling the cool air on her skin as she inhales. The breath comes slow at first, hesitant but then deepens, flowing through her body, expanding her chest, filling her lungs with the scent of ancient wood and light green light. She feels the weight of the world fall away with each exhale, the constant hum of her thoughts fading into the background, until there is only the pulse of the room and the rhythm of her breath.

"Focus on the space between your brows," Shantanu continues, his voice now a whisper "Feel the energy gathering there. Quiet the mind and let it settle like dust."

Kshipra feels it; a subtle tingling, a pull, as if her consciousness is drawn upward, toward the center of her forehead. It starts soft, almost imperceptible but with each breath it grows stronger. A warmth blooms beneath her skin, as if a fire is kindling in the very core of her being.

She breathes deeper, surrendering to the sensations; the warmth, the hum, the growing pressure. Her pulse quickens, but she does not resist it. She allows herself to be consumed by the sensation, her body becoming lighter, more fluid. The green glow of the statue seems to pulse along with her heart, matching the rhythm of her breath.

"Let go of everything that holds you back," Shantanu says softly, almost a mantra. "Let the light fill you. Let the vision come."

Kshipra's breath quickens now, a soft shudder running through her body as she feels the pressure between her brows intensify. It's as though her mind is opening, her perception stretching beyond the confines of her own body.

In the silence of her meditation, she feels her consciousness stretch into the vastness, as if something is unlocking inside her. The heat is now a fire but a fire that does not burn, one that illuminates. The space between her eyes begins to ache, then to throb, each beat like a soft drum calling her to the edge of a forgotten realm.

The light becomes more vivid, more real. Kshipra feels her awareness shifting, as if something ancient stirs, ready to reveal its secrets.

The first few days are restless. Each dawn, she enters the meditation chamber, sits in stillness, and fights the weight of her own thoughts. Images flicker like half-formed memories, fragments of dreams, the noise of a mind untrained in silence. At times, doubt creeps in, whispering in the quiet corners of her consciousness.

"Let go," Shantanu reminds her. "You are not your thoughts. You are the space between them."
Slowly, something shifts.

By the fourth day, her awareness deepens. The darkness behind her closed eyes is no longer empty. It has movement, a pulse of its own and flashes of violet and indigo swirl dissolving as soon as they appear. A ringing sound, subtle yet persistent fills the silence. It no longer feels like she's merely sitting, rather she's descending, layer by layer, into something vast.

By the seventh day, time loses meaning. The mornings stretch into eternity, and yet pass in the blink of an eye. Her body no longer feels like a boundary but a vessel, floating in currents of unseen energy. The vibrations within her forehead grow stronger, as though a door is trembling, waiting to open.

"You are close", Shantanu murmurs on the twelth day, His voice barely a breath "do not seek it. Let it come to you."
She surrenders completely. No striving, no grasping, only presence.

And then, the night of the full moon arrives. Shantanu moves closer to her, placing his hand gently on her forehead. She feels his touch like a warm current of energy flowing into her, dissolving the last remnants of hesitation. His voice weaves through the silence, rhythmic and unwavering, like the pulse of the universe itself "Close your eyes, breathe."

She obeys, drawing in a slow breath. The air feels more different now; denser, charged. As she exhales, the boundaries of her body begin to blur.

Shantanu's voice continues to chant, his words growing more intense, more powerful.

Kshipra's closed eyes, focusing on the sensations coursing through her body. There is a heat in her chest, a pressure between her eyes as if her third eye is slowly waking up.

"Focus, Kshipra," Shantanu whispers, his voice is a grounding force. "Feel the energy as it moves through you. Let go of your fear."

The pressure between her eyes intensifies, and Kshipra gasps, feeling a rush of energy surge through her. It's as if her mind is expanding, opening to realms she has never known. Her vision flashes with vivid images; blurred, distant, yet intensely real. She can feel the weight of Rajan's pain, his bitterness, his unresolved emotions. Ajay's resentment feels sharp, biting, and cruel. The darkness between them feels like a shadow, growing and pulling at Kshipra from every direction.

Her head spins as she feels the weight of their negative feelings; those deep, hidden wounds that have festered for lifetimes. She feels the anger that binds them, the guilt that holds them prisoner, and the untold stories that remain buried in their hearts.

But through it all, there is a quiet, steady presence of a grounding force holding her, guiding her through the darkness. She knows that she is not alone. She feels the connection to Lakshmi, and to Shantanu, their energy supporting her, anchoring her as she faces the truth.

Shantanu's voice grows softer, more melodic, as he guides her deeper. "You are safe, Kshipra. Trust the process. Let the truth reveal itself fully when the time is right."

As Kshipra sinks further into the ritual, she feels herself unraveling, shedding the layers of illusion and fear. She is becoming one with the truth; the painful, powerful truth that lies beyond the surface. And as she begins to see the reality of Rajan and Ajay's past, the clarity she has been searching for slowly starts to unfold.

"Close your eyes, Kshipra," Shantanu's voice is a soft whisper, yet it carries the weight of ages. "Trust the process. Let go of everything."

Kshipra's breathe trembles in her throat as she closes her eyes. The room around her seems to dissolve into a vast, infinite nothingness. The world outside fades and all that exists is the sensation of her own body, her skin, her breathe and the endless space within her mind. The stillness envelops her like a thick blanket, cocooning her in peace and a deep, unwavering quiet.

Beneath the stillness, there is something stirring, an energy. It begins as a soft pulse, like the beat of a distant drum. Her heart syncs with it, the rhythm of her own life merging with the energy that surrounds her. It grows, deepens, and she feels the pull in the center of her chest, at the very core of her being.

Shantanu moves with purpose, his steps graceful, deliberate. He circles around her, a figure of wisdom and quiet strength. His voice fills the air now, not with words, but with sound, a chant that seems to come from a place beyond time. The syllables flow like a river of light, each sound resonating with her soul, vibrating through her very bones.

The chant resonates through her body, vibrating from the tips of her toes to the top of her head, a sacred vibration that sets every fiber of her being alight. Kshipra can feel it deep within her spine, the sound weaving itself into her very DNA, unlocking the hidden chambers of her mind. It's as if the words are a key, unlocking something ancient and buried within her, something that has been waiting to awaken.

She feels her breath slow, the rhythm of the chant intertwining with her heartbeat. The pull at her chest intensifies, and then slowly, almost imperceptibly she feels a pressure between her eyebrows, at the point of her third eye. It is not painful but rather a deep subtle pressure, like the gentle nudge of the universe itself urging her to open, to awaken.

Shantanu's hands hover above her, not touching but close enough that Kshipra can feel the warmth of his energy radiating from his palms. He moves in a circular motion, his fingers tracing invisible patterns in the air. With each movement, the pressure between her eyes intensifies, and Kshipra feels as though she is being pulled into a vortex, spinning toward a cosmic center.

"Allow yourself to surrender," Shantanu's voice comes to her from the depths of her consciousness. "Let go of everything. Release the fears, the doubts. Let the light in."

As Kshipra breathes deeply, the pressure at her third eye becomes almost unbearable, and for a moment, she feels as if she might break open from the inside out. Her skin tingles, her scalp prickles with an electric charge. She can feel the energy building inside her, swirling like a storm within her being, gathering power, preparing to erupt.

And then, with a sudden flash, her third eye opens.

The sensation is nothing like what she expected. It is as if the very fabric of her mind is torn open, exposing her to the raw, unfiltered truth of the universe. A flood of light pours into her from every direction, illuminating every dim corner of her soul. Her body tenses, her muscles aching from the intensity, but there is no pain; only an overwhelming rush of pure energy. The light is blinding, all-encompassing, and yet somehow, it is familiar, as if she has always known it.

Kshipra gasps, her breath catching in her throat as the visions come.

They come like a torrent images and sensations flooding her mind in rapid succession. The world spins around her, dissolving into a kaleidoscope of colors, shapes, and sounds. She sees herself as a child, running through fields of tall grass, the sun warm on her skin. She sees her ancestors, their faces blurry and distant, their lives unfolding in fragments moments of joy, of sorrow, of pain.

And then the visions shift.

She sees Rajan, his face twisted in anger, his eyes dark with unspoken pain. She feels the heaviness of his emotions, the deep, unrelenting bitterness that has followed him through lifetimes. She sees Ajay too, equally burdened, his soul clouded with resentment and regret. The two of them are locked in a dance of conflict with her soul, their energies clashing in a way that feels ancient, almost predestined.

Kshipra's heart aches as she feels the weight of their emotions, the tangled threads that bind her together with each one in an endless cycle of suffering. She feels the resentment with them like a tangible force, a wall that cannot be broken, a knot that cannot be undone.

But the visions continue to shift, and Kshipra's mind expands further, seeing beyond the surface. She sees the root of the conflict, an ancestral wound, passed down through generations, like a thread woven into the very fabric of her family's existence. She feels the pain of generations past, the unresolved issues that have haunted her lineage, passed down from one life to the next, each soul carrying the burden, until it lands upon her.

And in that moment, Kshipra understands.

She sees the patterns the invisible forces that have shaped the course of her life, the lives of countless others. She understands that the pain is not personal but it is ancestral, a chain of unresolved emotions that has wrapped itself around their hearts, holding them captive.

But with this understanding comes a profound sense of liberation. She realizes that she is not bound to this cycle. She can break the chain. She can heal.

Her breath quickens as she feels herself being drawn back into her body. The light begins to fade, the visions slowing as the energy settles. The pressure at her third eye releases, and with it, the intensity of the experience begins to wane.

Shantanu's hands are on her now, steady and grounding, his energy like a steady anchor pulling her back into the present. Slowly, the world comes back into focus. The light fades, and Kshipra opens her eyes, blinking against the sudden dimness of the room.

For a moment, she sits in stunned silence, her mind still reeling from the immense flood of visions. The world feels different now; vast, expansive, and full of endless possibilities. She feels a profound sense of clarity, a deep knowing that she has touched something beyond herself, something sacred, something eternal.

Shantanu stands before her, his eyes full of quiet understanding. He smiles gently, as though he has been waiting for this moment, for her to fully awaken.

"You have seen, Kshipra," he says softly. "The truth is now within you. You know what you must do."

Kshipra nods slowly, her heart full of gratitude and awe. She feels an overwhelming sense of peace, as though the universe itself has embraced her, guiding her to a place of healing. The path ahead may still be uncertain, but now, she carries the wisdom of lifetimes within her. She has opened her third eye and with it, the eyes of her soul. And in this moment, she knows that nothing will ever be the same again.

As the light from the third eye opening fades and Kshipra begins to regain her senses, she feels the vastness of the experience settle within her. Her body feels lighter, her mind clearer, as though she has unlocked a door to a higher level of awareness. The weight of the universe, which seemed so heavy just moments ago, now feels like it's gently cradling her. She looks up at Shantanu, her heart still racing, but there is peace in her eyes.

Shantanu raises his palm, signaling Kshipra to remain in this state of mind, allowing the moment to envelop her completely. Kshipra closes her eyes once more, surrendering to the experience, letting it wash over her in waves. Time seems to stretch, and she is immersed in the tranquility of this profound stillness.

Now, Kshipra is ready to confront the unseen, the unknown and the unrevealed. She feels an inner strength, a sense of readiness to step beyond the veil. Shantanu, sensing her transformation, gently guides her to continue refining this state of mind, to practice it for a few more days, until she can slip into it effortlessly.

This morning, Kshipra approaches Shantanu as he sits in his study, his calm demeanor radiats the understanding. He senses the change within her, recognizing that the moment has come for her to move into the next phase of her journey. He meets her gaze, filled with hope and curiosity, and simply says, "We begin tomorrow."

"I shall be there before dawn," she responds with a quiet determination in her voice.

Shantanu exhales slowly, his expression soft yet resolute. "No," he says, "it won't be our usual meditation place."

Kshipra's brows furrow in confusion. "Then where?" she asks.

Without answering, Shantanu turns and walks away, expecting her to follow. She does and together they leave the Ashram, stepping deeper into the forest. The air grows colder as they venture farther from familiar grounds, but Kshipra feels a strange pull, an energy guiding them.

After a short walk, they arrive at a large, imposing dome nestled in the forest's heart. The structure appears ancient, covered in moss and vines, yet it radiates an undeniable energy. Shantanu opens the door, and Kshipra steps inside.

The room she enters feels as though it belongs to a different world, far removed from the ordinary. The air inside is thick with a palpable stillness, almost as if time itself has slowed. The walls of the dome are adorned with intricate carvings, their patterns swirling in harmonious geometry, exuding an ancient wisdom.

In the center, a large green idol stands, softly glowing with an ethereal light. The light emanates from the idol casts reflections on the walls, creating an aura of deep peace and reverence. Kshipra has never seen this idol before anytime, anywhere. She is unable to utter a word or ask anything about it. The glance of a divine idol gives her calm wrapped in the divinity.

The temperature inside the room is cool, but there is distinct warmth that seems to come from the very space itself, as though the room itself is alive with an unseen presence.

The scent of earth and ancient wood fills the air, grounding Kshipra in a way that feels both humbling and awe-inspiring.

There are no windows, only the faintest sliver of light entering through the door, but the room is lit by the soft glow of the idol. It feels sacred, timeless, as if it has witnessed countless spiritual journeys. The vibrations in the air hum with a quiet, otherworldly resonance, sending shivers down her spine.

As Kshipra takes it all in, she feels her senses sharpen, her awareness feels expanding beyond the confines of her body. The room seems to invite her to let go of the material world, to surrender to the deeper, unseen forces at play.

Shantanu stands beside her, silent as though he is guiding her into this sacred space of transformation. He doesn't need to speak, she already understands. This is the moment. This is the place where she will confront the unseen and the unknown.

Kshipra looks around looking at the walls carved with delicate symbols, twist and weave like the threads of an ancient tapestry. Each engraving pulses, as if alive, subtly shifting in the dim light. The patterns aren't random; they feel purposeful; like a language, a code waiting to be deciphered by those who are ready. The stone itself, dark and smooth, breathes with a life of its own, warm to the touch, yet cooling as she moves farther into the room.

Kshipra's gaze fixes at the idol. The figure, towers with a fierce grace; her wide, unblinking eyes seem to pierce through the veils of time, while a faint, knowing smile curves her lips.

Her form, seated upon a lotus, is draped in a garment whose stone-carved folds cascade like liquid emerald, rippling and clinging to her frame with graceful ease. From beneath the swirling attire, one leg extends, bent gently at the knee, toes pointed downward in effortless poise, caught between dance and flight, weightless yet anchored in a deeper power.

Her other leg stands firm, strong and steady, anchoring her to the earth while the upper body leans slightly forward, a gesture of unstoppable motion. Ornate anklets, meticulously carved, cling to her ankles, and the hem of her robe flutters around them, frozen in an eternal breeze. The air thrums with a subtle, electric reverence, and Kshipra feels as if the figure might, at any moment, step down and wrap the world in her outstretched arms; mother, warrior, protector, destroyer.

For a heartbeat, Kshipra forgets to breathe. A deep, ancient tremor passes through her chest, as if some sleeping part of her has just been called awake.

She stands rooted to the spot, unable to tear her eyes away from the radiant figure. Reverence floods her senses, not the gentle kind born of temples and prayers, but a raw, overwhelming certainty that she is in the presence of something far older and far greater.

Her knees feel weak, her palms damp with an invisible heat. Every carved fold of the flowing garment, every sharp glint of the statue's eyes, seems alive, watching her, weighing her. She feels seen, stripped bare, judged, and yet somehow, fiercely protected all at once.

A lump rises in her throat, emotions too tangled to name. Fear, devotion, longing, and a strange, wild joy swirl inside her, pulling her closer to the ancient green light. In that moment, Kshipra is filled with an aching awe, as if she has stumbled not upon a sculpture, but into the presence of something awake, something eternal.

Before Kshipra can form a thought, Shantanu's voice threads into the silence, steady and grave, as if echoing from a place beyond time.

"This is where the veils are thinnest," he says, his gaze unwavering on the luminous figure, "Ma Tara, here, the unseen waits, heavy with the stories forgotten, the wounds unhealed."

He steps closer to an idol, his words slow and deliberate almost like a chant, "You do not ask for visions, you offer yourself for truth. You do not seek to see; you seek to bear, witness, even to what was hidden from your own soul.

Shantanu looks at the idol and begins the chant. Kshipra joins as if she knew already, **"Om Tare Tuttare Ture Soha…"**

The chant continues moving through the air. The chant isn't loud rather it is alive.

As chant continues, the ache behind Kshipra's ribcage opens like a lotus, ready to uncoil, buried truths. She closes her eyes and now she doesn't see Ma Tara in form, yet the presence presses in cool and vast, like a moonlit river, yet sharp enough to sever illusion.

Kshipra no longer seeks the light.
She **is** the light.

As Kshipra continues to chant, Shantanu guides her "bow your spirit and offer your longing, your sorrow, your strength. Only then will the third eye open. Only then will the broken paths be revealed, so you may walk them back into the light."

The room breathes around her, ancient and alive, and Kshipra feels the weight of her journey, not just for herself, but for the souls bound to her by blood and betrayal.

Memories flicker at the edges of her mind, her husband's eyes, burning with a hatred he could never explain; her brother's back turning away from her without a word. Wounds she had carried like stones in

236

her chest, heavy and sharp.

Kshipra draws a slow breath. This is not a place for hesitation, not a place for pride.

Closing her eyes, she surrenders herself to the silence, feeling it seep into her bones. She lets her longing rise, not for revenge, not even for answers, but for healing, for peace. For the weaving back of threads that were torn before she even understood they existed.

When she opens her eyes, they shimmer with unshed tears. With a heart laid bare, Kshipra kneels before the glowing figure, head bowed, hands pressed together in silent offering then she slowly slips in meditation pstsure.

And somewhere beyond sight, something ancient begins to stir.

The silence inside is deep, profound. It's not the kind of silence one would hear in a secluded place, but a silence that pulses with life, with the breath of the world, a hum so subtle it is almost imperceptible, yet Kshipra feels it inside her very bones. The vibrations from the crystal idol move through her, drawing her energy closer aligning her with something much larger than anything.

Shantanu stands beside her, a still presence in the midst of all this cosmic beauty, as though he is part of the room itself, a part of the unseen forces that have guided her here. His gaze is calm, expectant, as if this moment, this room, has been waiting for her to arrive, to step beyond the boundaries of the known and into a space where the visible and invisible merge.

Kshipra breathes in the room's energy, feeling her senses sharpen, her very awareness expand as though the walls are no longer just stone and wood but portals to other realms. The room is not just a space; it is a living being, an entity that speaks in frequencies, in light and sound, in whispers that only the soul can understand.

It is here, in this room, that Kshipra realizes she is not just a person in a room. She is the room. She is the ancient symbol, the moss, the stars above, the crystal's pulse. The boundaries between her and the world blur.

Everything here is interconnected; timeless, endless, and infinite.

The air seems to hold its breath, waiting for the moment when she will step deeper, closer to the core of her own being. It's not just a meditation space, it is a place where worlds collide, where the unseen is made visible, and where Kshipra will confront what lies beyond the veil.

Shantanu says gently, "you will now see what was hidden from you, not because it was kept from you, but because you were never present at those moments in time. You will finally understand Ajay's hatred, its true source, and what fuels it. You will also see why Rajan, as your husband, treats you the way he does. You have tried to reach their souls, to convey your love, to mend the bonds, but you were blind to the real reasons behind their actions. Now, you will see clearly."

Kshipra's fingers tighten around the edge of her shawl. The thought of witnessing the truth, truth she has longed for yet feared, sends a shiver down her spine.

Shantanu continues, his voice sounds firm yet compassionate. "But before you heal them, you must first break the ancestral patterns. Until you do that, the pain will keep repeating across generations. The burdens of the past will continue to weigh down the present."

Kshipra looks up curiosity flickering in her eyes. Shantanu nods. "Yes. These patterns are woven into your lineage passed down like an invisible curse. They shape destinies, create wounds, and keep souls trapped in cycles of suffering. If you want to heal Ajay, if you want to heal Rajan, you must first heal the root. You must reach out to your ancestral souls and see where this curse began. Only then can you break it."

A deep silence settles between them. Kshipra feels the truth of his words sinking into her being. She has already identified the pattern on Lakshmi's advice so she immediately connects with what Shantanu says.

Shantanu gazes at Kshipra with unwavering certainty. "You must go beyond time. You must see the origin of the wound. And then, you must be the one to end it."

Breaking the Pattern

The wind rustles through the trees outside, as if the universe itself is listening. Kshipra closes her eyes, preparing herself for the journey ahead; the journey into the past, into the very core of her lineage's suffering.

"You must reach out to the ancestral souls the ones who carry pain, sorrow, and the weight of unfinished destinies. These are the souls bound by the suffering of your lineage. Some remain trapped in grief, others in anger. And one among them holds the curse that has passed through generations. Your task is to find this soul."

Kshipra nods, her heart pounding with both anticipation and reverence.

"Set your intention," Shantanu instructs. "Be clear, you seek the soul who has placed the ancestral curse, the one whose pain has echoed through your family's bloodline. Go with an open heart, with no fear, only understanding."

She closes her eyes. Her spine is straight and her palms rest upward on her knees. The familiar pressure between her brows returns pulsing and drawing her deeper.

Her breath gradually slows down. The world around her fades. She descends into a vast, boundless space; neither dark nor light, neither empty nor full, a realm beyond time.

At first, there is silence. Then, shapes begin to form. Faint whispers, sighs of sorrow, the murmurs of forgotten voices, one by one, souls appear. Some flicker like fading embers, others loom like heavy shadows. Faces distorted in pain, eyes hollow with longing. They drift, lost in their anguish seeping into the very air around her.

A mother asking for help clutching a child who never grew up, a man whose hands are stained with regret, a warrior who died with betrayal in his heart, so many souls, so much suffering, so much hatred, so much anger, so much pain. A Sharp pressure blooms beneath her ribs, as if her heart itself is caged and struggling to break free. She wants to reach out, to soothe them all, but she remembers Shantanu's words "find the one."

She concentrates, deeper and deeper. The souls swirl around her, restless, searching. Then her body tenses her soul calls, calls for the one she need to confront.

One presence pulls at her, a force unlike the others. A figure stands at a distance, shrouded in a dull, faded light. An old woman, wrinkled face, sorrowful eyes, her back slightly bent as if weighed down by centuries of grief.

The moment Kshipra's gaze meets hers, something shifts, a wave of recognition, though they have never met and the other souls fade into the background. This is the one, Kshipra's soul marks it, 'the bearer of the curse, the source of the ancestral suffering.'

Kshipra takes a deep breath, steadying herself. She has found her. Now, she must listen. Now, she must understand, now she must heal!

Kshipra steps forward, the old woman stands before her, a flickering presence, her face twisted with grief and fury.

"Mother," Kshipra says softly, "Will you tell me what happened? What caused this pain?"

The woman's face darkens. Her lips curl into a bitter snarl as she lets out a piercing scream. The force of it shakes the very space around them.

"You dare ask me? You who belong to his lineage? You will suffer, just as I have made them all suffer!"

Kshipra doesn't flinch. She watches the spirit, her eyes filled with compassion rather than fear. But the woman refuses to speak. Rage radiates from her like fire, and she turns away, as if shutting out the past itself.

Kshipra closes her eyes. If the woman will not speak, then she must find the truth herself.

She takes a deep breath and sinks into deep meditation once more, descending beyond the layers of thought and emotion, into the vast ocean of memory of the Universe that stretches beyond time.

She sets her intention. "Show me what happened. Show me her pain, for I need to heal my linage, I need to break the ancestral pattern and free all the further generations from this curse."

The air shifts. A strange pull tugs at her consciousness. And suddenly she sees.

The scene around her transforms. The spirit world dissolves, replaced by a small, dimly lit hut in an old village. The scent of damp earth and burning oil lamps fills the air. A young woman; frail but beautiful, sits by the fire, her hands trembling as she clutches a thin shawl around her shoulders.

A man stumbles into the hut. His eyes are bloodshot, his breath reeks of alcohol. Without a word, he raises his hand and strikes her across the face. She falls, clutching her cheek, but she does not cry out. She has learned long ago that there is no use, this is her husband.

Kshipra watches, her heart twisting every moment.

The days pass, the beatings continue. The woman, once full of life, grows hollow. She no longer speaks of dreams. She no longer hopes.

Then, one night, the pain becomes too much and she just runs, barefoot and wounded through the dark streets, through the cold and rain. She stumbles but does not stop until she reaches her brother's house.

A man opens the half broken wooden door. His face is kind and lined with worry. He sees her bruises and, without a word, pulls her inside.

"You will stay here," he says and she does.

Her brother takes care of her. He shares what little food he has, but the weight of the household is heavy. He has a wife and two children. Feeding another mouth stretches his limits.

And the woman, she is no longer herself. The suffering has changed her. She sits in silence for hours, staring into nothingness. She does not help with the chores. She does not laugh with the children, she is broken.

One eveing children eat their meal, small hands cupping the last of the rice. The woman finishes what is served to her and then watches with weird expressions at the younger child as her hunger is yet unbearable.

She reaches out, snatches food from the children. "No!" the boy cries, pulling it back, something inside her snaps. Her hands strike him, over and over, until he collapses. The boy lies motionless.

Her brother rushes in, horror filling his face, he lifts his son, shakes, calls him and cries aloud as the kid doesn't respond.

The boy's mother too rushes and snatches the boy from his father, shakes him. She takes some water and sprinkles on his face, continuing shakeing him.

Suddenly, the kid's body jerks taking a long but shallow breath. The child stirs, weak but alive.

His father turns to his sister, "you are no longer my blood." The words cut deeper than any wound "Leave, just leave at once." The woman shakes from inside, not expecting this, "leave? Where will I go?" don't ask me to leave please, I will just sit in one corner, won't even ask for any food. Just let me stay here."

Boy's mother comes to her husband and in a calm tone tells him "either she lives here or we live. If you can't leave your sister then I will leave this house with my kids". The woman approaches her sister-in law, "no no, please don't say so. I hit him by mistake." Then making the fists of her both palms she hits her stomach continuously "My stomach aches as my hunger never subsides but you don't worry, I will just be there outside the hut. Don't give me anything to eat but let me stay here."

She cries and cries until she falls down. Not sure if she is unconscious or asleep, her brother watches her throughout the night in the dim light occasionally gazing at his kids and his wife. He feels the pain of all of them and feels helpness for not sufficing their basic needs.

He sits there as it is, the whole night. Just before the sunrise, he gets up and approaches his sister, shakes her. She opens her eyes and with frightened expressions looks at him trying to spread a smile on her face but fails.

He holds her shoulders and makes her sit. Wiping the wound on her foreheads looks into her eyes "you are hurt come I will take you to doctor" Her heart fills with emotions hearing this and eyes spills as she responds "doctor? You are taking me to doctor? Ok ok". She immediately gets up, washes her face and walks behind him murmuring "you are my brother , how will you leave me, I know you will always take care of me, now you see , I will take medicine and I will be healthy then I will work in fields and earn you food.".

Her voice is low but her brother is able to catch it as she continues "you don't worry; now I will take medicines and I will be fine and I will my self feed your children. You are my brother, how will you leave me. You wont't leave me." His wife watch them walking out while she still lay down cuddling both her kids.

They walk and then take a bullock cart and travel throughout the day. They get down and she holds his hand feeling insecure as it gets dark. He looks down at their hands and also feels the warmth of her touch. He knows the hold gives her comfort and trust.

By now they both are tired and reach at the outskirts of some village. He makes her sit on one big stone "You wait here I will get you something to eat". She is not willing to leave his hand but her stomach also aches with hunger "ok, but come soon. I feel alone". He nods and turns while she traces him till he disappears.

Feeling uneasy as he goes out of sight, she again murmers "you are my brother, you won't leave me, I know you won't leave me". She clutches her both palms together and is about to cry out of fear but suddenly he appears with a small packet and opens it for her. She feels releaved and literally gulps the flattened rice from the packet. She gets hiccups, he taps her back saying "eat slowly, wait I will get you some water." She nods continuing to eat looking at the rice and he leaves to get water.

Her hiccups intensifie making her breathless, she looks here and there and finds a small mud pot filled with water just there. She picks itup and drinks all at once and she realizes, where did this pot come from? Where is her brother? He kept this pot before leaving?

He is gone leaving her all alone in this dark, at this place, which she doesn't even know where this is.

She realizes and gets crazy. She runs here and there calling for him "I am your sister, you can't leave me. I took care of you while you were a kid, I feed you. Your family came later, we are a family first". She runs and runs searching for him. But he is not there.

She wanders the village like a ghost, no home, no love, no identity.

And in her grief, she speaks the words that will bind generations to her pain

"If I am to suffer alone, so shall your lineage. They will never know peace. They will turn against each other, just as you turned away from me." She repeats and repeats "None of the siblings will be able to help each other and they will leave each others back when they need each others the most, just as you did to me."

Her loneliness clouds so much so that she loses her senses and dies in a very painful condition eventualy.

Kshipra gasps, her body trembling as she returns from the vision and there, before her, the spirit of the old woman watches.

For the first time, there is something other than rage in her eyes. There is sorrow.

Kshipra breathes in deeply as the weight of the past feels too heavy. She understands now that the curse was never about revenge. It was about abandonment. It was a cry for love.

"Mother," Kshipra says gently, "You were not abandoned out of cruelty. Your brother did not hate you. He was afraid and he was helpless just as you were."

The old woman's lips tremble. The curse wavers, standing on the edge of being undone.

Kshipra kneels, her breath flows shallow. The old woman's sorrow hangs in the air, thick and heavy. Around her, countless other souls linger, silent witnesses of their own suffering, their own pain echoing through generations.

She now understands. This was never about hatred alone. It was about abandonment and betrayal. A wound left to fester through time.

A deep stillness takes over Kshipra's mind "I take your pain."

Her voice is barely above a whisper, but it carries the intension through the space like a command. The spirits waver.

"I take all of it, yours and the pain of every soul bound by this curse. I will carry it, so you may be free."

A low hum builds in the air. The spirits tremble. Then, the first wave hits her. A searing ache rushes through her chest. It feels as if a thousand knives pierce her ribs at once. Her body stiffens. Sweat beads on her forehead. But she does not break.

The old woman gasps, her presence feels flickering. A thread of dark energy unravels from her form; grief turned tangible and flows into Kshipra.

Then another soul steps forward. A man, his face lined with the exhaustion of an unlived life. Then another woman her sorrow so deep it drowns the very air around her.

One by one, they come, their pain latching onto Kshipra like molten iron. Her hands shake. Her spine curves, the agony pressing her down. Her breathing turns ragged and her limbs convulsing as unseen wounds etch themselves into her being, her body rebels.

The weight of centuries is too much. Her skin burns, fever rising, her muscles locking under the torment. Her lips part in a silent scream.

Still, she does not stop.

More pain, more suffering. It floods into her, twisting her insides, pressing against her ribs like a force determined to crush her. The darkness coils around her soul, seeking to pull her under.

Her vision blurs. The souls are almost free, but she is drowning.

She needs light. Kshipra clenches her fists, pulling whatever strength remains within her "Divine Light," she whispers. Then louder "Divine Light, I call upon you!" The space trembles.

A radiant glow flickers above her, soft at first like dawn breaking through mist. Then grows brighter and brighter.

A pillar of golden light crashes down, engulfing her completely. Her body, burning like molten metal, now glows white-hot. The pain, unbearable just moments ago, begins to shift. It lightens.

The agony flows out of her, rising toward the light. From her veins, from her skin, from the very depths of her soul, it is lifted.

The souls around her watch in awe. The darkness that bound them dissolves into nothingness.

The old woman gasps. The bitterness in her face softens. Tears, centuries old trace down her spectral cheeks.

She looks at Kshipra, her lips trembling. "I… am free, and so are you my dear."

One by one, the spirits ascend as their burdens are finally lifted, their suffering no longer tethered to the living world.

Kshipra exhales, her body sagging. The last of the pain drains from her, seeping into the earth beneath. Mother Earth takes it in its core, transforms it and heals it.

The ancestral curse is broken, the weight is gone. The lineage is free.

Kshipra collapses forward, her palms pressing against the earth, her breath shaky but steady and deep and in that moment peace settles over generations.

Throughout the night, Kshipra lies still on the sacred ground where she completed her ancestral healing.

Shantanu's diciple creates a serene atmosphere by placing aromatic herbs around Kshipra and covering her with comforting clothes. Sitting beside her, Shantanu gently rests her hand on Kshipra's forehead, offering reassurance and stability.

Kshipra healed all her anchesters and her linage but the process has taken a toll on her body. She lies down motionless, surrendering to the moment. Shantanu's disciple carefully prepares a herbal paste and apply it to her forehead, while another, different blend is gently spread over her feet.

They let her rest, allowing the remedies to work their magic. By morning, she awakes unchanged in form, yet transformed in essence. She is the same yet different, as though freed from her limitations.

He begins chanting a mantra softly, its soothing tones resonating through the air. The chant is a gentle melody that calms Kshipra's soul, easing the lingering echoes of ancestral pain.

As the night deepens, the chant continues, a beacon of tranquility amidst the profound stillness of the night.

Under the protective care of Shantanu and the healing vibrations of the chant, Kshipra rests peacefully, her breathing slow and steady. The healing energies of the night embrace her, nurturing her body, mind, and soul as she begins to recover from the intense spiritual journey she undertook.

Healing the souls

Morning breaks with a gentle light filtering through the trees, signaling a new dawn for Kshipra and her ancestral lineage.

Shantanu continues to sit vigilantly beside her, his presence a pillar of support and compassion through the night's silent vigil.

Where Kshipra feels partially releaved, she is yet to counter the unease of her relationship with Ajay and Rajan. She doesn't want to wait until she resolves this.

Shantanu is firm that unless she is physically and mentally and emotionally stable, it will atleast take two more days. Finally, the day arrives.

Kshipra sits for meditation, her breathing steady and calm as she allows herself to sink deeper and deeper into the stillness. A strong pull tugs at her from within, guiding her into an intense, immersive state. Her mind sharpens with intent she wants to see everything from both her perspective and Sujay's perspective in that pivotal birth. She wants to understand what transpired to create the negativity he holds against her.

As her meditation intensifies, the visions begin to unfold vividly.

She sees a village thrown into chaos. British soldiers storm through, their brutal cries blending with the terrified screams of the villagers. The close-knit village is suddenly scattered, people fleeing in every direction, desperately clutching their loved ones. A wave of dread washes over Kshipra as she watches the villagers run toward the dense jungle for refuge.

But safety eludes them. The British soldiers follow relentlessly, dragging villagers out of hiding, one by one. Kshipra's heart tightens as she sees them tied and hung from trees, their lifeless bodies swaying in the breeze.

The haunting scene triggers a flash of memory; her present life, where she has often been tormented by dreams of people hanging from trees.

The vision moves forward. The jungle is eerily quiet now, except for the rustling leaves and the flapping wings of pigeons.

Among the chaos, a small girl, no older than seven or eight, stumbles out from her hiding place. Her face is streaked with mud, her tear-streaked cheeks glistening faintly. She looks around, crying, searching desperately for someone, practically anyone. Her cries echo through the forest, a heart-wrenching plea that goes unanswered.

Kshipra feels the girl's terror as it is her own. The pigeons dart overhead, their sudden movements startling the girl. She flinches, retreating instinctively, her small frame trembling with fear. Another wave of recognition washes over Kshipra her present life flashes before her eyes, where she has always been inexplicably afraid of pigeons.

The girl cries and cries, her tiny hands clutching at her chest, her knees sinking into the muddy ground. The jungle stretches endlessly around her, devoid of life except for the birds and the trees holding their grim burden.

And then, silence. The vision begins to fade, but the overwhelming sadness lingers. Kshipra's heart aches for the girl, for the hopelessness and fear that consumed her in that moment.

She begins to rise out of the meditation, tears streaming down her cheeks as she processes the emotions and memories that have surfaced. The clarity she sought has only begun to unfold.

As the scene of chaos and despair gradually fades, Kshipra feels herself pulled forward, her vision shifting to a new moment. The small girl, still covered in mud and tears, trudges weakly through a path that leads to another village. Her tiny legs wobble with exhaustion, her steps slow and uneven, but she keeps moving, driven by some faint hope of finding safety.

The faint sounds of chatter and laughter guide her to a clearing where a well stands, surrounded by four or five women drawing water. Their brightly colored attire moves gently in the breeze as they talk and work. The girl stops a short distance away, her small frame swaying from fatigue. She looks at the women with wide, frightened eyes but doesn't dare to move closer.

The women notices her frail figure caked in mud, her

tear-streaked face barely visible beneath the grime. For a moment, they exchange puzzled looks, their laughter quieting. The girl freezes under their gaze, clutching her small hands together. By now her cry and her tears are driedup.

Before any of the women can approach her, another figure emerges from behind the girl, a woman with a soft but commanding presence. She walks up to the child and gently places her hand on the girl's head. The girl flinches slightly at the touch, her eyes darting up to meet the woman's face, her fear plain to see.

The woman crouches slightly to meet her gaze. "Who are you?" she asks gently, her voice is filled with concern. "What is your name? Where are your parents?"

But the girl remains silent. Her lips quiver, but no words come. Her body trembles with exhaustion, her eyes heavy and on the verge of closing. The woman, sensing her frailty, takes her hand firmly but kindly and leads her to the well.

She fetches a small pot of water, using it to carefully clean the girl's face. Her dry lips part apart to sip the drops instantly. The mud washes away, revealing the child's pale, tear-streaked skin beneath.

The woman's expression softens with understanding as she begins to piece together what might have happened to this girl.

Scooping more water from the well, she holds it to the

girl's lips, "drink," she says softly. The girl hesitates for a moment then obeys, taking small, shaky sips "where are your parents?" the woman asks again.

Still, the girl does not respond. Her eyes flicker as if she's struggling to stay awake, her body giving in to the overwhelming fatigue.

The woman straightens, determination settling in her features. Without another word, she takes the child into her arms. She is strong but moves with care, holding the girl close as she begins walking toward her home. The other women at the well watch in silence, their earlier curiosity replaced by quiet respect.

The woman doesn't look back. She knows the child needs more than questions; she needs shelter, food, and care. And for now, she will provide it.

The woman carries the exhausted girl carefully with steps steady as she approaches her humble little hut at the edge of the village. The roof is thatched, the walls uneven but sturdy, and a faint wisp of smoke rises from the outdoor cooking fire nearby. Just outside the hut, two children are playing; a boy and a girl, their laughter echoing in the quiet surroundings.

The boy, slightly older, runs circles around the girl, teasing her with a stick as she giggles and tries to snatch it. The woman's voice rings out as she calls to them, "Karan! Gauri! Come here."

The boy stops abruptly and turns toward his mother, his

curious gaze shifting to the small figure she carries.

Kshipra, deep in meditation, focuses intently on his face. A sudden jolt of recognition hits her; this boy is Ajay, her brother from her current life. Her heart clenches as she realizes the connection.

Karan looks at the girl in his mother's arms with suspicion. "Who is she?" he asks bluntly.

"She will stay with us now," the woman says firmly, her tone brooking no argument "but why?" Karan's voice grows louder, laced with disapproval. "She's not part of our family!"

The woman kneels to place the girl gently on the ground and straightens to face her son. "Because she has no one else," she replies, her eyes narrowing. "And I expect you to treat her like your sister."

Karan scowls but says nothing. Gauri, on the other hand, runs forward and crouches beside the girl, her small hands brushing against the mud-streaked clothes. "What's your name?" she asks brightly, her innocence untainted by prejudice.

The girl looks up but doesn't answer, her exhaustion is too great. The woman shoos the children aside and carries the girl into the hut.

Kshipra, watches as the scene shifts. Days pass in this life from long ago. The girl, now known as Arya, slowly adapts to her new surroundings. She helps the family with household chores, sweeping the floor, grinding grains, and cooking simple meals. She even begins tending to the small field outside their home, her hands pulling weeds and watering the plants.

Her foster parents grow fond of her, their pride evident in the way they praise her diligence and kindness. "You're a blessing," her foster mother says one evening, placing a gentle hand on her head as they all sit for a meal.

But Karan remains distant. He watches from a corner as Arya works in the field, his arms crossed, face set in a hard line. He refuses to join her, even when their mother urges him to help.

One evening, the family gathers outside the hut under the fading light of the setting sun. The foster father, trying to mend the growing rift, says, "Karan, she is your sister now. You must accept her."

Karan's jaw tightens, and his eyes flash with resentment. "She is not my sister," he says sharply, his voice cutting through the evening air. He storms away, leaving the family in silence.

The memory intensifies Kshipra's meditation. She feels Arya's pain as it's her own; the sting of rejection, the longing for acceptance and the weight of trying to belong where she isn't wanted.

Years pass in the vision, and Arya continues to dedicate herself to the household and the small farm. She cooks meals, repairs the torn roof after storms, and tends to the crops with quiet determination. Karan grows, but his resentment does not fade. He watches her silently, never offering help or comfort.

As Kshipra witnesses this in her meditative state, she begins to feel Karan's emotions as well; the jealousy, the bitterness of having his family's attention divided and the insecurity that made him push Arya away. It's a mix of emotions so intense that Kshipra feels it pierce her heart.

Arya is a young girl yet but grows quite rebellion as she witnesses the Britisher's acts.

Many a times they cross her way and mark her attitude.

One such day the market is alive with the rhythm of daily life. The vibrant calls of vendors fill the air as they hawk their goods, the sweet aroma of fried pakoras drifting on the warm breeze. Arya moves through the crowd with a basket of vegetables balanced on her hip, her stride confident yet unhurried. Her eyes, however, remain sharp, scanning the street, always aware of the ebb and flow of both the market and the tension in the air. Life in this village is simple, but that doesn't mean it's without its threats.

Arya knows the subtle whispers of rebellion are spreading like wildfire, even here in the heart of British-controlled territory. But it's not just the rebellion that keeps her alert; it's her family, her people, the land she's sworn to protect. She walks with a quiet resolve, balancing the demands of her life as a daughter, sister, and worker, while carrying the weight of a patriot's spirit that grows fiercer with each passing day.

At home, her days are spent tending to the fields and her hands calloused from the endless work. The sun beats down, but Arya is unbothered by the sweat dripping from her brow.

She enjoys the rhythm of the plow as it slices through the earth, the smell of the soil, the satisfaction of watching the crops grow strong under her care. It's a life of simple pleasures, the laughter of her younger brother as they tend to the garden; the quiet hum of her foster mother singing as she prepares meals and the occasional exchange of stories from the elders in the village.

But no matter how peaceful it seems, Arya feels the weight of the world pressing against her. The British soldiers are always present, always watching, always reminding the villagers of who holds power. Arya can't ignore it, no matter how much she longs for a world where her family is safe, where the land is theirs to nourish and protect.

One day, as Arya walks through the market, balancing the basket of vegetables against her side, she is suddenly stopped by a tall British soldier. His presence is almost a physical block, a stark contrast to the bustling warmth of the market around them. He tilts his head with that all-too-familiar smirk, his fingers reaching for the edge of her dupatta, an unwelcome gesture of dominance.

"Ah, look at this one," he says, eyes running over her form with a mixture of disdain and amusement. "Fierce eyes for a mere village girl."

Arya doesn't hesitate. Her basket swings with a practiced ease, and the edge strikes him across the face with such force that the tomatoes burst, staining his crisp white uniform a deep blood-red. For a moment, the market falls silent.

The soldier stumbles back, his hand swiping at his face in a futile attempt to clean it. His face turns crimson with rage. "You little creature..." he spits, his words dripping with humiliation.

Arya stands her ground, her voice calm, steady. "These are not for you. If you want food, pay for it like everyone else."

A ripple of laughter runs through the crowd. People shift nervously, but their smiles are hard to suppress. The soldier, his pride wounded, glares at Arya one last time before storming off. She watches him leave, but in the pit of her stomach, she knows this moment this small victory will not go unnoticed. The British will remember.

The sun is sinking low over the riverbank as Arya bends down to scoop salt into baskets, her hands moving with steady precision. Around her, the women of the village work in silence, their hearts united in quiet defiance. They know that gathering salt, which the British have taxed and claimed as their own, is an act of rebellion.

But they also know that the river does not belong to the British. It is a gift from the land, something that cannot be taken.

Arya's foster father, an old man whose back has long since bowed under the weight of years, works beside her. His hands tremble slightly as he gathers the salt, but his eyes are proud. He may not have the strength of youth, but his heart burns with the same fire as his daughter's.

Suddenly, a thudding of hooves breaks the quiet. Arya's eyes snap up, and she sees the red-coated officers approaching, their horses kicking up dust as they ride toward the women. She stands tall, her posture proud despite the danger she knows they face.

One officer dismounts with sharp, calculated movements. His cold eyes sweep over the gathered women. "This salt belongs to the Crown," he announces, his voice loud and authoritative. "Hand it over."

Arya steps forward, her fingers tightening around a handful of salt. She feels the weight of the land beneath her, the silent strength of her ancestors that course through her veins. She speaks with a calmness that betrays the fire within. "The river belongs to no king," she says firmly. "It belongs to the land."

A murmur rises among the women, a soft undercurrent of agreement. The officer's gaze hardens, narrowing as it lands on her. "Who dares defy British law?" he spits, his voice sharp with authority.

"The land defies you," Arya replies, letting the salt slip through her fingers like a small, deliberate act of rebellion.

The officer's eyes narrow and he gestures sharply to his men. Without hesitation, they move in, grabbing the baskets from the women and shoving them aside. Arya clenches her fists, her body tensing, but she remains where she stands, refusing to back down. Her heart races with anger, but her voice remains steady. She will remember this. She will not forgive this.

Later that evening, when the sun has dipped beneath the horizon and the world has settled into the quiet of night, there is a sharp, insistent knock at the door. Arya's foster father opens it, his face pale with fear. British soldiers force their way inside, their boots heavy against the floorboards.

"You've raised a rebel," one of them sneers, his eyes filled with malice as he eyes Arya. "This one thinks she's clever." He grabs her arm roughly, pulling her toward him, his grip bruising.

Arya wrenches free, her chin lifting in defiance. "Or maybe it will teach you fear," she retorts, her voice cold and unwavering.

The officer strikes her then, a swift slap that echoes through the small house. Arya stumbles but doesn't fall, her fire burning brighter than ever in her chest. Her eyes lock with his, defiant and fierce.

Her foster father steps forward, trembling. "She is just a girl," he says, his voice breaking with fear.
The officer smirks, his cold gaze never leaving Arya. "Not for long."
With that, they turn and leave, knocking over a lamp on their way out. The house smells of spilled oil, of anger, and of promises broken. Arya kneels to pick up the shards of glass, her hands steady as she gathers the broken pieces.

Her foster mother, watching from the doorway, speaks in a voice laced with worry. "Why do you provoke them?"

Arya doesn't answer immediately. Her fingers linger over the sharp edges of the glass. She feels the weight of the moment, the heaviness of the decision she has made. And then, quietly, she speaks, "because someone must."

She stands, the fire in her chest never wavering. Her family, her people, the land; these are the things worth fighting for. Even when the cost is high, even when the British strike at her with cruelty and power, Arya knows she will not back down. Not now. Not ever.

And so, the rebellion continues, not just in the fields and the markets, but in the quiet resolve of a girl who has chosen to stand tall against the Empire, no matter the price.

This day, Arya's hands are still raw from the day's work, but the satisfaction of tilled soil beneath her fingers and the crops growing under her care dulls the ache. She walks back toward the small house she shares with her foster family, the cool evening air ruffling her hair, a slight smile playing on her lips. Life has been simple, albeit hard, but the bonds she shares with her family make every challenge worth facing.

But as she nears the gate, her heart sinks. There is a sharp, unexpected noise; a voice calling out to her, a voice she recognizes all too well, "Arya," the voice purrs. "Arya, come here."

She freezes. She knows that voice. It's the same voice that made her blood run cold the last time she heard it, The British officer, Thornton.

She turns slowly, meeting his gaze with a cold, unwavering stare. He stands at the edge of her yard, leaning against his horse, his uniform immaculate, the scarlet of his coat gleaming in the fading light. There is something in his eyes, a dangerous mix of arrogance and something darker. He watches her as though she's a possession he intends to claim.

"You," he says, his lips curling into a smirk, "you are a fascinating creature."

Arya's pulse quickens, but she doesn't let it show. She stands tall, her hands at her sides, despite the way his gaze lingers on her as though it might consume her. She's faced his kind before, and she will face him again.

"What do you want, Officer Thornton?" Her voice is steady, but the undercurrent of anger is unmistakable.

He steps forward, closing the distance between them with slow, deliberate strides. "You are too bold for someone in your position, Arya," he says, his voice soft, almost coaxing, "Perhaps you need to learn what happens to those who defy us."

Before she can respond, he raises a hand, signaling to the two guards who stand behind him "take her father and brother inside."

Her stomach drops as two armed guards move swiftly toward her home. Arya steps forward, her heart racing. "No! Leave them alone!" she shouts.

Thornton's smile widens "They will be fine, Arya, as long as you do what I say. Do you understand?"

He watches her closely, a glimmer of something dangerous in his eyes. She swallows hard, but she can't let fear show "You can't do this," she says, her voice trembling, but defiant.

The words hit her like a physical blow. She feels the pressure of the situation closing in around her. Her parents and her brother, innocent as they are, will suffer. The thought of them in pain, helpless, sends a surge of desperation through her.

Thornton steps closer still, his hand brushing lightly against her arm, his fingers trailing along the length of her wrist. His touch is light, almost casual, but there is a menace in it, a warning.

"Come with me," he murmurs, his voice low and seductive, "work for me in my house, in my garden. Show me you're willing to do what's necessary."

Arya clenches her fists, struggling to keep her composure. She wants to scream, to fight, but the weight of his words presses down on her. She knows what he's capable of, what he's already done to her family. Her gaze flits to her house, where the guards are already pulling her father inside, her younger brother stands at the threshold with fear in his eyes. She knows then that she has no choice.

"I'll go," she says, her voice barely a whisper, but firm. "But you leave them alone. Promise me."

Thornton leans in closer, his breath warm against her ear. "I promise," he says, though the promise rings hollow. "As long as you do as I ask."

Next morning, as Arya arrives at Thornton's estate, her heart beats erratically. She's led through the gates by one of his guards, the grand house looming in front of her like a fortress. The smell of fresh herbs and flowers fills the air, but it's not the kind of scent that brings comfort. She feels like she's stepping into the lion's den.

Thornton greets her at the door, his presence more commanding than ever. His eyes rove over her as though she is an object on display.

"Come, Arya," he says, motioning toward the garden. "You'll work here, I expect results. And remember, your family's well-being depends on you."

Arya clenches her jaw as she follows him, walking through the sprawling estate. Every step feels heavier than the last, but she won't show weakness. She won't let him see how much his control over her cuts deep.

As she works, Thornton watches her closely, his gaze never straying far from her movements. His presence is a constant shadow, his eyes following her every step as she tends to the plants in the garden.

"Arya" he utters, his voice too smooth, too intimate. "You are a beauty, aren't you?"

She ignores him, focusing on the soil beneath her fingers, trying to block out the uncomfortable feeling of his eyes on her. But then, she feels his presence behind her, too close. His fingers graze the small of her back, and she jerks away, her breath catching in her throat.

"Don't touch me," she snaps with sharp voice.

Thornton chuckles, "You are a firebrand, but that only makes me want you more."

His words hit her like a poky wind. She feels sick to her stomach, but she won't give him the satisfaction of seeing her break.

"You'll learn," he murmurs, almost to himself. "I like

them feisty."

Over the next few days, Arya is forced into labor under his watchful eye. She spends hours in his garden, pulling weeds and planting new crops, all while Thornton hovers, his gaze constantly trained on her. He makes sure she knows that he's always there, always watching. At night, the sound of his voice echoes through the halls of the estate, calling her to him. "Arya" he says, his voice a command. "Come to my room."

She ignores him at first, refusing to let his presence dominate her. But one evening, as she passes his door, she finds it ajar. The flicker of light from inside the room illuminates his figure, leaning casually against the doorframe.

"Just a moment of your time, Arya," he says with a grin. "Come in" she stops, her body rigid with defiance. "I'm not your plaything."

He steps toward her, his eyes dark with desire. "No, but you will be. You'll learn your place, one way or another."

He reaches for her, but she pulls away, her breath ragged. She knows that as long as her family is under his control, she has no choice. She has to endure this. But that doesn't mean she'll ever give him what he wants.

The weeks drag on, each one blending into the next. Thornton continues his relentless pursuit, his eyes never leaving Arya, his demands never ending. He tries to get closer, to break her spirit, but Arya is stubborn. She resists with every fiber of her being, even as she works day after day in his garden, under his watchful eye.

He keeps trying to touch her, to bring her to his side, but Arya pushes him away with every ounce of her strength. She may be bound by the chains he's placed on her family, but she will not bow to him. She will fight, even if it's in the quietest ways, even if it costs her everything. She refuses to be his possession.

And one thing is clear, Thornton will stop at nothing to break her, to make her his, but Arya will never stop fighting. No matter how long it takes, she knows that the rebellion inside her will burn hotter than any of his cruel advances.

And one day, one day soon, she will find a way to make him pay for everything he's done.

With trembling breaths, Kshipra lets the vision settle into her heart, knowing she has more to confront, more to heal. But for now, she holds onto the connection she has rediscovered, no matter how painful it might be. Her intention to understand the reality intensifies and takes her vision to this dense Jungle.

The jungle path looks twisted through the dense undergrowth, the evening sun casting long shadows as Arya walk barefoot over the damp earth.

She often wandered here after finishing her work at the British estate, drawn to the wild silence that offered a strange solace.

That evening, however, the silence feels different to her. Somewhere amidst the thick foliage, voices murmurs in hush urgency. She pause, her ears catch the low tones of men speaking in rapid whispers. Arya edge closer, her heart thudding as she crouch behind a cluster of dense leaves, "their movements are fast. We need to strike before the next shipment reaches the port."

"They've doubled their patrols near the railway lines..."

Arya's breathe hitches. She had only heard about them in passing; brave men and women fighting for a cause that stirred something deep within her. Now, here they were, planning in secret while the jungle bore witness. Before she could retreat, strong hands grab her arms. "Who are you?" a rough voice demands.

Arya gasps as she gets pulled forward, her pulse sounds hammering. Four men stand before her, their faces hardened by struggle, their eyes sharp with suspicion. One held gun, the others carried satchels slung over their shoulders.

"I... I was just passing through," she stammered, her gaze darting from one face to another. One of them, a tall man with piercing eyes, stepped closer. "Then why were you listening?"

Arya hesitates, but something inside her refused to cower. She straightened, meeting his gaze. "Because I wanted to, because I feel connected to this mission."

The men exchanged wary glances. "I work at the estate," she continues, her voice sounds steady, "at the British commander's residence. I hear things, important things. If you let me, I can help."

A tense silence follows. Then, the tall man nods "Come with us."

They led her deeper into the jungle, where a hidden camp flickered with lantern light. The smell of burnt wood and damp earth fills the air. More men and a few women worked silently, rolling up maps, tending to supplies.

Arya knew, with every fiber of her being, that this was where she was meant to be, she knows it from heart and even she doesn't know from when?

The first time they tested her, it was with a simple message.

A man scribbles a note on a scrap of paper. "Read this once and repeat it back to me exactly." His voice is strong and crisp with a typical accent. Arya glances at the words, they look foreign to her. Then, she closes her eyes and takes a deep breath and utters exactly as the man said "Read this once and repeat it back to me exactly." Her voice, her tone, her accent just the same as his!

They all look at her , ones sitting stand up, rest all turn towards her in curiosity a she continues "I cant read, or write or understand english but I can replicate what I hear, I will listen to the officers and relay it to you as it is, will that help?"

The man and women there get surprised and murmer amoungst themselves while Arya stands waiting for their judgement.

A lady comes forward and places her palm on Arya's shoulders "This will be very valuable if you do it. Let's try it out, we meet here again tomorrow same time and you relay us what you hear". Arya nods and runs away.

Next day she arrives earier than decided and waits for one of them to take her to their secret place. He comes and she follows him.

She enters the room and look at all of them as their faces depict the curiosity as she straightens her posture, clears her throat and in exaggerated imitation of Thornton she mimicks, "Gentlemen! I tell you, the heat in this country is unbearable! My boots are melting, my tea tastes like bathwater, and worst of all, my mustache is refusing to stay in place! I shall write to the Queen herself! If we are to rule this land, we must first learn to survive its horrors!"

For a moment, there is silence. Then, the entire camp bursts into laughter. One of the men wipes his eyes "his mustache! The poor fellow is fighting his own battle!" Another chuckles, "Maybe we should let the sun defeat him before we do!"

The laughter fades, replaced by quiet determination.

The fight is on.

From that day, Arya became their silent courier. No ink, no parchment, only her voice and memory carried secrets through enemy lines.

This was the quality developed within her which she realized few years a go but she had hiden it from everyone. Least she knew that it could be used this.

Now, she did not fight with guns or swords. But she fought with her ability which was unique! And that was just as powerful.

Arya presses herself against the cold stone wall, her breath shallow as she watches Thornton through the small gap in the curtain. His silhouette sways as he lifts a bottle, taking long, indulgent swigs. The dim candlelight flickers, casting distorted shadows on the walls, and his voice slurs as he murmurs her name, "Arya... Arya...I want you but not forcefully, rather with your wish. Till then.."

She inches forward, her heart keeps pounding. This is the closest she has ever been to him, and she knows the risk is great. But the freedom fighters need the information. They are counting on her. Just as she is about to move closer, she senses another presence in the room.

A faint rustle, a whisper of movement, Arya stiffens. In the dim light, she spots the figure of a woman slipping closer to Thornton. Unlike the other British officers' women, this one is not here to entertain. Her grip is firm around the handle of a sharp knife. Arya realizes the woman has come with an intention far deadlier than hers.

Before she can react, Arya shifts slightly, and their shoulders brush. The woman gasps, her body stiffening and Arya instantly clamps a hand over her mouth. The knife gleams, held rigid in the woman's tense grip. Arya locks eyes with her; wide, startled, and filled with both fear and determination.

Thornton stirs at the sound, groaning as he shifts in his chair. Arya presses her finger to her lips, signaling the woman to stay silent. The woman hesitates then nods slightly. The tension between them is electric; two strangers caught in the same storm, each with their own mission, each now forced into an uneasy alliance.

Outside, the wind howls through the night, but inside this room, silence reigns, heavy with danger.

Arya's grip tightens around the woman's wrist, her fingers pressing against the cold metal of the knife. The flickering lamp casts jagged shadows across their faces as their eyes lock.

"What are you going to do?" Arya whispers, barely moving her lips. The woman pulls back slightly but Arya does not release her hold.

"Kill him," the woman says without hesitation, her voice carries years of bottled rage. "He has taken everything from me."

Arya studies her, noting the quiver in her voice, the raw emotion barely concealed behind her hardened expression. Slowly, she lets go of her wrist but keeps her gaze fixed on her. "Who are you?"

The woman exhales sharply, straightening her shoulders "Divya."Arya nods as the name settle in her mind like a puzzle piece falling into place. Divya's eyes narrow as realization dawns "Thornton," she murmurs "He calls for Arya. That's you."

Arya hesitates then nods. "I need information. Something important is being planned against my people." Divya scoffs "and you risk yourself for that?" Arya does not flinch "Yes" Divya studies her for a long moment before stepping closer. "Let me go to him. He has already destroyed me, I can take this risk."

Arya shakes her head, uncertain. But Divya places a hand on her shoulder, firm and resolute. "I will make him drink and speak. You wait here and Listen."

Before Arya can argue, Divya turns, gathering her composure. She adjusts her scarf, masking herself further, and steps out into the dimly lit chamber. Thornton is slouched in his chair, a half-empty bottle in his grip. His eyes, red with intoxication, light up as he sees her.

"Arya," he murmurs, reaching out, a drunken grin spreading across his face.

Divya steps closer, lowering her head slightly to keep her face in shadows. "Yes, I am Arya," she says softly. Thornton chuckles pouring another drink for himself "You're a slippery one," he slurs. "But you came back." He takes a long sip, his eyes drooping. "You see, Arya, you cannot run forever. And neither can those fools in your village."

Divya tilts her head. "What do you mean?"

He laughs making a dry, rasping sound. "Tomorrow a lesson, your people will learn what happens when they defy the Crown. We're torching the grain stores. No food. No harvest. Let's see how long they survive without their precious crops."

Behind the curtain, Arya stiffens, her pulse hammering in her ears, she has to rely what she heard as quickly as possible.

Thornton leans forward, gripping Divya's arm "but enough of that, you're here now."

Divya forces a smile, pouring him another drink. "Yes, drink more," she coaxes.

Moments later, Thornton collapses into a drunken stupor. Divya pries his fingers off her wrist and slips back into the shadows. Arya is already gone.

Outside, under the cover of darkness, they meet the freedom fighters near the village outskirts. Arya relays everything in hurried whispers. Divya too listens understanding their working pattern then takes a deep breath. Looking at the Freedom fighters leave Divya utters, "this isn't over. If he speaks when drunk, then we make sure he drinks."

Arya nods. "Now they will stop the fire before it starts." Divya looks toward the flickering lights of the British quarters, "you have got a unique talent, can't imagine using this against these crooks. Let's do it together. I'll get him to drink, talk, and you convey it to the freedom fighters".

From that night, their pact is sealed. Divya will play the role of Arya in Thornton's chamber, drawing out secrets, while Arya listens and delivers them to the freedom fighters. The resistance has found an unlikely pair of spies, and Thornton, in his drunken arrogance, has no idea that his own lips are his undoing.

Kshipra's face gets red, as she continues to feel and absorb as she sees all that. Her heart feels for Divya as if she knows her by heart! This feeling makes her gasp for breath at times. She concentrates deep into in intention set and this navigates her to that night …

This night is thick with silence, the kind that wraps around shadows and secrets. Arya and Divya slip through the darkness as planned. They have been informed that earlier this morning there was a meeting of top officials and all that need to be known by the freedom fighters.

Thornton is slumped in his chair, a half-empty bottle of

whiskey dangling from his fingers. His eyes are glassy, unfocused, yet a slurred murmur escapes his lips; Arya's name, again and again, like an obsession that refuses to fade.

Now as always, both are dressed like Arya does, Divya throws Arya a quick glance, the unspoken agreement passing between them. She steps forward with calculated movements, her voice laced with an imitation of coyness. "I am here," she whispers, her head lowered, the shadows of the dimly lit room keeps disguising her face.

Thornton grins, pleased yet suspicious. His fingers clutch her wrist, pulling her down onto his lap. "You've been different these nights…something about you," he mutters, pressing his face close to hers. Divya stiffens, but she forces herself to stay calm, to lull him deeper into his drunken haze.

Arya is hidden behind the thick curtain, watches in mounting dread. She has learned to steel herself against the things she witnesses in this room, but tonight, something shifts. Thornton's grip tightens. His fingers tangle in Divya's hair, yanking her head back. Her silent plea reaches Arya, run. But Arya is frozen, her breath caught in her throat as she sees what is about to happen. The night stretches unbearably long. Thornton takes what he wants, and Arya, helpless behind the curtain, chokes back silent sobs. Her nails dig into her palms as guilt swallows her whole. This is because of me. She swore to fight, but she never imagined the price would be this steep.

The night grows thick with the scent of liquor and smoke. Arya still waits in the shadows, heart pounding as she listens to Thornton slur her name in drunken obsession. He grins, believing Divya to be Arya, and pulls her close. But as he pushes her onto the bed, the dim candlelight flickers over her face, revealing the deception.

His drunken haze clears for a brief moment, his grip tightening. "Who the hell are you?" he snarls, his fingers digging into her arms. Realization dawns in his bloodshot eyes. "You're not Arya... You've been fooling me!"

Divya gasps, struggling against his grip. Danger fills the air. Arya, still behind the curtain, clenches her fists, her body rigid with fear and fury. The British officer's fury morphs into something worse, a predatory rage. He slams Divya down, determined to punish her for the deception.

Arya cannot stay hidden any longer. She lunges, knocking over a candle stand as she barrels into Thornton, shoving him away from Divya. He stumbles but quickly regains his footing, eyes gleaming with sadistic amusement. "Ah, the real Arya," he sneers "how convenient."

Divya scrambles up, grabbing a dagger from the officer's belt in a desperate bid to protect Arya. But he is faster and his gun is drawn before she can strike. A deafening shot shatters the tense air. Divya staggers, blood blooming through her dress. She gasps, her hands trembling as she reaches for Arya. "Run!" she chokes out, collapsing to the floor.

Arya hesitates for a fraction of a second, agony twisting inside her. But she knows she has no time, she turns and flees. Thornton roars behind her, but Divya, with the last of her strength, grips his leg, slowing him just enough for Arya to slip through the door and disappear into the night.

Arya's legs trembling beneath her, she needs to get away before Thornton reaches her. She steps outside and it's the first rays of dawn slicing through the sky.

Now with all her power to see the unseen reality Kshipra sees, Suyog is there, standing a few feet away, his face twisting in disbelief. His eyes move from the officer's quarters to Arya's disheveled form, realization dawning in the worst possible way.

Now, Kshipra can hear his voice as he murmers with something unreadable, hurt? disgust? "Arya was inside all night? Did she surrender to his riches? Is this the reason she doesn't acknowledge my love? He loses his balance due to this load of feeling.

He recollects all those times he thought he silently caught Arya entering Thorton's room and kept watch.

This night his worst fear came in light, he feels.

Kshipra also witnesses that Arya is unaware that Suyog saw this and misinterpreted. Now she understands the real hatered comes from here. He doesn't know. He doesn't understand. But how could she explain? Suyog's stare burns into her, his expression hardening as he turns away. He runs away not able to tolerate what he saw and what his mind interpreted. He doesn't even witness all about Divya and Arya's collaboration, their mission, their purpose. He try to reachout to Arya but the news spread like fire that she ran with a strange person, not from this village.

Suyog gets lost in the false delution so badly that he reach out to the hill top and thinking all wrong about Arya, his heart filled with hatred and pain his soul gets so much soaked in these fillings that it carries these fealings beyond the mortal realm.

Kshipra's heart is at the verge of bursting and her soul shakes after knowing the unknown. She is not able to move forward. She gets locked, she sees Suyog approaching the tip of the mountain when she realizes that this is the moment she has to call for the divine light and she does.

Her physical form flushes with the divine light as she embraces all the hurts and hatred of Suyog for her. It burns her inside out before it drains to the core of the earth. It's not less than the lighteneing passing through her and she has to remain unshakable as it passes through.

Kshipra watch Suyog's expressions change as his soul is liberated of all the hurt and hate, while Kshipra too feels the peace of his soul and wants another moment to continue feeling this way, Suyog surrenders his body to the valley. Kshipra loses a heart beat and her body gives up and falls. Shantanu holds her delicately.

Shantanu looks at her with deep admiration, tenderness, and reverence. As he watches Kshipra collapse from sheer exhaustion, his eyes soften with an ache only a healer understands; the weight of witnessing someone sacrifice themselves for love.

There is awe in his expression, for he knows the depth of her strength, the purity of her intention. He sees her not as fragile, but as someone who has carried the unbearable and transmuted it into light. His looks hold gratitude, for she has done what many cannot; chosen selfless healing over resentment.

Yet, there is also be sorrow, a quiet sadness that she had to endure so much pain to free souls of her loved ones. His fingers, as they cradle her limp form are gentle, reverent, as if touching something sacred and somewhere, beneath it all, a silent promise; he would be there to support her, to ensure she is not alone in her own healing.

Back home, both Kshipra's families are absolutely unaware about her journey.

This morning feels dull and sad and within the walls of the house, a different kind of heaviness lingers. Rajan walks through the rooms, the familiar, yet hauntingly empty, corners of the house that once buzzed with life, with laughter. Kshipra's absence presses down on him like a thousand-pound weight. He cannot ignore it any longer. The silence that drapes over everything is suffocating, like the house itself is mourning her. His mind drifts back to the memories of her, the gentle laughter, her soft whispers at night and the warmth of her presence that made everything feel alive.

But today, Rajan is restless, a gnawing ache in his chest. It's almost as if the air itself is trying to tell him something. His thoughts swirl in frenzy. "Kshipra", he whispers to himself, almost as if she could hear him, "come back?"

He feels it; the pull, the quiet urgency that forces him to act. The house seems to echo with a longing, a quiet, almost inaudible whisper calling her back. It's the kind of feeling he's never experienced before, a strange and unshakable sensation that maybe, just maybe, Madhu is calling for her, urging her to return.

Rajan, for the first time in months, feels a stirring in his heart. The pride that usually shields him, the arrogance that keeps him distanced from his feelings, falters. For once, he wants to reach her. He has to, how long would he ignore her?

Without another thought, he decides, he's going to her parent's place. It's been nearly a month.

As Rajan reaches Kshipra's childhood home, the door creaks open. Inside, Ajay stands in the dim light, halfway dressed, his brow furrowed. He doesn't expect Rajan, especially not alone, and especially not looking as haggard as he does. There is a silence between them, a space that feels thick with unspoken words.

Rajan's voice breaks the stillness, hoarse with an emotion he's never allowed himself to show. "Can you call Kshipra? I can't live with this uncertainty anymore."

Ajay looks at him, his expression unreadable at first. The realization dawns on him too late, call her, means? Kshipra is not here!

They exchange quiet words, both confirming the same terrible truth. Kshipra left without a word, without a trace and nobody knows where she went. They are both consumed by the same rising panic. For now, they decide to hide tis from Vasanti and Madhukar.

Couple of days pass in restless searching, they go to every person she could possibly be. But they don't find her.

At the Ashram, Kshipra knows that she has to gets ready for her final encounter, confronting her brother's soul journey. She takes few days to gather her energy and her strength back as Shantanu guides so.

Kshipra steps out of her room, ready for her daily meditation, as the early morning light spills over the ashram. The air carries a different kind of stillness today; subtle, yet undeniable. The familiar sounds of birdsong and the soft rustle of trees remain, but something else lingers in the air, something unspoken. She pauses, frowning slightly. Why does everything feel so... different? She glances around. The disciples move with an unusual quietness, their gestures more measured, their voices hushed. Even the breeze seems gentler, as though the world itself is preparing for something. She spots one of the younger disciples, Aniket, arranging fresh flowers near the meditation hall. Without hesitation, she approaches him.

"Aniket," she says, keeping her voice low, "why does everything feel different today? What is happening?"
Aniket looks up from his task, a small smile playing on his lips. "Bhikkhuni Sampriya is visiting," he says simply. "She will be staying here for a few days."

Kshipra nods slowly, allowing the name to settle in her mind. She has heard of Bhikkhuni Sampriya few days back; a revered Buddhist monk known for her profound wisdom. But hearing about someone and experiencing their presence are two different things. Perhaps that is what she senses; a shift in the very air, as though the ashram itself has aligned with a deeper rhythm.

After breakfast, the disciples and seekers gather in the meditation hall, sitting cross-legged on woven mats. The hall, usually filled with murmured conversations and soft laughter, is now enveloped in a sacred hush. The golden light filtering through the high windows paints gentle patterns on the stone floor, flickering like whispered blessings.

Kshipra settles into her place, her eyes drawn toward the front of the hall. And then, she sees her.

Bhikkhuni Sampriya, her presence is unlike anything Kshipra has ever witnessed. The simplicity of her ochre robe enhances, rather than diminishes, the quiet grace she carries. Her head is shaven, her features unadorned, yet there is an undeniable radiance about her. She does not appear fragile, nor does she seem commanding. She simply is a presence, neither forceful nor passive, like a river flowing effortlessly towards the sea.

Kshipra watches her, captivated. There is something deeply soothing about the way she sits, unmoving, as if she belongs to time itself but is not bound by it. The weight of existence seems to rest lightly on her, as though she has learned the art of carrying nothing and, in doing so, holds everything.

A soft chime signals the beginning of the session. Bhikkhuni Sampriya opens her eyes; calm, deep, like the vast sky before dusk. When she speaks, her voice is gentle, yet it carries an unshakable strength, as if each word is drawn from a place beyond the world of fleeting concerns.

"Many of you seek peace," she begins. "But what is peace? Is it silence? Is it the absence of suffering? Is it a destination, waiting to be reached?"

She lets the question hang in the air. The listeners remain still, waiting, "no," she says softly. "Peace is not found outside of you. The world shifts; people come and go, seasons change, desires rise and fade. If you seek peace in things that move, you will always be lost." Her eyes sweep across the room, resting briefly on each listener, as though she is seeing something beyond their forms.

"There was once a bird caught in a storm," she continues. "The wind howled, the trees bent, the sky roared with anger. But the bird did not fight the storm. It spread its wings, allowed the wind to lift it, and in doing so, it became free. Not because the storm ended, but because it no longer resisted."

The room remains silent, yet something stirs within each listener; a recognition perhaps. A truth they have always known but never quite named.

"You suffer," Bhikkhuni Sampriya continues, "because you believe you are separate from others, from the world, from the vast unfolding of life itself. But this 'I' that you defend, the 'I' that fears, that longs, that clings, have you ever truly seen it? If you search for it, you will not find it. It is but a shadow cast by passing thoughts."

Kshipra listens, her breath steady. There is something indescribable in the way these words settle within her. Not as mere knowledge, but as something far deeper, like a forgotten memory awakening inside her.

"The world does not need you to be perfect," the bhikkhuni continues, "It does not ask you to be more, or less. A river does not struggle to reach the sea, nor does the sun doubt its rise. They simply are as they are. And so you too, must be."

For a long time, no one speaks. The stillness is not

empty rather it is full like the quiet of a forest before dawn, like the vastness of the sky before the first stars appear.

Kshipra lowers her gaze, letting the words settle in her heart. She does not try to define what she feels. There is no need. Some things are not meant to be understood. They are only meant to be lived.

The day rise when Kshipra feels ready to face Ajay's reasons for the hate and reason he keeps her away despite their evitable love for each other.

The room is ready to ground and hold Kshipra while she would let the wheels of time unfold as she would journey back, brave and bold for she has come again, to sow the love, fulfil the deeds.

With her emotions settling and her heart focusing, she looks at Shantanu, parting his wisdom. Their eyes meet briefly, his eyes saying a lot and her eyes acknowledging the same.

Kshipra sets an intention; a strong, "I want to understand what Ajay knows, what he believes, and what he misunderstood about me. I want to see into his soul, deep embedded emotions which are turned into this dislike."

This intention feels like a key unlocking her understanding. She takes a deep breath, allowing herself to sink into the meditation once more as Shantanu sits opposite she feels that wherever her soul wonder in search of the unseen, he will help her be grounded.

Her vision shifts. She drifts, back in time, to when she is still in their house as a little older child; growing, playing in the fields, and helping with chores.

As her meditation goes deeper, memories return to her, moments she did not experience first hand and things she could never have known. She begins to see that her hasty assumption of safety and isolation was false.

She spots the narrow path leading to her village and then she sees her home but before Arya can step onto the familiar path, the memory of that unfateful night at Thorston's place crashes over her again when she had managed to escape, but Sujoy had misunderstood everything.

As she comes out of Thorston's house, desperate and confused, she runs straight toward her home, only to find British soldiers already there, shouting her name. They are beating the other three mercilessly.

From a hidden distance, Arya watches in horror. Her instincts urge her forward, but just as she takes a step to rush to them, a hand yanks her back.

A fellow freedom fighter grips her arm tightly, his voice urgent and low, "If they catch you now," he warns, "they'll uncover everything; our mission, our people. They will kill your family as well. As long as you remain free, they'll keep them alive, hoping you'll return."

Arya's heart breaks under the weight of his words. Tears blur her vision as she gazes one last time at the home that gave shelter to an orphan like her. The freedom fighter pulls her away, and she stumbles along with him, her eyes fixed on her house until it disappears from sight.

Kshipra's vision takes her to the same place but months later.

It is not the same. The courtyard is dry, cracked. The mud floor has holes where water once stood. The tulsi plant looks withered, as if it has forgotten what rain feels like. Her foster mother sits on the verandah, her back bent, grinding something slowly with shaking hands. Her eyes look far away, like she's searching for something in the air.

Suddenly there is the sound of boots; loud, heavy, careless.

British soldiers enter the house. They look around as if they own everything. One of them pushes open the kitchen door with his gun. Another one kicks the storage box.

Her father rushes to the front yard. His face is tired, his beard is turning white, but he folds his hands politely. "We told you already," he says softly. "She is not here. We do not know where she is."

A soldier laughs "Lies," he says. "We'll see how long you keep lying."

The soldier hits him on the back with a thick stick. He falls to his knees, gasping. Her mother cries out and tries to help him, but another soldier pushes her back.

Kshipra flinches, still sitting in meditation. Her body is quiet, but her heart is screaming. She feels the pain in her father's bones as if it is her own. Her breath becomes shaky. She wants to open her eyes but she can't. She needs to see it all which she didn't witness.

Kshipra shifts her vision further, British soldier return again. They take everything. The little money her family hides under the floor, the copper vessels, even the grain kept for winter.

Once, when her mother cooks a simple meal; boiled rice and pumpkin, the soldiers take it from her hands and throw it on the floor. Then they laugh as they walk away.

Kshipra sees her mother kneel down and gather the food again, brushing the dirt off. Her hands shake, but her eyes are dry. She does not cry anymore.

Her brother sits outside, staring at the sky. His face is hard now. No more smiles. No more stories. When their father returns from the fields with a bruised leg he does not offer to help, "It's because of her," he says, almost spitting the words "Because of Arya we are suffering and she... she must be hiding somewhere.

Eating, sleeping. She doesn't care."

Their mother says nothing. She just presses her fingers to her forehead and closes her eyes. But her lips move in silent prayer.

Kshipra hears's voice. It cuts her deeply.

"She left us. She destroyed us. Let her suffer too. Let her feel what hunger is. What pain is, how it feels to lose everything and then get nothing, nothing at all. Even if she has it, she won't be able to have it. No food, no help."

One day, after months of waiting, hope arrives in the form of a good crop. The field glows golden. Her father smiles for the first time in weeks. Her mother prepares sweet rice with jiggery, even helps with the harvest.

But just as they gather the grain, the soldiers return. No warning, No questions. They set fire to the field. Flames rise like angry arms into the sky. Her father runs, tries to stop it with a cloth, but the fire doesn't care, he throws sand, his face red with helpless rage.

Kshipra feels the heat on her skin. She can't move, but tears roll down her cheeks in her meditation. The flames dance in her closed eyes.

That night, the house is quiet. Her father sits by the door, staring at the ashes. He doesn't speak. He doesn't blink. He just rocks slowly, as if the silence can comfort him.

The next morning, he leaves. He walks through the village, limping slightly, using a stick. He passes the temple. He passes the pond where Arya used to sit. No one stops him. His face is blank, like already half gone. He hides near an old shed, trying to rest. But the soldiers find him.

They beat them, again and again. No one is there to stop them.

Later they finds his father's body; broken and Cold. His chest doesn't rise anymore.

Karan kneels beside him, his hands shaking. His face is filled with something beyond pain. It is rage. It is betrayal. His lips tremble. His teeth grind.

"Our family is finished," he whispers "because of her."
Her mother doesn't light the stove the next day. She doesn't eat. She doesn't cry. She sits beside her husband's bed, imagining stroking his face with trembling fingers.

The memories come with clarity. She sees her mother trying to convince to understand. "She is not responsible for this. What she is doing is good for the country and you must not hate her," the mother murmurs over and ove. Herr as's belly remains empty and his eyes glint with resentment.

But he doesn't undestand. His emotions fester. In her vision, Kshipra hears his words, sharp and bitter: "We are struggling every moment for food, for survival and it's because of you Arya. You will suffer just as we suffer. You will always suffer and you'll never find happiness. Its because of you I lost my father and feel alone now, you too will feel alone always, each and every moment you will feel alone."

That evening, the soldiers come again. This time, her mother stands. She picks up a sickle from the kitchen, holds it tight. "Enough," she says. Her voice is not loud, but it is firm. She charges. She doesn't reach. They shoot her. Right there, in the courtyard.

She falls slowly, her white saree blooming red like a flower no one wanted to grow.

Kshipra gasps seeing this. Her body bends forward as if something inside her is breaking. Her hands clutch the mat. Her breath comes in sobs. She doesn't open her eyes.

She sits back up, slowly. Her spine is still straight, but her soul has collapsed inside. Grief rises like smoke from the center of her being. She feels it, all of it. And it doesn't go away because pain doesn't leave when you run from it. It waits quietly until you are ready to feel it. And now she does!

In her meditative trance, Kshipra feels's emotions; his pain, his memories. She understands that each moment of suffering, each beat of his heart, was filled with the bitterness of injustice, the starvation, the fear, and the endless weight of helplessness, over the time grows more bitter, his young soul becomes hardened by these experiences, linking Arya to the violence and pain in his life.

Kshipra breakdown in her meditation, the weight of these realizations is crashing upon her. She gasps, tears streaming down her face as the memories wash over her like a storm. She hadn't understood the depth of this pain before. She hadn't understood how entwined his soul was with resentment and suffering, driven by repeated torture, fear and struggle for survival.

Now she knows why Ajay developed such animosity toward Arya. It wasn't just instinct, nor was it baseless hatred. His life was built on the memory of betrayal, loss and pain, his survival rooted in anger and frustration. The thread of her understanding stretches further.

She sits in the aftermath of the memory, heart pounding, overwhelmed with grief and understanding. "Oh my God," she murmurs softly. "This is what happened."

The weight is heavy in her chest. The knowledge, raw and brutal, makes her realize how much deeper their souls' entanglements run. She can feel pain, his suffering, his resentment toward Arya.

The moment she feels full of these emotions towards Arya, She ceases it and call for all his pain to herself, all at once. What suffered for months and years together, Kshipra's soul experiences in that very moment. It pricks all over her physical form, like thousands of thorns prick all at a time. Her soul screams but takes it till soul is free of all the resentments and hate and pain.

Just at the moment when she feels that her body is about to explode and her soul screams with ache, she calls for the divine light and allows it to pass through her and routing it to the core of the mother earth. Her body experiences the lightening passing through yet again, challenging her physical form to the level where her determination to heal the souls only makes her survive.

Lightening feels intense and intense till all the emotions are parted. Kshipra takes it all until the divine light cleanses the emotions and frees Ajay's soul from the hatred.

Gradually, very very gradually Kshipra gets calm but yet not ready to come to the present moment.

Releasing the darkness

Shantanu touches the blue lotus on her forehead and guides her further and she follows "all this healings you carried out need a proper closure and no trace of the curses and the lineage patterns should remain. Focus on all the conditions that prevailed and what exists now. Focus on the feeling of satisfaction as the burden is released". Kshipra's facial expressions shift to more calmer and content ones. She feels a tension released off her shoulders but feels as if a breath, a single breath holds something back. Shantanu notices this on her face "Exactly that one tinch need to be cleared, this is irrespective of any issues your soul carries. You need to visit the same place which took you to the door accessing your previous lives. Now on you will never revisit that place, your souls journey is now meant to be in only forward".

He continues "focus on the stairs leading you to this place and take a step at a time."

Kshipra takes a step at a time to reach the beautiful garden and the springs and the flower beds. She feels mesmerized like never before.

Shantanu guides her further. "Kshipra are you able to see the dark black cloud surrounding you? Kshipra in her meditative state looks up and is surprised to see the same, she takes a back as this cloud is thick and scary, it slowly approaches her and gradually picks up the speed. Shantanu asks her to stand still and take charge of it

Kshipra doesn't understand what that means. Shantanu's voice guides further, "dark cloud looks huge but you have the capability to control it and hold it in between both your palms. Raise your hands and hold it, the voice repeats and repeats, "Raise your hand, Kshipra, take control, crush it and drain it, now."

Kshipra feels that the cloud itself will blow but she manages to raise her hands and feels the density of the cloud as it settles in her palms she crushes it just like a burnt paper ball and continues looking at it. Shantanu's voice directs "Walk towards the sea. This is the same route you went through and you have seen the sea while going on the way to the truth. Go there and throw these crushed pieces into the sea and let it drain from your lifetime".

Kshipra looks at the sea which is at a distance, and she slowly walks. Though the crushed pieces are just a handful now, she is able to feel the weight of it. She struggles to walk while holding it, but she does as Shantanu's voice keep on encouraging her to balance herself and walk slowly without dropping a bit of it. Kshipra throws it into the sea. It floats on the water, and Kshipra conveys the same, "I threw it but it's not flowing, it's still there, it's floating" Shantanu tells her, it will settle, it will settle at the bottom and eventually disappear." Kshipra witnesses the same and feels relieved.

Kshipra asks "I am feeling very calm and peaceful here, it looks beautiful around. I didn't notice it while passing from here. Can I sit here on the rock for a while?".

Shantanu explains "No dear, you are not supposed to be there now. Past always attracts and attracts more once sorted but you can't be there. You are not meant to be there. You have to come back. You have to come back where you belong. You were there for a purpose and it is fulfilled. You need to be in the present and you need to leave behind the past. You have experienced the truth of the past and healed it and now you are free from its weight. Come back dear."

Kshipra walks through this beautiful path, through the bank, crossing the rocks, leaving behind the appealing trees, the warmth of the breeze, and the fragrance of the past.

While Kshipra takes up relaxing meditations to cool down mentally, physically and by soul; Ajay and Rajan fail to find trace of Kshipra yet. The weight of it; the sorrow, the emptiness floods them.

Ajay walks to the riverbank, the place where they spent endless hours as children, the place where memories were made, and now, the place where they are slowly unraveling.

The river is calm, its surface unbroken, but to Ajay, it feels like it's mocking him. He sits on one of the large stones, letting the chill of the morning seep into his bones. His mind drifts back to those days when Kshipra was always there, always laughing and guiding them with the lightness they took for granted. He had always seen her as a constant, a rock. But now, the river's whispering current too seems to ask him, where is she?

Ajay closes his eyes, his chest heavy with grief. He can't stop thinking about Kshipra. He can't stop wondering where she went, what happened to her. He feels tightness in his throat and his heart races with a nameless fear.

After what feels like an eternity, Ajay stands, his legs stiff from sitting too long. He turns to walk back home, his heart sinking with each step. But then something catches his eye, a faint glimmer, a flash of something in the corner of his vision.

He pauses.

There, by the edge of the river, something dark against the rocks, a bag. His breath catches in his throat realising that it's Kshipra's bag. A feeling like ice slides down his spine, his heart hammering in his chest. He rushes toward it, his feet nearly stumbling over the uneven terrain as he draws closer. It looks wrong. The bag is dirty, covered in dust and grime. It's been lying here for days, forgotten as if abandoned.

Ajay's hands tremble as he reaches down, fingers brushing the worn leather. It's hers, there's no mistaking it. The bag, the familiar design, the way it feels beneath his touch, is unmistakable. He identifies this bag, which he purchased for her just before her marriage and that small episode flashes in from of him, the way he teased her showing this bag and telling her to wrape up everything and take away!

In that moment, all the air seems to leave his lungs.

Panic sets in like a tidal wave as he looks at the river and its deep waters.

And then, from behind him, Rajan arrives. Seeing the bag, seeing Ajay's pale face, chaos erupts. Questions flood the air, what does this mean? Why is it here? Did she…?

Rajan's face twists in disbelief, his mind races. No. This can't be happening. Not like this.

Ajay's voice is a broken whisper, barely audible. "Do you think... do you think she...?"

Rajan's eyes flash with panic, but the answer hangs heavy in the air. They both know what they are thinking, but neither of them dares to voice it. The river seems to hum with an eerie silence as they stand there, frozen, surrounded by the awful uncertainty of it all.

By morning swimmers dive in for Kshipra's search as the crowd gather. Sudha is in terrible shock and doesn't leave Ajay's hand, search continues for hours. One of the divers comes up and confirms "there is a body of a lady but it's caught in between two stones and i am not able to pull it out". Ajay and Rajan collapse on their places.

Rajan cries aloud and runs towards the river. He is unconsolable and escapes from the hands of the villagers present there. He reaches the river and throughs his body into it. Two of young boys jump behind him and forcebly take him out of the river. He shouts on top of his voice looking up at the sky "Ma, I killed her. I couldn't value her love, I couldn't treasure her Ma".

Ajay goes speechless, Sudha shakes and shakes him but he just gives up on his body and lay down motionless as he falls. His hand and fore head bleeds but gives him no sensation over this grief. His eyes look like rocks, motionless and feelingless depicting nil expressions for all those watching him. But deep down his heart aches, shouts and calls for his sister. His pain is beyond expressions. Warm breeze spill all the dust on his face and his eyes they don't blink. Kshipra's voice echoes in his mind a sweet little girl running behind him taking a bowl of rice to feed him and shouting "Aja…y", a teenager showing him all the fire flies and jumping with him "Aja…y", a graceful bride as she runs back to him and hugs him tightly while leaving her maiden house calling "Ajay, how will I live without you".

Little far standing on the rock, Murli witnesses all this silently. He doesn't understand what his mind goes through. All the memories with Kshipra flash continuously untill her body is taken out and layed on the bank.

Someone shouts "It's not Kshipra, who is she?" Sudha runs towards the body leaving Ajay who catches a breath with a deep sigh and gets up and runs towards the body. Rajan too rushes towards the body and making way from the crowd stand still infront of the body, not identifying it. Sudha utters "Usha!"

Murli closes his eyes and his tears flow continuously "How could we think like that, I know you are strong Kshipra, you cannot finish yourself like this. I should have understood this. You won't run away like this, I should know this, I should have known this for sure."

All of them stand near Usha's body, trying to figure out the answer to the puzzle 'Why did Usha commit suicide and when? Her face looks just so fresh! Moreover why is Kshipra's bag lying here?"

They all visit Usha's house only to learn that, she was missing past few months and her parent's didn't bother to search her thinking she must have gone to her grandmother Lakshmi's place, whom the family have aboundened. Usha's mother slowly peeps out and hands over a chit to her which has Lakshmi's address written on it.

They feel relieved but tension still prevails. All that Ajay and Rajan wanted now was Kshipra's one glance which would assure that she is safe and they reachout to Lakshmi's place expecting Kshipra there.

Back home, Murli unable to express his sorrow and worry and desperate to see Kshipra, quietly opens the old photo album. His fingers move slowly across the worn pages, memories unfolding one by one. He not only misses his friend; he feels with sudden clarity, how wrong he had been to hate her.

His gaze freezes on a particular photo, a little boy,

maybe eight, laughing playfully, a small mark on his forehead.

Murli stares at it, strangely drawn. He doesn't know that this is the same photo Kshipra saw in her first past life regression, the boy who laughed at her as she tried to return from that other realm.

His heart twists as he flips to the next picture, Kshipra is feeding a sweet to Ajay, her face full of warmth. Murli, just behind them, stares with a quiet, almost forgotten hope. Lost in that sentimate he whispers to the silence, voice breaking "Kshipra… I always wanted to belong to you. As a brother, as a son, anything that meant I was yours. But I thought the only way to hold you would be as a lover. I didn't understand that I already belonged to you as your closest friend."

His fingers tremble on the page, "you shared your fears with me, your dreams, your pain, even things your family never knew and still… I wasn't there when you needed me most. I betrayed your love. Not the kind that asks, but the kind that gives."

Murli weeps softly, shoulders shaking.

In the doorway, Sudha stands still. She hears everything Murli murmurs.

Tears brim in her eyes, not just for Murli, but for Kshipra, her dearest friend, now seemed to be lost from all their hands. Her absence echoes around them; in their home, in their silence, in the space where her presence once lived.

This evening as Lakshmi lights up a lamp in her small temple, Ajay and Rajan stand outside the room. They both are desperate to know if Kshipra is here. Ajay is unable to wait patiently, "I am Ajay, and he is Kshipra's husband Rajan". Lakshmi lifts her gaze and look at them. Not saying much she says, tomorrow morning I will take you to her. You can rest in the adjustant room for this night". Rajan becomes desperate "She is not here? Where is she?" Lakshmi doesn't say anything, she just dims the lanterns and says "We leave tomorrow morning and shall reach there by noon".

Earling morning just after the dawn, they set to walk till Shantanu's Ashram, all that way Kshipra walked through. The path is the same but the motos so different.

The same morning Kshipra steps down from the bed, her feet brushing softly against the floor. The room feels still, bathed in the gentle glow of morning light. She walks slowly toward the window, her heart light, her body graceful, as if each step is a reflection of the calm she has just found. The cool air welcomes her as she pulls back the curtains and gazes out at the world beyond. The sun, just beginning to rise, casts a soft golden glow on everything it touches.

With a serene smile, Kshipra moves towards the well. The rhythmic sound of the rope unwinding fills the quiet space as she pulls the bucket up, feeling the weight of the water as it rises. Her hands are steady, open, almost as if offering something to the world. The water is clear and cool, and she feels a sense of purity and peace flowing through her as she walks back into the house.

In the bathroom, she stands before the mirror, feeling the calmness settle deep within her. She gently pours the cool water over her head, and it cascades down, her body. The water slides over her cheeks, her hair, and down her neck, like a river of renewal, washing away the remnants of the past. Her face, illuminated by the soft light streaming from the window, radiates with a soft glow, as if every drop of water is bringing her closer to her true self.

Her reflection in the mirror shows a woman transformed. The peace in her eyes, the quiet strength in her posture, tells the story of a soul that has found its way home. Each drop of water seems to cleanse not just her body, but her very essence, leaving her feeling reborn.

The tension in the air is palpable as Rajan and Ajay enter Shantanu's ashram, following Lakshmi closely. The peaceful surroundings of the ashram contrast sharply with the anxious expressions on their faces. They exchange wary glances, their minds filled with doubt and anticipation. The faint rustling of the trees outside seems louder in the silence between them, their footsteps echoing on the ground as they walk.

The Last Release

Lakshmi, unperturbed by their unease leads the way with quiet confidence. Her presence feels as a calm anchor amidst the turmoil swirling around the two men. They approach the central area of the ashram, where a few stone benches sit under the shade of ancient trees, inviting moments of reflection. Rajan and Ajay take their seats, their eyes never straying too far from Lakshmi, as they wait for the moment that might bring them closer to finding Kshipra.

Holding it for long Ajay breaks, "we found her," he says with a tight voice "Usha's body, in the river."

Rajan swallows hard, "She was gone days, probably months before we found her body cold and still…"

Lakshmi lowers her head, trying to cover her tears, "Usha, smiled quietly and left even more quietly. No one had truly seen the weight she carried, the sting of her parents' constant humiliation, the shame they cast on her skin being too dark, too unwanted, too difficult to marry. They just wanted to get rid of her.

She didn't come to me while alive but her soul did for her friend, Kshipra.

Ajay interrupts, "She committed suicide months ago? how is it possible, her body was not at all decomposed as if she was just sleeping".

Lakshmi's voice trembles with conviction: "She took her own life but I sensed it the moment it happened. Though she never came to me, we are always connected. I had to protect her body."

Kshipra's breathe hitches as she hears all this in the room behind the wall.The scene returns in Kshipra's vision, the crowded room, bright with guests. A baby wrapped in silk. Laughter, lights. Kshipra offers Usha to hold the baby but usha just says "No, I can't".

Kshipra remembers how no one looked at Usha. How no one responded when Kshipra thought Usha spoke. How she never touched anything

Kshipra's heart thuds as she sees it now; a dream, a memory herself walking alone down a village path, wind at her back and a presence behind her; gentle, familiar.

Lakshmi's, voice echos in her thought as Ksipra asks Lakshmi, "where is Usha? " She left, she couldn't wait".

Kshipra turn around on her position feeling a soothing cool breeze, Usha stands there with unspoken; not seen not heard but felt.

Chills run across Kshipra's body as she feels presence being not just of Usha but Divya as well.

Kshipra's eyes close as she leans into the feeling, sensing it more deeply. Here she is; a friend, extending her love and silent support, from lifetimes unknown.

Always near, sometimes beside Arya as Divya, sometimes beside Kshipra as Usha.

The air is filled with expectation, and after a brief pause, Shantanu emerges from a small room in the distance. His calm presence fills the space, and he walks toward Lakshmi. Lakshmi's quiet words to him are not audible, but the exchange sparks something between them, as if unspoken communication passes through the air, leaving Rajan and Ajay wondering what is unfolding in this sacred place.

Lakshmi's face softens into a small, knowing smile, signaling that something important is in motion. With a subtle gesture, Shantanu retreats back into the room, leaving the two men to grapple with their curiosity.

Lakshmi turns toward Ajay and Rajan, her steps deliberate as she walks toward them. "Follow me," she says softly. The three of them move toward a door at the far end of the ashram, a door that feels both familiar and unknown. As they approach, Shantanu emerges again, standing in the doorway, silently observing them.

Rajan's nerves are on edge. He feels the weight of the moment, "please, call Kshipra. I need to see her," Ajay's voice breaks the quiet, his desperation evident.

Shantanu exchanges a long look with Lakshmi, their connection unspoken but powerful. After a long pause, he steps aside, allowing them to pass. It's then that they see her, 'Kshipra'.

But she is no longer the woman they knew. The transformation is so stark, so complete, that neither Rajan nor Ajay can speak.

Kshipra stands before them, not as the wife or sister they had known but as a ….!

Her face looks serene with a slight, almost imperceptible smile and her head, shaved. She wears the simple orange robe, the attire symbolizing her journey of detachment and inner peace. Her eyes, once filled with uncertainty and turmoil, now reflect an undeniable calm.

The sight leaves Rajan and Ajay momentarily stunned. They cannot reconcile the person standing before them with the woman they came to find. She has changed, and in that change, she has found a peace they had not expected.

As she walks ahead, Ajay's eyes fall on the back of her shaven head.

He remembers her braid; the thick, black plait he used to hold on to when they ran through the fields. She never liked it as he pulled it, always brushed him off but lovingly. He held it like a lifeline, feeling secure and connected.

Now, it's gone.

The plait, the childhood, the sister he thought he'd always have, it has slipped from his hands without a sound.

He doesn't call her back, in that moment, he lets go.

Without saying a word, Kshipra; her true self, as she has now become, looks at Rajan and Ajay, her gaze soft yet distant. She doesn't speak, doesn't explain but the message is clear, she is no longer the woman they knew. She is something different, something beyond their understanding.

Kshipra pass by Ajay and her soul hears it what she promised herself, "If he cannot see me as a sister in this life, then let me return as his real one. Let me be born again, not to be loved, but to love. Not to be accepted, but to heal. This is my penance, my offering, my promise."

Kshipra walks toward the main entrance of the ashram. Both men, still rooted to their spot, watch her leave, their hearts heavy with emotions they can't fully grasp.

As Kshipra almost reaches the entrance, Bhikhuni Sampriya appears, guiding her toward the path beyond. Without a glance back, Kshipra follows, her steps slow but purposeful.

Rajan and Ajay stand motionless, watching as Kshipra walks away from them, disappearing into the serene world she has chosen.

She walks, not away from them, but toward herself.

The scene leaves them both with a mixture of awe, confusion, and sorrow. They came looking for a way to bring her back, but what they found is something far more profound. They had already mourned for her and now when she is in front and still not going to come back ever, they both just watch; no sorrow, no tears and probably just an unexpected shock!

As Kshipra walks behind Bhikkhuni Sampriya, her steps are filled with a quiet purpose, each movement releasing the weight of years of searching, struggling, and finally healing and letting go. The world around her seems to fade, the noise of the past falling away as she enters into a space of profound stillness. There is no rush, no need to hurry; just a calm surrender to what is.

Lakshmi utters looking Kshipra walk "Kshipra, your journey has reached its fulfillment, from the moment you chose to walk this path of healing. Your wish has been granted. You have fulfilled your commitments to the family that sheltered you in your last life. You took on their burdens, understood their pains, and guided their soul toward the healing of their hearts. Your love, your wisdom, and your care have mended what was broken."

A sacred voice fills the air reverberating in the space, "And now, dear soul, your task here is complete. Your mission to heal, to teach the value of true connection, is done. The time has come for you to move forward. Your soul is ready to step into its highest truth, beyond the limitations of this life, beyond the ties that once bound you. The road ahead is vast, and it calls to you, Kshipra. It calls to you as you walk into the light of your own becoming."

These words settling in the air are not simply an end. They are a beginning, a turning of a page that cannot be turned back.

The voice fades, leaving only the echo of its message, its truth. The story that once began with confusion, pain, and longing, now finds its conclusion not in finality, but in the endless journey of the soul.

In the stillness of the moment, a voice resonates, timeless and gentle. The words flow with the calm authority of ancient wisdom, a deep invocation that seems to echo through the very fabric of her being.

"Buddham Sharanam Gachami, Dhammam Sharanam Gachami, Sangham Sharanam Gachami."The words, "I go to the Buddha, I go to the Dhamma, I go to the Sangha" drift through the air, and suddenly, the world around Kshipra blurs.

In a flash, the present moment dissolves and gets transported to another time, another life and in that place which is dimly lit by the soft glow of the fading sun, old Arya lies on her deathbed. Her skin is weathered, and her eyes are closed. As the rays of the setting sun touch her wrinkled face, a soft smile curves her lips.

Arya's breath slows. Her body rests, fragile and still, but her soul stirs gently, ready to move on. The chant echoes one final time and she understands. Her life, her duty for now, is complete. In the stillness, she lets go.

In her final moments, she hears the chant which is clearly heard now, the same invocation,

"Buddham Sharanam Gachami, Dhammam Sharanam Gachami, Sangham Sharanam Gachami."

The words ring out carrying with them the echoes of a life lived with purpose, a life of commitment fulfilled. As she hears those sacred words, the light of the sun falls over her face, bathing her in golden warmth, and in that moment, she understands. She has done her duty for now, but much remains to be fulfilled yet. Her eyes close for the last time.

In that moment, she completes her journey, but in her next life, as Kshipra, the same soul returned.

As Arya's final breath fades into eternity, the soft chant becomes a bridge, guiding the same soul into a new body, a new moment. The rays of the sun touch her face, and she breathes deeply, feeling the sense of peace she attains for now.

She has come full circle.

Her soul has travelled from that old woman on her deathbed to this moment in time, fulfilling the commitment she made in her past life, the vows she took to heal, to guide, and to transform. The past and present are no longer separate rather they are one continuous journey, leading her to this moment of fulfillment.

With a final, steady step, Kshipra walks away from the ashram, no longer burdened, no longer bound by the past. She has completed her journey.

She is free to move forward, her soul now ready to embrace its true purpose.

She looks back once, not with longing but with reverence. Arya's fire and Vasanti's ache, the quiet strength of all she has been, they still live in her. But now, she isn't carrying them. She is them. And they have brought her here to peace, to choice, to love that doesn't bind, but frees.

To Vasanti, she owed voice, sacrificed once to silence. In this life, she returned as a daughter who listened. Who saw the pain beneath the service, who made space for softness without shame.

To Madhukar, she owed love returned, not worship, not duty but quiet, equal love. In this life, she did not ask for it, she lived it; in stillness, in truth.

They had once given everything to her and lost themselves. She returned to give it back, gently without fanfare, without needing to be seen.

Vasanti lights the lamp, her hands steady and her heart no longer reaching for answers. For the first time, Madhukar stands beside her not as a man hardened by years, but as a father who has learned to let go.

A cool breeze touches their feet, they pause. A subtle fragrance lingers in the air, unfamiliar, yet strangely known. They don't speak. They don't need to.

They both feel Kshipra's presence. It is yet for them to know, she is walking her own path. Not gone, only beyond their knowing.

And as Kshipra walks into the horizon, the voice lingers, softly fading into the distance, reminding us all that true peace is not the end, but a new beginning.

Beginning of the new journey!

Why I Wrote This Story

This story was born from a deep creative impulse; a need to explore pain, love, and healing that seem to stretch beyond what we understand in a single lifetime.

While the ideas of past lives and soul connections are central to the narrative, they are not presented as fact or belief, but as a lens through which to view emotional patterns, relationships, and unresolved wounds.

Through Kshipra's journey, I wanted to explore how healing can feel both deeply personal and strangely collective, how sometimes what we carry isn't just ours, but part of a much larger, unseen tapestry. This is a fictional exploration of soul-to-soul healing, of breaking the invisible patterns that bind us, and moving gently toward compassion and understanding.

This story is for those who resonate with emotional echoes they can't quite explain, who feel the weight of something unspoken, and who are courageous enough to seek clarity; not through answers, but through reflection.

About the Author

Anamika S Yadav is a writer who finds her spark in people, their stories, silences, quirks, and questions. Whether through chance conversations or quiet observation, she explores the emotional undercurrents that shape who we are and how we connect.

She believes storytelling is one of the oldest ways we make sense of the world. In India, stories have long been at the heart of several festivals and rituals; not just as entertainment, but as a way to pass on memory, meaning, and feeling. Anamika's writing carries forward that spirit, blending the everyday with the timeless.

When not writing, she loves singing, traveling, and getting lost in conversations that meander through laughter, wonder, and insight.

She's passionate about inspiring others through both words and presence.

If you'd like to connect for a invite Anamika for a motivational talk, author session, or just share your thoughts, feel free to connect at authoranamika17@gmail.com

Author's accomplishments

Debut Novel- **Down the Memory Lane**

□ **4.5 Stars** on Amazon, Recipient of the Emerging Author of the Year Award 2022, by Ukiyoto Publishing at the Kolkata Literary Carnival.

Synopsis: "Some journeys begin not on the road, but deep within the heart."

A young biomedical engineer's first solo tour becomes a journey of inner awakening. Amidst unfamiliar cities, kind strangers, and quiet reflections, she rediscovers love, courage, and her sense of self. Down the Memory Lane is a tender, nostalgic tale of growing up, letting go, and finding home within.

Second Novel - **Kasturi 'The Musk in You'**

□ **4.6 Stars** on Amazon, receipent of Golden Book Award by International Authors Association & Wings Publication International.

Synopsis: "Sometimes, the storm you fear becomes the path to your truth."

Kasturi, a spirited entrepreneur, builds a life of balance, until betrayal and loss dismantle everything. Through financial chaos, shattered trust, and spiritual trials, she rises with resilience. Kasturi is an inspiring story of grit, grace, and rediscovering the strength that always lived within.

□ A short story by Anamika S Yadav was selected and published in LitGleam, an international platform showcasing bold, original voices in fiction.

9 789334 313246